Praise for
BLUE LAKE

"*Blue Lake* is at once a legal thriller, a romance, a mystery, and a poignant defense of the waters, woods and wildlife of the Upper Midwest. Warm and generous, serious and comic, eloquent and thoughtful, the novel underscores the ongoing tension between humans and our environment and ultimately celebrates the natural beauty we continue to take for granted."

—**LINDSAY STARCK**, author, *Noah's Wife*

"*Blue Lake* is a thoughtful, entertaining, and insightful novel featuring refreshingly grownup characters who deal with complex, real-life issues of love and loss, set against a backdrop of murder, mystery, intrigue, and climate change. The novel's Wisconsin setting is beautifully rendered with lovely, evocative descriptions of the state's small towns, rural idylls, and natural attractions."

—**ELIZABETH RIDLEY**, author, *Searching for Celia*

"Part love story, courtroom drama, and thoughtful meditation on pressing environmental concerns, *Blue Lake* is also a well observed and stirring love letter to the Upper Midwest."

—**TED THOMPSON**, author, *The Land of Steady Habits*, which was adapted into a film for Netflix by Nicole Holofcener.

"The personal meets the political in spectacular fashion in Jeffrey Boldt's suspenseful tale about the lengths people will go to exploit and protect natural resources. Boldt's experience as an attorney and judge informs this taut, well-crafted legal thriller, and he provides an inside look at how competing interests duke it out while climate change looms and the stakes couldn't be higher."

—**CHRISTINA CLANCY**, author of *Shoulder Season*
and *The Second Home*

"A smart legal thriller. Boldt does for the wilds of the Upper Midwest what Grisham did to the backwoods of the Deep South."

—**STEPHAN EIRIK CLARK**, author of *Sweetness #9*

"*Blue Lake* takes the reader behind courtroom walls, where a love story battles greed and murderous intent. Jeffrey Boldt's novel is an insider story, offered to us by a writer who knows this world."

—**CASS DALGLISH**, author, *Nin*; poet, *Humming the Blues*

A Novel

BLUE LAKE

Jeffrey D. Boldt

RIVER GROVE
BOOKS

Published by River Grove Books
Austin, TX
www.rivergrovebooks.com

The author gratefully acknowledges that his poem *No Mutants Yet in Baxter's Hollow* first appeared in *J Journal*, Vol. 7, #1, John Jay College, CUNY, Spring 2014

Distributed by River Grove Books

Design and composition by Greenleaf Book Group
Cover design by Greenleaf Book Group

Grateful acknowledgment is made to the following sources
for permission to reproduce copyrighted material.

From "In Praise of Limestone" by W.H. Auden from *Horizon*, July 1948.
Copyright © Curtis Brown, Ltd. All rights reserved. Used by permission.

Cover Images: ©iStockphoto/SanderStock, ©iStockphoto/UmbertoPantalone, ©iStockphoto/Alex Potemkin

Publisher's Cataloging-in-Publication data is available.

Paperback ISBN: 978-1-63299-516-2

Hardcover ISBN: 978-1-63299-518-6

eBook ISBN: 978-1-63299-517-9

First Edition

For Allie and Anna and in memory of their mother, Rebecca

"So lovely was the loneliness
Of a wild lake, with black rock bound
And the tall pines that tower'd round."

—EDGAR ALLEN POE, *The Lake*

"Time wasted at the lake is time well spent."

—ANONYMOUS

PART ONE:

SAVAGE ELEMENTS

Why should we fear
To be crushed by savage elements,
We who are made up
Of the same elements?

—RALPH WALDO EMERSON

Prologue

~~~~~~~~~~~~~~~~

ON THE
TWISTED-SOMETHING
EXPRESS

A swirling flood of memory fragments. Fleeting, chaotic. Then little islands of recollection. A trial. The bathroom stall. Avoiding the hook on the inside door. That weirdly lettered envelope. Footsteps, but no one there. Running on the street toward the sheriff's department. The dude in the baseball cap.

He'd been shot by someone he didn't know. He was pretty sure of that.

There was a struggle, he vaguely remembered, but not with the man in the baseball cap who'd followed him. No, he was suffocating. Choking to death on his own blood. He'd fought with the ambulance guys. Had he really pulled off the oxygen mask to tell them that he couldn't breathe? Was that idiot him?

They must have sedated him at some point. He could recall little after the moment when two paramedics forced a fat needle into his chest. In for a second and then back out.

His memory whirled around aboard a wobbly state fair ride the name of which he couldn't remember. The Twisted-Something. Loved it as a kid.

Now, here he was at Grace Church in Lower Manhattan, happily marrying Madeline. Shit. Maddy was walking off with Walter. Her big, dumb banjo player.

Oh, but now there was Tara. Brown eyes. Blue Lake. Their white pine. That night in the hotel. Had Tara really been his lover?

Now, along came his little brother, Justin, tagging behind him in a purple stocking cap, pulling a wooden sled up a hill. Cute little fucker. Thump, the sled would land him back at the courthouse square.

He was presiding over a big trial. There was an afternoon break. He was standing in a stall in the men's room. Avoiding another sneak attack conversation at the urinal from Earl. A thick envelope was pushed under the door. JUDGE JASON ERICKSON was typed on the outside in mismatched letters. Jason flung open the stall just as the bathroom door was closing.

He ran to the door but there was no one there. He bolted from the bathroom and hurried down the old brownstone courthouse steps, so stately and beautiful. Jason ran past the enormous new jail. He had to get that envelope to the police. Suddenly, he was overtaken by the man in the baseball cap.

A black-and-white S. Was that a Chicago White Sox cap? The man was bearing down on him. Then he called out, "Jason, Jason!"

The man reached into a paper bag and pulled something out. A gun! The shock of it. That sound! That strangely familiar, terrifying sound. The dull thud of his body hitting the concrete.

He'd been shot by that skinny dude in the Sox cap. Fitting, since he'd always hated the White Sox. The banjo too!

The whole cycle would start over again. Struggling with the mask, highlights of his whole life circling the painful sequence, and off to other worlds.

At one point, Jason came to long enough to lift his head. He peered out at his circumstances. He was in a hospital. They were giving him oxygen. Cool, misty, and choking, all at the same time. Overhead, all around him, were bags of fluids, suction canisters, and hoses. That thick tube in his chest.

A woman was standing there. Grace? He was hoping for Tara.

Exhausted from having slightly lifted his head, he wobbled back aboard the Twisted-Something Express, and back to sleep.

Chapter One

~~~~~~~~~~~~~

ALONG THE UPPER
MISSISSIPPI

By the time Judge Jason Erikson had packed up and secured the exhibits, it was already past 10:00 p.m. and both of the local Alma motels were full. The parties had agreed to run the Dog Lover's pet food trial late so that everyone would be home in time for trick-or-treating tomorrow. It had been a long day. A woman had cried trying to describe what life was like living next to the sickening smells of the fat-rendering plant. *Fresh-roasted death,* she'd called it. *Twenty-four seven.*

They'd been on the record for more than twelve hours.

The night air was still unusually muggy and warm. Jason loaded the banker's boxes into the trunk of his car and put his suitcase in the back seat. He got into his trusty, state-issued Ford Focus and blasted a playlist from his phone to keep himself awake. Driving up from Madison this morning, the sandstone bluffs along the Mississippi had been aflame with the dazzling colors of late October.

Now, as Jason drove the narrow, winding road beside them, the dark hills filled him with gloom. He was tired, and both the season and this geography were fraught with memories. Down the river an hour or so, when Jason was just fourteen, his father's funeral was held on a snowy day just after Halloween.

Then, two years ago, Madeline had convinced him to go to Halloween Freak Fest on State Street in downtown Madison. In costume, of course. Jason went as a fairly decent Ace of Spades, and Maddy was a seductive Sexy Nurse. Freak Fest had settled down a lot since its near-riot days, and Jason had been ready to head home by 11:30. Madeline was surprisingly determined to stay, until she accidentally ran into Walter at the stroke of midnight.

Walter was in a brown bear costume that perfectly matched his auburn beard. The Sexy Nurse and the Grizzly Bear had shimmied together for the next hour. Jason had watched them warily as he danced with a group of college-aged Vampire Girls.

It was suddenly all clear to him.

Her new interest in country folk. Dragging Jason to see Blue Ox Bluegrass, Walter's band, a couple of times. The nights he'd called her from the road and she hadn't picked up. Madeline had at least shown the decency to wait until the next afternoon to confess to her ongoing affair.

But Halloween was now more or less a permanent Bummer Fest for him. Without someone to go home to, these days on the road could get a little bleak. This time of year made him feel like brittle kindling, in need of a fire.

There was a motel ahead. He pulled in, saw the No Vacancy light flicker, and got back on the dark highway. It was hard to believe that he'd been doing this for sixteen years now, traveling around Wisconsin to hear environmental cases.

At first, it was a great opportunity to have a real say about things that he cared about. Jason had convinced himself for years that the job was a great fit, but he was never home. He covered the whole state, and there was so much driving! Still, he felt some obligation to stay.

Since the new governor had taken office in 2011, there was constant political pressure on regulators to do what donors wanted rather than what the law required. His new boss had no backbone, and state politics now meant winner-take-all. It was demoralizing, but he tried to just keep calling balls and strikes. So far, the higher courts had mostly backed him up.

Ahead to his left was a sign that said Rooms in orange neon. Jason pulled his car around back. He remembered it now. It was a flophouse for the barge handlers who docked at all hours of the day or night. There was a black Prius parked in back as he pulled in. Please, not someone from the trial! The last thing he needed was to share a bathroom with someone lobbying him to do something.

The flophouse lobby was surprisingly clean and spacious with a high ceiling and lit by table lamps. Olive lampshades with knitted tassels. A large calico cat was perched on top of an old oak armoire, just above a sign that said: AFTER 11 PM, PLEASE DEPOSIT $10 CASH HERE. There was an arrow indicating a slot in a locked drawer.

Jason was pleased to see that, instead of the expected windbag, it was Tara Highsmith, that fine journalist, standing at the front desk. She was always insightful, accurate, and a bit shy.

"Hi, Tara, sorry we went so late. Pretty dull stuff," he said. "Anybody around?"

"No." She smiled. "And it's not quite eleven."

The proprietor came shuffling out, sporting a sleeveless white T-shirt and suspenders.

"One or two rooms?" the old man asked, looking them over.

"Oh, we're not together," Tara replied. She had a novel tucked under her purse, *Outline* by Rachel Cusk.

"Our trial went late," Jason offered.

"You're both here for a trial?"

"Yes, that rendering plant hearing," Jason said.

"Smells like hell. Just a brutal odor, like dead bodies," the old man said. He handed each of them oversize keys that were attached to ping-pong paddles. "Hard to lose these keys. You're in four and you're in five. You share a bath."

Damn, that was a little much. Close quarters. They walked down the hall together with their bags.

"Ladies first on the bath."

"Thanks, Judge."

"Call me Jason, please."

"Okay. Sure," Tara said as he turned down the hall. "Hey, Jason, you don't happen to have any Benadryl, do you? I'm really allergic to cats."

"I think so. It helps me sleep. Meet me in the lobby in ten minutes?" Was he overplaying his hand? "I've got two cold ales to wash it down with."

She nodded. "See you in ten!"

They sat down together beside one of the little olive lamps and matching antique chairs in the front of the lobby facing the Mississippi. The old house had been built on high ground, and the large window had an expansive view of the river and lights on the dock below. The window was propped open with a title-less old book.

Tara was probably a few years younger than him. Late thirties to early forties. She looked youthful, in her skinny jeans, white top, and an earth-toned, green-and-brown plaid jacket that brought out her big brown eyes. He handed her a couple of Benadryl and a bottle of Moon Man pale ale.

"Nice and cold," Tara said.

"I keep a little cooler in my trunk."

"Great. I like this one. Cheers, Jud . . . Jason!"

"Cheers, Tara. Thought today would never end."

"So many descriptions of the foul odor!"

"I think nauseating is pretty accurate," Jason said.

"Putrid, I had that in my story. Revolting is good, too."

"Rendering plants—God—let's talk about something else." He

shook his head. "I noticed your book—how do you like the Rachel Cusk?"

"You know her?" Tara asked.

He nodded. "I try to keep up a little. I was an English major."

"Me too."

They both paused to enjoy a long freight train rumbling below them along the Upper Mississippi. His father used to make Jason and his brother count the cars on these river freighters. There was now a cooling breeze coming off the river.

"Better view from here than at the motel."

"I love this area. So, where are you from?" Tara asked.

"Milwaukee, the east side. Three blocks from Lake Michigan. And you?"

"Grew up in Minneapolis, grad school in Boston, and now six newspaper jobs since I got my Science Journalism MS."

"I spent some time out east too. New York, mostly. Sometimes wonder why I came back!"

He'd married Madeline and lived happily in Park Slope, but returned to Wisconsin for grad school. Law for him, social work for her. They'd settled in Madison and found good jobs. Time, his life, glided by.

"At least you're in Madison. You should try Green Bay." She smiled. "There's the Packers and the bay, the Packers and Door County."

"Don't forget the Cheeseheads and the Packers." Jason looked at her hand. No ring.

"This is nice," she said. "We've done all of those trials together, but never really talked."

"We did the CDF in Green Bay that was denied."

"Yes, the landfill in the bay next to the kids' park!" Tara smirked. "Thanks for denying that harebrained idea."

"Your stories on that were great, by the way. They probably made it easier for me to do that."

She nodded.

"Tough time to be in the environmental field in this state."

"Yes, the governor from hell," Tara replied, sipping her ale. "And of course, print journalism is thriving right now."

"Well, I never thought I'd be making the world safe for pet food."

Tara smiled. "You do a lot more than that."

"Something has kept me doing this for so long." Part of it was inertia, but he also worried that whoever took his place wouldn't stand up to the political pressure as well. However decent or deluded his intentions, he sometimes felt the job sucking the very sap of life out of him. Giant, rattling pans of it. But probably a lot of people felt that way.

"In a nineteenth-century novel, they'd call me *a mid-level functionary in the provincial capital.*"

She had an honest, earthy laugh that he recognized from the trial.

"One thing I've always wondered," she began. "Do you get pressure from the governor's office?"

"This is all off the record, right?" Jason looked directly into Tara's brown eyes. Eyes that would be so easy to get lost in.

"Of course!"

"I do, but I just ignore it," he replied. Sometimes they made that hard, threatening to discipline him. "So far, the higher courts have sustained. But they're getting so partisan, too. It's depressing." He sighed. "But you know, a couple of weeks ago, I was jogging in the university arboretum and a student ran along with me. The young man told me that he wanted to go to law school someday to become an environmental decision-maker. It was good to remember that I had someone's dream job. How about your job?"

"I'm not sure how many more local environmental cases they'll let me cover." She shook her head. "It's gotten way more difficult since the merger."

"Do you still like the job?"

"I like the work, but for me it's the hours."

"Me too, not great for the home life." He didn't want to get into his divorce. Madeline had said it was hard to be married to someone who was gone so much. He'd done fifty-five overnight trips that last year. How many had she shared with Walter?

"I got kicked out of my book club because I'm never there for the meetings!" Tara said.

"You're kidding. That sucks."

"It was a hard blow." She shook her head with a smile and kicked off her shoes.

It was true, he was brittle kindling in need of a book club. "Maybe we should start our own?"

"I'd like that," she agreed. "But we'd have to do it by email."

"Works for me." He extended his hand. She gave him hers and he held it. She had long fingers and a delicate wrist.

"First up, *Outline*. I'm only five pages in."

"Deal." Jason let go of her hand.

There was another long flash of lights from below, but quieter than a train. A barge was approaching, its bright searchlight panning from port to starboard.

"Beautiful, the lights on the black water."

"Yes, lovely." Her head swayed toward him a bit as she spoke.

She looked out at the river and he glanced at her. Her eyes were the color of his favorite dark chocolate bar.

They quietly watched the barge approach and then dock. He liked sitting there next to Tara, someone so familiar and yet unknown. He'd always admired her professionalism and talent. They'd smiled at each other a couple of times over the long day. She was shy, but confident and witty.

"Shall we have a toast?" he asked.

"I'm afraid that I've already finished mine."

"I've got two more." Jason didn't want their night to end. "What do you say?"

"Why not?" Tara shrugged. She stepped back into her shoes. "I'll hit the bathroom while you get them."

That meant they both were going down the same narrow hallway that led to their rooms and the shared bath. Their arms touched briefly before Tara went ahead. Jason went into his room and found his cooler. He stopped at the bathroom before bringing the cooler out to the front room where Tara was waiting.

"You brought the whole cooler this time," she joked.

"There are a couple of waters in there, too."

He opened two beers and they clinked the bottles.

"Cheers," he said.

"Cheers," she agreed, smiling. "Do you come to this area much for work?"

"Some. Air cases, mostly. They're taking down some of these bluffs for fracking sand. It's supposed to be the perfect weight for it."

"What a shame. This area is so unique. Minnesota has a moratorium."

"Minnesota has common sense," Jason said. "My dad would've been so upset! He was obsessed with this area. He grew up in La Crosse, and used to drag us over here a lot when we were kids." He paused. "We lost him thirty years ago, more or less today."

"I'm sorry. I'm lucky to have both of my parents. Most of the time, that is."

"Yes." Jason let out a slightly embarrassing laugh. "And I'm lucky to know this beautiful area pretty well, even if this time of year makes me a little sad." He was on the verge of telling her about Madeline, but Tara seemed excited to talk about something.

"Have you ever run into Phil Lewis at any of your hearings?"

"Is that the landscape professor, the Circle Cities guy?"

"Yes! Lewis talks a lot about this area and the Driftless Area bluffs being the natural center of the whole area between Chicago and Minneapolis. He said that they should be preserved, kind of like the Adirondacks."

"I agree. Taking them down for fracking sand is pretty shortsighted." He smiled. "All of this is still off the record, right?"

"Hah, of course! For me as well?"

He nodded. She took his hand to shake on it this time. But soon she checked her phone.

"Oh my God," she said. "It's almost midnight. I'd better get settled before the barge handlers arrive." She stood up and handed him a card with her personal email on it. "But I'm excited about our book club!"

"Me, too."

Jason wondered if he should get up and give her a hug, but she was gone before he decided. He lingered in the lucky olive chair until he heard footsteps and voices approaching from the river. He didn't want to meet any barge handlers tonight, and didn't want to spoil the mellow mood. He got up and headed into the bathroom and then room number five.

He'd just pulled off his tie when he heard a knock. Could it be? Yes, it *was* Tara.

"Look, there's something I should've told you." She paused. "I'm married."

"Of course," he replied, trying not to betray his disappointment. "I'm divorced."

"I hope it's not a deal breaker for our book club." She looked disappointed too. Or maybe she was just tired?

Chapter Two

~~~~~~~~

A FRIEND FROM WORK

The Benadryl Jason had given Tara put her right to sleep. The trial started at eight o'clock the next morning. There was some rot-gut coffee in the lobby, which she diluted with sugar and some nasty chemicals masquerading as non-dairy creamer. She was pretty sure that Jason was already out and on his way to court. She'd heard the squawking shower run at some ungodly hour.

Tara quickly showered and dressed. Last night was a rare moment of connection in her lonely life. It was a bit ironic because this might be one of their last trials together.

Last week, corporate headquarters had arrived, with their expensive suits and sweaty palms, to lecture them on how to maximize profits, or at least minimize the bleeding. Tara had been specifically singled out as an anachronism—a local environmental reporter? No, the story now was climate change—not local issues that couldn't fit in national papers.

The suits said that Tara was a talented reporter, but that there may well be a need for her to change her practice and try to find a national perspective in a majority of her articles, so that content could be shared by others with similar concerns. Fine. Tara was okay with that.

But there might also be a "need" for Tara to cover other areas of readership concern. Health, food, wellness, all of it involved science. These stories, too, could lead to nationally syndicated bylines. There was a bottomless appetite for it among readers, the suits said. But Tara had no desire to write fluffy Lifestyle clickbait pushing super foods, float therapy, or CBD oil. She'd rather be out in the field with the putrid odors, dead fish, and brown water that were part of people's lives.

When Tara arrived at court with one minute to spare, Jason greeted her with a nod and a smile. The judge looked fresh in his dark suit, white shirt, and a bright blue tie the same color as his eyes. He had thick, wavy black hair. Sitting close last night, she'd noticed his long eyelashes. They'd stood out in the soft light of the table lamp.

She spent the morning rewriting her story about the rendering plant, adding telling little details in real time as they came in. She had it filed before lunch and had even included some background to give the story a national angle. Take that, suits.

At lunchtime, Jason approached her. "I'm heading to Emma's downtown for lunch if you care to join me."

"Sure." Her husband, Michael, was always amazed that she went to lunch with local judges and mayors all the time, but it was part of her job. Not usually her favorite part, to be sure.

It was four blocks away in downtown Alma, and they were able to walk down the steep hill toward the Mississippi. The sky was an inviting blue and the river a darker indigo, the color of a pair of earrings Michael had given her.

"Last night was fun," she said. "Sorry if I startled you in your room."

"No, I'm glad you did," Jason said. "Otherwise, I'd be nervous as hell right now and wondering if this was a date."

"Ha." No comment. Tara knew the wisdom of that simple phrase. "Well, there's no doubt we have a lot in common."

"Yes, two English majors made pretty good."

They arrived at Emma's, where there were pictures of Mark Twain everywhere. Young and dashing with a dark moustache. Old and ironic with hair as white as his suit. There was one photo from around the time Twain wrote about the bluffs and fine architecture of La Crosse in *Life on the Mississippi*. Tara took a picture of the quote with her phone.

"What's up with the Mark Twain theme?" she asked as they waited.

"Emma told me her whole life story one time. Grew up in East Germany loving Mark Twain's novels and wit. As soon as she could, she moved here and found a place to buy on the Mississippi."

Emma turned to them. "Yes, that man lured me here." She pointed at the younger Mr. Clemens. "Damn him." She seated them with a flourish. "You're back," Emma said to the judge as he sat down. "And you've brought your lovely wife."

"No, a friend from work," he replied casually.

Yes, that's what they were, like Michael and his colleague Susan.

Tara wasn't thrilled when she saw the menu. It was almost all pork and beef, and she didn't eat red meat. Schweinelendchen in a Pfefferahm Sauce, Schweine Haxen and Bavarian Weisswurst.

"I don't eat my fellow mammals," Tara said, trying not to sound snotty.

"Me either. I usually just get fried eggs and home fries here."

They ordered the same.

"I gave up red meat in 2000 after I read this article about climate change," Jason said.

"That's amazing. Because I did too. A *New York Times* article that said quitting red meat did as much as not driving your car to work!"

"We probably read the same one." Jason grinned. "So why Green Bay?"

"Michael, my husband, got a job, and I was able to transfer there. One of the few benefits of chain newspapers." But Michael's job took him to California and the east coast, and Tara went to Alma and West Bend, Wisconsin. "He still gets to fly all over the country."

"And you get to drive here?"

She nodded, as they began to wolf down their eggs. There was just enough time to eat them and dash back to the courthouse together.

"I ordered a copy of *Outline* during a break," Jason said, as they hit the sidewalk.

"Aww, that's great. You get to pick the next one."

She was trying to normalize it, with him and in her own mind. Would she tell Michael?

The afternoon passed quickly. It was amazing how fast lawyers could work when they were rushing to get home to their kids in costumes. They wrapped up around 3:30 p.m.

It was a four-and-a-half-hour drive from Alma back to Green Bay. From the west coast of Wisconsin, the Mississippi, back to the east coast of Green Bay and Lake Michigan.

Tara called Michael on her way home.

"Hey, Michael. I'm glad I caught you."

"How was Alma?" he asked.

"It's cute. A little strip of classic small-town shops between some big sandstone bluffs and the Mississippi. Pretty. There are a few hilly streets, but not much else. I had to stay in a flophouse because the trial went so late." Should she tell him about the judge? About the book club? "The judge was staying there, too, and we had a beer together in the lobby."

"That's a nice contact to have made," Michael replied.

"Yes, we're going—"

"—Look, my plane is boarding," Michael said abruptly. "Let's talk tonight; I'll call you if it doesn't get too late. Otherwise, I'll text you."

That night, she told Michael about the book club and their lunch. No reaction. Michael said he'd gone out with a colleague that day as well. Tara had a pretty clear idea of which one. Susan Gunderson. Mike seemed to have a slight crush on her. He'd told Tara that he thought Susan looked like the actress Elisabeth Moss. Tara didn't like to be catty, but Elisabeth Moss was kind of a stretch!

And about six months ago, she and Mike had gone to a friend's

fortieth birthday party. Michael had spent the evening basically cud-
dling with Susan, who had an arm around him all night. Tara had made
it pretty plain that she didn't approve. But Mike was oblivious to her
entreaties, and Tara didn't want to make a scene.

"How can you be mad?' he asked her on the drive home. "I never
touched her!"

"She had her arms around you all night. Would you say the same
thing if I'd done it?"

Not in a million years. They were growing apart in so many ways.

Michael's recent focus on making money was slightly alarming too.
He'd even done consulting work on the side for one of the mortgage
companies that had been sued several times for fraud and contributed
to the crash of 2008.

"I haven't done anything wrong." Michael dismissed her concerns.
"I've just done their IT. If not me, they'd find some other techie."

"Well, then it would be on that person that they're propping up
these greedy bastards." They didn't have the same personal ethics.

Tara had been surprised to hear herself agree to Jason's book club
idea. It was pretty clearly a flirtatious joke. But Michael did what he
wanted, and she was going to start doing that too. It was just a book
club, after all.

Within the week, she'd received an email from Jason with the subject heading Jason's Outline of *Outline*. He'd hit the highlights of the
novel narrator's engrossing conversations with sometimes complete
strangers who shared their most intimate secrets. They casually put
forth their best rationalizations for their failed marriages, careers, and
doomed families.

One theme Cusk gleaned from this was the idea that a marriage
was mostly a shared vision and story. When that was gone, it seemed
the marriage was doomed to fail. Jason had written just two sentences
about his own divorce, but their story seemed to fit the pattern.

He admitted that maybe his wife had chosen her new partner

because he was everything that Jason was not. Jason was serious and intellectualized his feelings. Walter was fun-loving and an open book. After being offended, he'd come around to understanding her choice and accepting that they probably weren't right for each other. Was there such a thing as being right for each other? He wasn't sure.

Tara wasn't, either. Suddenly she was telling Jason about her own marriage. About Mike's lack of curiosity and increasing obsession with material success. She was trying to keep a shared vision but it seemed to be getting harder and harder.

Michael had stopped reading books several years ago, even as her own reading had seemed more essential to her now than ever. She'd seen where journalism was heading and was now writing poems and essays too. A friend of hers from the Milwaukee paper was writing a book about the Great Lakes. Maybe she'd end up doing something like that.

Tara was spilling her most intimate secrets to her new friend. Well, some of them. She didn't tell him about Susan, Michael's work friend. Tara didn't want to rationalize in the way of Cusk's characters. People talked themselves into and out of affairs so easily, but that was not her style.

Nor did she mention that she was still open to having kids—something that Michael wouldn't even consider. She was thirty-eight and heard the clock ticking. She boldly asked Jason if he ever heard it too.

She was playing with fire! But the warmth of it made her feel more alive.

Chapter Three

~~~~~~~~~~

HALLOWEEN SALMON

Grace Clarkson tried to take her mother to lunch once a week. Her mom was eighty and used a walker. But Grace didn't have two hours to spare that week, so they made it an early dinner at her mom's favorite, the Waterfront, for Thursday. Grace hadn't realized then that Thursday was Halloween. She left out a huge bowl of candy at her house before going to get her mom.

Grace got her mother in and out of her car and seated at a prime table, with enough space to stash her mom's walker out of the way of the waitress.

"Oh, there's still lots of color," her mom observed pleasantly. She was looking out at the river and looking spry in a dark orange sweater and black silk scarf. "I love this view."

"Me too, Mom. And the salmon, too."

"You can't beat the salmon here." That was at least as much an article of faith for her as the Lutheran Book of Worship. "The Waterfront does an excellent salmon."

"I agree," said Grace.

The food was terrific, and the view of the tree-lined Mississippi and blue bridge over it never got old for either of them.

A tall man in his mid-forties was being seated near them. He looked vaguely familiar in his dark suit, white shirt, and blue tie. Some lawyer she knew? Or had he been at one of those lame speed dating lunches?

"Do you see what I see?" her mother sang out cheerfully. "No ring, either."

"Your eyes are amazing since that surgery." Hopefully, the man couldn't hear.

Her mother had been literally praying for Grace to find a new love for almost twenty years now, after her tragic early marriage. Her mom's generation couldn't feel complete without a partner and kids. Grace thought she could, most of the time, anyway.

Losing Jon, she'd lost the whole life she'd planned. That they'd planned together. They were not going to sell anything, buy, or process anything—as the John Cusack character says in *Say Anything*, one of Jon's favorite movies.

They'd planned instead to be two ass-kicking lawyers who were going to do good but have way more fun than any do-gooder they'd ever known. They'd shared so much. An attitude toward life, most of all. For one thing, there was no way they would have wound up in La Crosse.

Grace had started working for her Uncle Ray in downtown La Crosse just after Jon's death, after her second summer of law school. Ray gave her a safe place to land. She was just a summer law clerk, but he kindly put her on the firm's health insurance.

You and your mom are my only family.

Ray himself was unmarried. He "came out" to her one night after she'd joined the firm that next summer. For many years, he'd loved Chris, a man who'd been his college roommate and who lived 30 miles up the Mississippi in Winona, Minnesota. They both lived alone and regularly but discreetly saw each other. Ray was known for his love of theater. He'd acted in the Winona Shakespeare Festival and was in many plays there with Chris.

"Gracie, do you want to know my deepest, darkest secret?" he'd asked that night at the bar. They were both a little drunk. Whiskey sours.

"Of course, the deeper the better!" She assumed it was the setup for a joke.

"I've had two great passions in my life—Will and Chris."

"Will, meaning Shakespeare?"

He nodded.

"And Chris, meaning the love of your life?" Grace asked.

He nodded again, playfully. Vintage Ray. It wasn't a huge surprise. His friend had been around enough that she'd called him Uncle Chris as a girl.

"That's wonderful," she said. "Thanks for trusting me. You know I adore Chris."

At the hospital just before Ray died, he pulled her close.

"It's all yours now, Gracie, the practice and the building. Do what you want with them. They're your inheritance and not meant to be a burden." But, of course, they'd both helped keep Grace in La Crosse. In her hometown.

Grace had plenty of opportunities and even a couple of marriage proposals. The first had come too soon, or she might have happily accepted it. The second had felt like it would be settling, and that was hard to do after the legacy of her first love. None of her new relationships had lasted. She was still waiting for lightning to strike again rather than settle into something she'd regret.

Her mom needed her. Her clients too. Was it enough? Was being a hometown hero what she wanted?

Grace and her mom both ordered the salmon and were clinking glasses when the man in the suit slowly approached them.

"Excuse me," the man said. "Is your name Grace?"

"It certainly is!" her mom said.

"I'm Jason Erickson, from law school."

"Nice to see you, Jason." Grace got up and they embraced. She turned to her mom. "We were in a couple of study groups together."

"Would you like to join us, Jason?" her mom asked.

"Oh, no. I don't want to crash your dinner," he said. "I need to catch up on my work emails. I just wanted to say hi to Grace. What kind of practice do you have these days?"

"Litigation, lots of trials," she replied. He still had the wavy dark hair and bright blue eyes that she remembered from law school. Grace had always liked the calm way he answered questions in Civil Procedure. He'd even asked her out once, not knowing she and Jon were married. "And you?" Grace asked.

"I'm an ALJ, mostly for the state EPA. I was just coming from a case up in Alma, but I thought I'd stop in for some of the salmon."

"Now, there's a man with good taste," her mother put in promptly. "You can't beat the salmon at the Waterfront."

Chapter Four

<center>~~~~~~~~~</center>

WEEDS, WILDFLOWERS, AND PAINTED TREES

Jason was trying to focus on the boring but important late afternoon testimony of a water chemist, but it was the third day of the Christmas tree trial. He was tired and a little distracted. For one thing, he couldn't get his mind off Tara, who was seated in the front row to his right. This was becoming a problem whenever his journalist friend was covering one of his newsworthy cases.

They always wound up spending so much time together. On and off the record. She was married but he was nonetheless taken with her. But if he turned his head away from Tara to focus on the witness, he saw the shimmering waters of Blue Lake.

It was early May, and even this northern lake was gloriously open, still and deep. No motorboats were allowed, just the odd canoe. Diving birds: heron, osprey, and loons. The play of sunlight on the deep blue water. After a couple of long days on the record, it was easy enough to get distracted.

The past two nights, Jason had walked with Tara along the public access path that wound around the maple-and-birch-lined lakefront. Hundreds of acres of undisturbed wetlands teeming with birds, shrubby bog laurel, and lush grasses. Together they'd identified wild raspberry, sarsaparilla, and numerous other flowering bushes that dotted the scrubby underbrush just off the path.

They'd made plans, again, for tonight after the hearing.

"Why does the Christmas tree farm need a water permit to paint the trees?" asked Mark Strand, the frequently sarcastic attorney for the objectors.

"Because it discharges into a stream within a thousand feet of the lake, and it's not a good idea to let paint solvents into the streams that feed this pristine lake," the water chemist replied.

Jason had heard him testify numerous times in recent years. He was a persuasive, if slightly monotone, witness.

"Are all Christmas trees painted?" Strand's face betrayed a smirk.

"I'm a water chemist and not a tree farm guy, but my understanding is that the colorant is applied to most commercially sold Christmas trees." His face betrayed no humor. "It helps them retain moisture and last longer, too." Of course Christmas trees are painted.

"Is it an accident that Blue Lake is pristine, while so many others are not?" Strand asked.

"Objection, vague," the tree farm's attorney, Cindy Northrup, said.

"Go ahead," Jason said. Please, put us all out of our misery sooner.

"No, Blue Lakers banned the clear-cutting of trees within the village one hundred years ago and prohibited building too close to the lake. That's why you still have all of these wetlands and such great water quality." The chemist looked directly at the crowd. "And the turnout at this hearing has shown how much people care about this lake. That's pretty exceptional too."

Yesterday had been best practices in paint application day—the intricacies and pros and cons of spraying (generates an even coat but also lots of runoff called *overspray*) and dipping (less paint waste but more variation in colors and perhaps impractical with trees) had been discussed ad nauseam. They'd also considered the ins and outs of electrostatic sprays and powder coating and water-wash versus dry-filter booths.

The usual grinding battle of experts.

Most of the time the angry crowds fled the tedious testimony, but yesterday they'd started off at 8:30 a.m. and, damn, if there weren't still fifty local residents there when Jason finally shut it down at 6:45 p.m. He and Tara had marveled at the passion and brute chair-sitting ass-chops of the Blue Lakers over dinner last night.

Jason snuck a glance at Tara now. Those bright brown eyes, slightly amused, as always. Maybe she was also excited about the outing they were planning tonight?

They were both intrigued by old-growth trees, and there was said to be a world-record white pine just a half-hour's drive outside of Blue Lake. He was going to try to shut the hearing down at five to make sure they could get there and back before dark.

Karen Jones, a local science teacher who'd just arrived, began cross-examining the chemist. "Why is it important to keep paint solvents out of the air and water, Dr. Benson?"

"Objection." Strand stood. "We spent all morning on that, Your Honor. And it's almost five o'clock."

"Sustained. I'm sorry, Ms. Jones, but we've covered this extensively. Let's try to finish up with this witness and break for the day at five o'clock."

Tara sought out his eyes and gave him a conspiratorial smile. Her thick lips naturally curled upward, always seemingly on the verge of a wisecrack. Her articles about the Christmas tree case were incisive and clever. The one with the corny headline, *Painted Trees Have Blue Lake Greens Seeing Red*, also had all of the water chemistry right.

"I just have one more question, Your Honor."

"Go ahead."

"Couldn't you cut them and spray them somewhere farther away from the lake?"

"Objection," Strand said.

"Sustained. It's another great question, but I'm sure we spent several hours on that point as well."

"I'm glad that's being considered." Ms. Jones looked disappointed rather than glad. Everyone always wanted to ask the question that changed everything. "Okay, that's all the questions I have. Thanks."

"Anyone else?" Jason asked, packing up his things. No one else came forward, and the day mercifully came to an end.

Jason ran to his hotel room, changed into jeans and his running shoes, and gobbled down a veggie sandwich in the hotel lobby. Tara showed up just as he'd finished. She looked relaxed in her jeans and purple Patagonia windbreaker. She'd pulled her hair into a simple ponytail.

"Ready to find that world champion pine?" she asked.

He nodded, and they set out for the old tree together in her messy Prius. It was a disaster. There was dog hair everywhere and a pile of books strewn about the backseat.

"Google Maps is pretty useless out there, but the National Forest Map should be back there somewhere," Tara said. "Sorry for the mess."

"Yeah, no problem. Just go out 49 North for now. Here it is. These maps are always a little confusing."

"Tell me about it," she replied. "The Forest Service is coming out with digital maps this fall."

Their way to Old Sven, as the locals had named the champion white pine, was full of sharp turns and winding gravel roads. Jason reached into the back seat and began sorting through the books. There were four or five on weeds of the Upper Midwest.

"*Minnesota Weeds and Wildflowers* . . . You like weeds, huh?"

"Some of them." Tara laughed. "I'm just trying to learn more about plants, and a whole lot of them are what we call weeds. I read that the average American can identify one thousand corporate logos but only ten native plants and animals . . . So, I'm trying to work my way up."

"I'm probably a bad American because I doubt if I know that many logos. But I've learned about a bunch of plants doing this job." He held up a photo of a little pink flower with brown-mottled leaves, his hand over the text. "Do you know this one? Hint, it has a very cool name."

"I am driving here, Jason." She glanced at it carefully. "Is that the white trout lily?"

"Yes!" Jason said. "Well done."

Tara was beaming. She kept her back very straight while driving. Her posture was impeccable. He tried not to notice her lovely neck.

"It sometimes seems that we don't understand the natural world simply because we don't know it," she said.

"These Blue Lakers sure do. Did you notice how much of the crowd stayed all day again?"

"Yes, I counted almost forty. The only other place where I've seen people come out and stay like that is Green Lake," Tara said. "After our conversation last night, I was thinking about it. People have some deep need to be by water. Some connection there."

"Well, if you live by a lake, you have lots of reasons to care about water quality. But, living next to water, you're forced to deal with the weather, the seasons, flooding, the unpredictability of nature. Lakes are real, part of the natural order." The natural order? He heard himself waxing eloquent, a sure sign that he was trying to impress her. And Tara had a way of disabusing him of his creeping cynicism. She was earnest, almost guileless at times.

"People need and expect more from nature these days." She bobbed her head in the distinctive way she did when she was happy. "There's a line from Stanley Krutch, 'St. Francis preached to the birds, but now people expect the birds to preach to them.'"

"Nice!" Jason looked up from the map. "I think we turn right here and it should be just down this road. There's a sign."

"Old Sven Please Park Here," she read, pulling in.

Tara hopped out of the car and was halfway down the short path to the champion tree. Jason hurried after her.

"Oh, no!" she cried. "Look!"

The record pine they'd been searching for had been battered. The smell of fire still lingered. Old Sven had suffered a devastating lightning strike. The giant tree had been hit about halfway up, and everything above its thick midsection was shorn off. The downed branches had already been hauled away. There were undignified tire tracks all around the majestic old tree.

"What a tragedy!" His hand went to her shoulder. Tara was silent. "What a grand life it had."

"It's been there for so long," she said at last.

They stood there for a few minutes, paying their respects to Old Sven. Tara was in his arms now, her head upon his shoulder. Just a friendly hug, he rationalized, but a longish one amid the blue smell of the pines.

Not long enough.

On the drive back, Tara put on a solemn Gregorian chant and turned up the volume. Jason found it slightly overwrought at first. He was no medievalist. But then he lost himself in the rhythmic music. In the moment. The memory of having her in his arms.

"Turn right there," he said, "and it's a straight shot to the hotel."

The orangey sunset was now behind them. He tried to resist taking her hand in his, but soon she offered it to him. Neither said anything all the way back to the hotel. Holding hands.

It was almost dark now. She pulled into the parking lot and they both got out and hugged.

"Good night," he said, glad to have her in his arms again.

"Good night, Jason." She gave him a fierce squeeze and mumbled something into his shoulder. Did she say, "I need you?" Or was it, "Thank you?"

He would have asked her which, but she'd already hurried into her room.

Chapter Five

~~~~~~~~~~~~~~

MAFIOSO?

T he next morning was a surprise. Off the record, the science teacher made a very practical suggestion for off-site spraying at another property that the experts agreed would be feasible. The tree farm guy ran some numbers and said it would add only a dollar to the cost of every tree. When Jason asked them about it, they said they could live with it to keep goodwill in the community. Within the hour, they'd formally agreed to paint the trees away from any streams, at another site that would not need a water permit.

Everyone seemed relieved. Jason put the settlement terms on the record, said goodbye to Tara, and drove back to his office in Madison. He arrived a little before lunch. His boss, Chief Judge Steve Hayman, was surprised to see him and quickly came into Jason's office.

Hayman was tall and stout. He still wore the kind of fat mustache that was popular in the 1970s, around the time Robert Redford played the Sundance Kid. The state's green metal office furniture was also a vestige from that era. The low ceilings of Jason's office made Hayman seem enormous, with his protruding belly and pleated pants.

"So, the famous Christmas tree case settled?" Hayman asked.

"Yes, they're outsourcing the tree painting to another site they own," Jason replied.

Hayman swayed nervously from foot to foot, like he was waiting to say something important.

"The timing is good because I have another Expedited Case for you," Hayman began. "It looks like a real bear. Earl Franks is representing this guy, Tommy Calandro, who is kind of an infamous Chicago-area wheeler-dealer."

"The Earl Franks?"

"I'm afraid so," Hayman replied.

"There goes my summer," Jason groaned. "You know what a pain in the ass he is. He files motions every other day."

Earl Franks had been a starting middle linebacker at the University of Michigan and that was how he practiced law. He was very old-school and aggressive, given to exaggerated facial expressions. Earl would bellow out *Objection!* without stating any substantive reason for it.

"Earl's a big personality, but you've handled him before," Hayman said. "It's actually a pretty interesting case."

"Oh yeah?"

"Tommy Calandro wants to convert the individual boat slips into condominiums known as 'slipominiums.' The legal arguments are about whether this would amount to selling the waters of the state, which belong to the public. It's clear under the law that you can rent out a boat slip each summer. But can you sell a permanent one? The decision could mean tens of millions of dollars to Calandro."

"Feel free to take it, Steve. It's all yours." Of course, his new boss wouldn't touch it. Hayman was obsessed with not jeopardizing his retirement.

"Nah, I've got that family reunion in Montana. But you'll be great. And look, in a few years you'll be the one assigning cases with the tough-guy lawyers and their Mafioso clients."

"Mafioso?" Jason asked. Great.

"Just kidding," Hayman dodged. "Really. Chicago and all that. People say all kinds of stuff. Anyway, they want to do the site inspection at the same time as the Water Law Conference."

"That's in two weeks, Steve."

"It's just convenient since you'll be there anyway," Hayman replied.

"How long of a hearing are they talking about?" Jason asked.

"They said two to three weeks in the request."

Jason knew that Tara's paper would never let her be there that long.

"Oh, they also want it expedited. The new forty-day rule and all that."

"This is going to eat up the whole summer," Jason lamented.

"You're the only one I trust with this." Hayman turned around to see himself out of Jason's office.

"Next time trust me a little less," Jason called.

Chapter Six

~~~~~~~~~~~~~~~~

PATHETIC

"Tampa Bay Derby. A thousand bucks on Timber Rattler to show," Earl Franks said, checking the time on his phone. Ten minutes before the cutoff. It was spring, at last, and big-time horse racing was back in Vegas.

"Good luck," said the bearded guy behind the window.

"Thanks. I need these Derby Prep ponies to produce."

"'Tis the season. Next!"

Earl checked his wallet. He still had all three tickets. He'd already put down thousand-dollar bets on the same horse to win and place. They gave you less grief about the size of your bets if you separated them. Otherwise, they sometimes went to get the manager when you put one big bet down. Even five thousand dollars. If only Tony Rossi and his other bookies had those kinds of limits. Earl wouldn't be sitting in the Sportsman's Video Lounge in Las Vegas.

Whenever he was short of money to pay off his Chicago obligations, he'd fly to Vegas and make legal bets on live simulcast horse races. Earl had listened to the Las Vegas Horse Racing podcast this morning and read and reread the Racing Forum and blogs. They were all very high on Timber Rattler to not only win Tampa Bay but also to be a threat all the way to Churchill Downs.

The video lounge had seven large screens and the feel of an airport bar. That same crappy appetizer smell, which Earl loved. He ordered a gin-and-tonic and found a seat as the Tampa Bay race came up on four of the video screens. Three of them had a soccer match on. Too bad he didn't know more about that. Maybe six or seven groaning soccer lovers under those and a dozen or so sweating it out with the ponies.

They were off—with a nice starting burst for Timber Rattler, who was running second around the first turn. Earl would be fine with either a place or a show, but a win would ease his present liquidity crisis.

"Go, Rattlesnake!" he called out. A popular sentiment in the lounge, and the horse must have heard them. Timber Rattler surged ahead to take the lead.

Soon, the other horses all made their move. Timber Rattler was back in second, then Miles Ahead surged past him and the lead horse too.

"Hang in there. It's only a mile!" the guy next to him yelled.

Mile races went by so fast. Hang in there, for sure. Please! Placing would be fine. What would he do if he lost?

Two horses came galloping from the middle track past him for a photo finish. Did he stay at third by a nose? The *Photo Finish* sign flashed on the screen. The guys next to him were split.

"Timber Rattler got toasted. And that means me, too."

"I think he held on," one of them hoped.

But the photo was clear. The tentative winners came up: Miles Ahead, Pickled Beets, and Go Lightly. Timber Rattler was fourth!

"Fixed!" the other losers cried.

It was supposed to be a sure thing. But these things *were* sometimes fixed, he had no doubt. Whenever he lost, he thought of Maggie, his ex-wife, looking at him with both pity and contempt. He marinated his losses in those memories.

"You're not the man I married," she'd said at the end. "You're not the man I thought you were." He'd gotten bombed and kissed one of her old friends on the lips.

"I'm sorry, Maggie. I was drunk. And I couldn't just sit there and pretend that we were the world's happiest couple, when you're dragging me to counseling."

"So that justifies it?" she asked. "I don't even know who you are anymore."

When they first got married, Earl had been a leader in the movement to ban PCBs in the state. There were glowing articles about him in all of the statewide newspapers, and the next thing he knew, he was the state attorney general. The youngest ever. He was just twenty-nine years old.

But now he'd begun to doubt if any of that activism had been real.

The idea to ban PCBs had come to him when 12,500 cans of PCB-contaminated salmon from Lake Michigan were seized by the Feds. After Rachel Carson, people were starting to get paranoid about toxic substances in the air and water. He knew he'd gotten lucky—the right place at the right time—and had ridden the *Silent Spring* train to state-wide office.

Ten years later, he was sworn in as a Wisconsin Supreme Court Justice when a Democratic governor appointed him to fill a vacancy.

"You don't even have the ambition anymore," Maggie said, shaking her head.

"I made $645,000 last year, plus my bonus."

"And there were three liens on your partnership bonus. Liens from people I've never heard of," Maggie reminded him.

Earl said nothing. It was better not to.

"Do you really love the horses, the numbers—all of that *stupid shit*—more than you love the kids and me?"

"Nah, don't talk like that." It was rare for her to swear, and it was wounding to hear it.

It'd been horse racing that had gotten him hooked on gambling.

Betting Belmont Park races at OTBs in New York in 1980, to be precise. There was a number you would call and a trumpet would play just before they announced the winners and payouts. That feeling of winning, of hearing your horse's name after the blast of the horn! It was the only thing he'd ever experienced that compared to sex. Even in his twenties.

Earl was then a law student at New York Law School—not NYU, for which half of his partners still gave him credit—where he'd hoped to go into the legal gambling offered on Wall Street. He'd hoped to buy a couple of brownstones in Brooklyn. Get into real estate a bit.

But the best job he could land was at the third-biggest firm in Milwaukee, back in his home state of Wisconsin. That's where he and Maggie had settled at first and had Laurie.

"Please don't leave me," he pleaded. "You *have* been the woman I thought you were for this whole time—" He'd reached something in her, because tears were now streaming down her face. But she was pissed. There was a steely look on her face he'd never seen.

"Don't try to give me any of your bull, Earl; I'm just not buying it anymore."

"You used to love what you called my roguish charm, my ungovernable spirit."

"It was charming when you were twenty-five—but it's pathetic now." Maggie shook her head and repeated. "Pathetic, there's no other word."

The next day Maggie set about packing with the same purposeful efficiency she might have given a church garage sale. By the next night, she was gone, and their house was listed.

The word "pathetic" was never more than ten words out of his mind for the next two or three years. It rang in his head again now, as he went up to the window to place his bets on the Florida Cup race tomorrow.

He had to get his juice back.

Chapter Seven

~~~~~~~~

HOW COULD SHE SAY
NO TO THAT HAIR?

On a particularly busy late-May day at Clarkson Law Office SC, the new office manager, Tom, came into Grace's office. "Grace, I hope you don't mind, but I told some folks, a big group, that they could talk to you for fifteen minutes about a potential hourly case."

"Great. We need some hourly cases if we're going to be doing all of these new contingency cases."

Tom was looking at her. He had thick blond eyebrows over piercing green eyes.

"What is it?" Grace asked.

"It's a group of neighbors who have wells that they believe have been contaminated with dairy manure."

"Groundwater cases can be kind of specialized."

"Yes, but it's basically just a public nuisance case like that Harris one you did a couple of years ago." Tom smiled, pleased with his own resourcefulness.

"You've been reading our old files." There were some major differences, of course, including the fact that the trial date would already be set. But Grace may have finally found someone to really help her run the office. "When are they coming?"

"Now. If that works—"

"Okay, that's fine. But please print out my calendar for the next four months. These cases go really fast," Grace replied. Being more efficient meant losing some control. "Just let me get these things signed first."

When Grace made it back to the conference room, there was a group of eight farmers, two married couples and four farm women, waiting for her return. She shook their hands and then mostly listened, though she found herself distracted by one of the women's hair. It was the sort of country bouffant favored by one of Grace's own aunts. It had been laboriously teased up and then hair-sprayed down to give it the appearance of indestructibility.

"My name is Irene Douglas," the woman said.

Midwestern women didn't wear them quite as big as their flashier Southern sisters. They just wanted to have their hair *done*—crossed off their endless list of chores—not to stand out in a crowd.

"I'm Grace Clarkson. You look familiar, Irene."

"Good memory. You helped my late husband, Jack, and me with a consumer credit issue a few years ago."

"I'm so sorry for your loss. I read about Jack in the Sunday paper."

"And I'm sorry for yours, too," Irene said.

The others nodded. Ray Clarkson, Grace's mentor and uncle, had been gone for a year and a half. The last time she'd seen one of those old-school bouffants had been at his funeral.

"Thank you. Why don't we all go around and say our names?" Grace suggested.

They did, as Grace carefully took notes. Then Irene, their apparent leader, explained that her husband, Jack, had just passed and that he was convinced the bad water had helped kill him. He'd left some money in his will for legal action to try to get the drinking water problem fixed. Jack had even recommended Grace and her late uncle as the people to do it.

"You're very kind. Uncle Ray would have been pleased. But Ray was our leading litigator. I've done some trials but not big ones like Ray."

"No disrespect to Ray," Irene said, smiling, "but Jack said you were the brains of the place anyway." She let out a little laugh.

"Tell me about your water," Grace replied. "Each of you."

They were from nearby Keegan County and had come to La Crosse to interview lawyers to help them fight the huge factory dairies that had destroyed their water quality and property values. They were all using bottled water already.

One of the women, about Grace's age and dressed in nursing scrubs, worried when her toddler took a bath in contaminated, well-drawn bathwater. "I mean, isn't it absurd that I have to worry that Molly will swallow a couple of drops of her bathwater? It's just ridiculous."

"Yes, ridiculous," Grace agreed. "Has anyone had their water tested to prove that it's coming from the cow manure?"

A humble older man raised his hand like a schoolboy to speak and Grace nodded at him to go ahead. "I have. I was eating Imodium like it was candy . . . had diarrhea so bad. I had my well tested by the university lab and it came back as bovine-manure-based fecal matter."

The nurse added, "But the regulators say it's still not good enough, because Bart there hasn't done a DNA test to prove which cow it came from, and there's so many cows in Keegan County. We have fourteen CAFOs—"

"Concentrated Animal Feeding Operations," Grace said. "I've done one nuisance case against one in your area; there was a large spill right next to a new subdivision."

"We know," said the nurse. "And you won."

The old man, Bart, laughed and this appeared to open him up enough to speak without raising his hand. "We also know that there are fourteen CAFOs with between eight and twelve thousand head in Keegan County, and that we have cracked bedrock," he said with conviction. "It's a recipe for a groundwater disaster."

"Half the wells in the county are contaminated," Irene said angrily. "That's what Jack always said, anyway."

"That's about right," said the nurse. "Forty-seven percent in one study."

"If you hire me, I will want that study and the results of all your water tests," Grace said soberly. "We will need experts and at least a couple of those DNA tests. And whether you hire me or not, you should all start keeping a diary of how the water problems impact your day-to-day life." Grace could hear her Uncle Ray in her own voice. It was always better to undersell rather than oversell them. "You'd probably be better off with one of the big Milwaukee or Minneapolis firms rather than me or, frankly, anyone else in La Crosse."

"You're being modest," Irene said.

"No, it's true." Grace felt a little overwhelmed by it all and the prospect of this complex case. One of the farmers handed her a Notice of Hearing, and she realized that the administrative law judge was Jason Erikson.

"The judge is a good guy," Grace said. "He was in my law class. And I just ran into him last fall."

Would she take their case if they wanted her? Grace knew that her Uncle Ray, with all of his successful trials, probably wouldn't have touched it. *Don't try to be a hero. Know your limits. Do a few things well. Always get money up front for costs.* Those were her uncle's mantras in the days when he must have known he was ill and was coaching Grace about taking over his practice. That was all really good advice.

But Irene looked and sounded like one of Grace's own country relatives—how could she say *no* to that hair?

"Grace, would you mind leaving the room for a minute?" Irene said suddenly. "We'd like to talk among ourselves about how we want to proceed."

"Sure thing, tell Tom when you're ready. I'll be in the conference room."

"That handsome young man who showed us in?" one of the other women said slyly. "You bet we will!"

"Sorry, but he's married." And to a man, Grace added to herself.

She sat alone in her office, thinking about her Uncle Ray. And that she might soon try a case with Jason Erickson.

Tom came for her in a matter of minutes, and they went back to the conference room. They wanted to retain her. Writing the check, Irene got a little emphatic.

"Jack always trusted your Uncle Ray, and you, Grace. Jack would have come here—I know that's what he'd have done." She had teared up, but her voice was still strong and assured. "It will just put my mind at peace if I know I have you working on it, Grace."

Chapter Eight

~~~~~~~~~~

BOGS, FROGS, AND BRIBES

J ason was in a lousy mood that wasn't helped by the construc-
tion and single-lane traffic that was snaking on the interstate
southeast toward Chicago. Last year the conference had been
held in Bayfield up on Lake Superior, at a big resort with an indoor
pool. Everyone but the speakers was in shorts and bright sundresses.
The whole thing had a low-key and summery vibe, with the smell of
chlorine and the sounds of excited kids running around.

But this year, on this beautiful June day, Jason was wearing a suit
and tie because he had to do the slipominium site inspection.

When he finally arrived, he grabbed a cup of coffee and walked around
to get a feel for the place. Its piers and "campus" buildings sprawled
around an entire bay. There were three restaurants on-site, two pools, a
nightclub with a large dance floor, a sports bar, a spa, a lavish workout
area, and several game and recreational rooms for kids. There was nothing
this grand, on this scale, anywhere else in the Upper Midwest.

There were pier slips for hundreds of large boats, many of them
small yachts capable of navigating the Great Lakes. The view from the
hill above the resort was all gray piers and white boats—all wealth and

concrete—so much so that even the shining ten thousand acres of Lake Joseph seemed small by comparison.

In his starchy white shirt, Jason sat down in the back of the large conference room overlooking the piers, grumpily missing both Blue Lake and Tara. The coffee was cold, and he was dreading the site inspection. But Rachel Eisenberg's presentation drew him in with a picture of a frog.

"This is what we're really talking about when we're talking about developing near-shore areas. It's about whether we're going to have any frogs left in this state." She paused for effect. "EPA researchers surveyed dozens of developed and undeveloped lakes in North Woods counties last summer. Among the species most affected by development are green frogs and loons. The study found that undeveloped lakes averaged one frog every one hundred and sixteen feet of lakeshore and one frog every four hundred and seventy feet on densely developed lakes."

Rachel was a former Olympic runner, now in her late fifties. She represented the State EPA in the slipominium case. She had a degree in biology and knew the science as well as she knew the law. Her trial style was serious and to the point, with an occasional burst of her dry wit. Rachel Eisenberg had quietly spent her professional life defending the "bogs and frogs" of the state, as she'd once put it.

"Amphibians are an important link in the food chain. If we're losing green frogs, we're probably losing a lot of other species too."

Rachel hadn't even mentioned the scariest part of the study. The researchers had found evidence that there were more mutant frogs, the ones with gimpy legs, in the developed areas.

The next slide was a picture of an advertisement for a lakefront development at a place known, appropriately enough, as Loon Lake. Every square foot of the lakefront area had been subdivided, and there were large Xs marking the last three available lots.

"Loons are also in danger because they tend to make their nests within three feet of the shoreline, and there are so many disruptions when people come in with motorboats and piers and dogs and cats. In North Lake County, a new house is started each day of the building season. The trend now is for people to buy old cabins, bulldoze them, and build larger summer homes. As more and more habitats are altered, we're losing some of the most-loved features of lakes: like the calling of loons, and the night chorus of frogs in the summer."

Up next, Earl Franks, who was now a partner at a prominent Chicago-based firm. The second Franks stood up, Jason remembered how much he'd loathed working with the guy. Still buff in his mid-sixties, Franks was a large and charming Irishman. Earl was given to verbal manspreading. He had a booming voice that commanded, or at least attempted to command, center stage in any room he was in.

True to form, Franks was out for blood in his "counterpoint." Jason's blood, in particular. Franks didn't talk about frogs, or frog-eating condominiums, but about the environmental review process.

"Everything is now a federal case, but these are state ALJs. One of them is here," Franks said, more than a bit derisively. "I like Judge Erickson. He works hard and is a friend of mine. But my clients spend way too much time with Judge Erickson every year."

According to Franks, the environmental hearing process had to be "streamlined." This brought Jason a wink from Rachel Eisenberg. Any case involving Earl Franks took twice as long and was at least three times as combative.

Franks went on about a leaner and meaner hearing process that the Republican governor and legislature were contemplating. Listening to Earl Franks attack public input into environmental matters, Jason had to fight off an injudicious urge to tell him where to shove it. But then he did raise his hand when it was time for questions.

"This is your good friend Jason Erickson."

Franks scowled at some scattered guffaws.

"I think that parties might play a part in streamlining the hearing process themselves. For example, not filing as many motions. I have one pending case that had twenty-two pre-hearing motions, the majority filed by you and your firm." Franks had filed all of those motions in Calandro's case at the first prehearing conference a couple of weeks ago. "How does this match your vision of a leaner hearing process?"

"Attorneys have the ethical obligation to zealously represent their clients," Franks replied. "And as long as the process remains so formal, good lawyers will do that."

Maybe Franks was peeved because his client was present in the audience? Jason could only push back so far and stay neutral. As usual, he regretted speaking up.

But at the next break, Grace Clarkson turned up. She was in jeans and a bright green blouse.

"Very funny reply, Judge."

"How are you, Grace? I don't see you for twenty years and then twice in a few months?"

"I know. Nice to see you again. I actually have a case before you coming up in the next couple of weeks. I'm here mostly for the groundwater contamination section." Grace had an appealing, slightly gap-toothed smile. "But it's all very interesting to me."

"Oh, you must have one of the White Farms Dairy cases then."

"Yep, the big one," she said. "Fourteen thousand cows."

"I've got to run, but it's great to see you, and I look forward to working with you."

"Me, too," she said.

In law school, her outlines were frequently the best of anyone in their group. Jason remembered now that he'd asked her out then, before he knew she was married. Her husband had later died in a tragic motorcycle accident while they were still in law school. It would be good for Jason to think of someone besides Tara, someone who just might actually be single and available.

Perhaps she was even thinking something similar? No, she was more likely just sucking up to him because he was presiding over her case—which meant that they were not ethically allowed to be too friendly. His job wasn't the best for his social life.

Soon, it was time to do the slipominium dock site inspection. All of the parties—Franks, Sharpe and Calandro, Eisenberg and a water expert, the title company attorney, an environmental group that opposed issuing the permits, and a retired mailman—were to meet at the resort clubhouse.

"The whole crew here?" Judge Erickson asked.

"No, we need Mr. Borker," said Rachel Eisenberg.

Richard Borker was a retired mailman. He'd grown up on Lake Joseph. He knew and loved the lake, but was set on trying to put in a bunch of largely irrelevant historical documents. Jason was very unlikely to allow them in to the record.

"There he is."

"Judge, Counsel, good afternoon," said Mr. Borker.

Tommy Calandro looked away. Calandro, as a point of honor, wouldn't look at, nor speak to, Borker. Borker had once used the word *mafia* to describe Tommy C. in one of the local newspapers. At the prehearing conference, it had been amusing to watch Calandro so conspicuously avoiding Borker's eyes. When Borker got into his historical evidence, Calandro pointedly got up and went to the men's room.

Now, Tommy Calandro was playing the gracious host. He was a short and burly man with a thick neck and close-set eyes. He greeted Jason with a hearty handshake.

"Are you enjoying the conference, Your Honor? A beautiful spot for it, no?" Everyone laughed.

First Earl Franks and then his associate Courtney Sharpe shook Jason's hand. Now, Jason felt obliged to shake the hands of everyone in the room. The often-tedious necessities of appearing neutral.

"Well, now that we're all here, why don't we get started?" They all followed the judge out into the brisk lake air. "So where are these famous lockboxes?"

"Don't you want the full tour?" Earl Franks asked.

"Here we are," said Calandro, leading them across a patio dotted with blue-and-white-striped lounge chairs.

The so-called slipominiums, the legal basis for selling the boat slips, were the kind of small locked boxes one might find at any post office. There was row after row of shiny steel boxes with numbers on them: Every dozen or so of them represented a million dollars to Calandro. Yet, even if the condominium scheme were approved, he would still own the resort and have a controlling interest in the condominium association. It was a brilliant scheme, and all it lacked was the right set of permits.

"Seventy thousand bucks for that?" Borker exclaimed. Many of them were probably thinking the same thing. "Come on."

"No editorializing, please," Jason said firmly.

Jason looked wistfully at some gulls loafing on the docks farthest out into the channel, enjoying the sunny day and their leisure. Meanwhile, the assembled humans spent a good half hour trying to get a precise idea of the dimensions, or "footprint," of the strip of riparian land that was being transferred to the condominium association. Poring over the ninety-five-page condominium declaration, they finally got it straight.

"So, you don't own this stretch along here?" Jason asked Calandro. He was trying to assess Tommy's feel for the complicated legal fictions that rationalized the slip sales.

Calandro smiled and shrugged. "This is the common area that belongs to the condominium association, right, Earl?"

"That's right," replied Franks.

Calandro smiled broadly, playing the buffoon, but he had the smug look of a man used to getting what he wanted.

They all reassembled in the clubhouse and drank another cup of coffee. Jason felt more relaxed, looking out at the lake from his big clubhouse wicker chair. He could go put on shorts now and enjoy the rest of the conference.

"Well, thanks for the tour." He stood up.

As Jason was heading across the parking lot toward his car, Earl Franks pointedly walked out with him.

"He's a decent guy," Earl observed. He was in his cryptically confidential mode. Jason had seen it before.

"Who?" Jason asked. It was always better to make Earl Franks spell things out.

"Tommy opened this place with nothing," Earl continued. "Now, it's The Place on Lake Joseph."

"I know."

"He's just trying to keep it afloat." Franks's bushy eyebrows took on a reddish tint in the sunlight. "And there's a lot of money involved. It helps all the people of this area."

"We can't talk about the merits, as you well know, Earl."

"I *wasn't* talking about the merits, Jason, I was talking about the money." Earl paused and looked him in the eye. "Those are two very different things."

"What does that mean?"

"There's plenty of money to go around, Jay," Earl replied.

"I'm not sure that I understand." Jason couldn't conceal the anger in his voice.

"You're a bright guy. You'll figure it out."

Earl Franks waltzed away, whistling some song that Jason couldn't make out.

Chapter Nine

~~~~~~~~~~~~~~~

NO SUGAR, NO PERMIT

E arl Franks was in a fine mood after hitting not one but two big winners in the Florida Cup. Not feeling pathetic, either. He had his juice back. Being single had some advantages, too.

One recent advantage was Courtney Sharpe.

He'd been on the committee that hired Courtney as an associate at Higgins and Clark, the large Chicago law firm where he was a partner. Earl immediately liked her matter-of-fact manner and style. She was ambitious, too. Before law school, Courtney had earned a chemistry degree. Now, she had no apparent qualms about putting it to use doing environmental cases for the firm's large corporate clients.

"I don't want to live on a public interest or government salary," she said, sensibly enough. "I didn't go to law school to be poor."

The truth was that law school had *made* her poor. Courtney was deeply in debt. Earl knew this because he'd asked her during the job interview. It was one of the legally borderline questions he always asked new associates, especially the attractive young women.

Courtney Sharpe was striking rather than beautiful. Her long blonde hair and height drew you in, and then you made your own judgment about her longish nose and pale lips. It worked for Earl Franks. Boy, did it work.

Their relationship had remained strictly professional for a couple of years. He was her mentor, her legal father figure. He hadn't really made much of an effort with her. Though he was still buff, Earl was thirty-three years older than Courtney.

He'd only recently resigned himself to only looking at the younger new associates who'd gone straight through law school. There were always the older new hires—the ex-teachers, ex-nurses, the ex-stay-at-home-wives—upon whom he might successfully employ his charms.

But one day, after they'd won a big ruling, he and Courtney went out for a drink to celebrate. Two G-and-Ts in, she gave him a couple of compliments. That he was "handsome in his own, old way." That "he had a lot of animal energy."

"You've got some juice yourself, Courtney," he said simply. She laughed and they clinked glasses. A woman of his generation might have blushed or gotten offended.

But Courtney just smiled. "So?"

"So, what kind of animal do you think I am? A big monkey?"

"That'd be a very fine monkey." Courtney drew up closer to him. "Stop fishing, Earl. You've already got a bite."

What the hell did that mean? Who knew what she was willing to do to make partner? "I've told you, you're a striking woman," he said as he kissed her.

She didn't flinch. Rather, she kissed him back, all out, and purring like a cat.

"A woman who really wants to make partner, and soon!" she replied.

"We understand each other." His heart sank even as his loins stirred. "I like a woman—a lawyer—who is direct. This firm needs people like you."

The next day she gave him her phone number and a note: "Come over for dinner tonight around eight?"

That first night, they ate dinner together in her hip apartment in Rogers Park. They flirted and talked and drank wine. Her forthrightness was refreshing. He told her so and they kissed.

"Do you want to go to bed?" she asked bluntly.

Earl nodded, a little stunned. He'd never known a woman to so matter-of-factly take off all her clothes, hop into bed, and start touching herself. But that was how it went on that first night together.

"Now, I get to watch you undress, Mr. Justice."

Did she have some kind of a father thing? It almost creeped him out. But only almost. It didn't really matter what her thing was.

Earl was more than happy to give her all the animal fury she was looking for, or at least willing to endure for the prospect of making partner. She cried out like it was something she needed, but it was hard to tell.

By the time of the annual Midwest Water Law Conference, Courtney and Earl were steady lovers, seeing each other once or twice a week. They booked rooms next to each other at the Lake Joseph Resort and spent hours discussing the case.

Earl's client, Tommy Calandro, was trying to sell his boat docking slips as slipominiums. The state EPA said the pier slips were on public waters and could only stay there at the pleasure of the state. They also took the position that if he sold the pier slips, he was really selling the public waters. The EPA was afraid that any bozo with a hundred feet of lake frontage would start selling pier slips on every popular lake, and then there would be no near-shore areas left for the frogs and fish. But Tommy C. wasn't just any bozo.

All of Tommy's resort boats and piers were already there, row after row of them. The plan wouldn't harm a soul—everything would remain exactly as it was—except Calandro would be twenty-five million bucks richer.

Tommy was used to the old Chicago ways of doing business. He wanted, he expected, the fix to be in. The judge, Jason Erickson, was relatively young and priggish, a Boy Scout. Pretty unlikely to be receptive to any kind of bribe. It would more likely lead to trouble.

Still, Tommy insisted that Earl make it known to Erickson that Tommy was expecting to have his permits. It wasn't something Earl enjoyed doing, even to an earnest little prick like Erickson. He really didn't see the need to bribe Erickson. Earl thought he could win the case on his own.

But Tommy couldn't live with that uncertainty. His people were used to having things set up. It made them nervous to have any chance of not getting their way. Part of it was a generational thing. In the old days, days Earl still remembered, some "sugar" was expected for any serious permit.

On one of his first big cases in private practice, Earl had represented an up-and-coming real estate developer. The local regulator came in, put his empty briefcase down on the table and then left the room for half an hour. When he came back and saw his still-empty briefcase, he was really steamed.

"No sugar, no permit," he'd said to Earl, shaking his head.

But Erickson was part of the new breed, and just righteous enough to blow the whole thing wide open. Earl hadn't looked forward to messing with Judge Jason Erickson, but he'd learned a long time ago that there was no point arguing with Tommy C. when he'd made up his mind.

The dreaded conversation with Judge Erickson went fairly well—though when it was over, Erickson stormed off. Earl was left alone in the clubhouse with Tommy C., who was in a surly mood.

"Did you talk to him?" Tommy snarled.

"Yes."

"And?"

"I told you, he's Mr. Clean," Earl said.

"You've got to make him understand that he doesn't have a choice." Tommy wasn't playing.

"I'll try, Tommy, I'll try."

"Trying's not good enough." Calandro raised his voice. "I've got too much fucking money riding on this thing. I've already spent most of it—do you hear me?"

"Calm down. I hear you. We're on the same side here." Earl grasped for something to mollify Calandro. "There's got to be a way to this guy; maybe you should have Stan Simpson get to know him better, so we know how Erickson's vulnerable."

"That's an idea," said Tommy, suddenly all sweetness and light. "That's my expensive lawyer talking."

Like all bullies, Tommy C. could turn on a dime. Earl had seen him shift from screaming insults at him to ass-kissing compliments while his ears were still ringing from the chewing out.

When Earl had left the state supreme court to try his hand at private practice, he was mostly hoping to pay off old gambling debts. Tommy C. was quick to see the benefit of having such a well-known and seasoned lawyer over a barrel. People used the leverage you gave them; it was the same as between Earl and Courtney.

But the whole bribe thing was something new.

Franks was a little rattled as he called Stan Simpson, the private investigator he used for any sleazy operation.

"Hello, Stan, it's Earl Franks. I'm representing Tommy Calandro again."

"Big surprise." Stan stifled a laugh. "I hear he owns you."

"Whatever. Don't believe everything you hear."

A couple more good days like his last in Las Vegas and maybe not. He'd tell them both where to stuff it.

"I need some dirt on someone, an administrative judge on environmental cases up in Madison. His name is Jason Erickson. I want to know everything. Kinks, family, weak spots."

"You got it," Stan said. "But Wisconsin ain't usually all that kinky."

Chapter Ten

~~~~~~~~~~~

SLIGHTLY
DANGEROUS

Tara had soon set up a private email account for her book club correspondence with Jason. Over time, these missives seemed to be less and less about books even as they became more and more frequent, from once a week to almost daily, to a couple of times daily.

Getting an email from Jason every morning was like having a good novel to read, a novel where you eventually become one of the main characters and the author is an ever closer, slightly dangerous personal friend. There was a delicious and absorbing rhythm to it all.

Jason was a night owl and Tara was a morning lark. Sometimes, Tara would be up reading his latest installment with her morning coffee just three or four hours after he'd sent it off. He was single and a little bohemian, and sometimes even wrote after a wayward night out on the town. She was married—perhaps a little unconventionally so. She would read Jason's epistles as the morning coffee brewed, then ponder her response as she brought Michael his favorite mug.

Their correspondence was intoxicating. She wasn't just a main character in their little literary novel, but an equal coauthor. There wasn't anything wrong with any of that— was there? Tara went back and forth on that part.

She and Jason were building some intimacy, for sure. He listened and gave her ideas and suggestions, and he came to her for advice.

One morning she saw in their private email the heading "Am I Just Being Paranoid?" It was a somewhat cryptic message alluding to a possible bribe attempt made on behalf of Tommy Calandro by his attorney, Earl Franks. Tara had resisted the urge to call Jason immediately. They did occasionally talk on the phone but usually with their work phones.

Instead, she sent him a reply:

"I'm so sorry to hear about this! And, no, I don't think you're being paranoid. I'm going to dig into both of them!"

That day at work she used her most powerful Lexus/Nexus search tool to find everything in news stories or legal filings about either Tommy or Earl. Since she was covering the trial, this was entirely appropriate background research. What she found wasn't pretty.

There was this city landfill site that Calandro was involved in—the city sold a huge tract of land for a dollar and then later resold it to some of Tommy's associates for over a million dollars. Earl Franks had represented Tommy through the whole crooked deal, and one of his partners had picked up the case when there was a public outcry and a sham criminal investigation. One key witness seemed to have died suspiciously. No charges were ever issued.

Earl himself had been through a bankruptcy and then a divorce. He was making a lot of money but was down to a small condo in Skokie and a family property in Blue Lake that was now in his daughter's name. Blue Lake, of all places!

Tommy Calandro seemed to have something over Earl. She put it all down in an email and then confirmed their meeting in Blue Lake.

Jason:
I'm worried about you!
   See you Sunday at the local place in Blue Lake.

Best,
Tara

Of course it felt a little shady, becoming so close to Jason. Tara dealt with it by doing what she'd always done—she read up on the subject. In this case, she consumed several How to Save Your Marriage-type books. One of them talked about the three Cs of a happy marriage—chemistry, communication, and commitment.

By chemistry Tara understood not just the obvious physical kind, but the feeling you get at the prospect of spending an evening together. Does it fill you with excitement or boredom, dread or comfort? Also, if your chemistry and commitment carry you that far, kids are part of chemistry too. What was more chemical than that feeling of *rightness* that is a keen part of any family?

For Tara, chemistry also included all of the unconscious things that drive human beings that no one ever wants to talk about. *Do I like his voice, his scent, his way of being angry or sad? Does it feel like home when we're together?* She would have to answer *yes* to Jason and *no* to Michael on all of those. Those damn marriage books cut both ways!

Tara also took communication more broadly than the relationship books might have it. Not only whether they could talk about money and sex and the division of labor, but also whether they liked to talk about the same stuff in the first place. Did they feel some need to share their lives with each other on a daily basis? Did they resolve conflicts well? Could they read each other's nonverbal cues?

Deep down, Michael was a computer coder—a man of numbers, not words. The most disturbing possibility was that they didn't understand each other in the way each of them communicated best. Maybe Michael could communicate more deeply with Susan than with her?

And there was no denying that Tara and Jason shared the slightly dangerous things that made her feel understood the way she wanted to be understood.

Finally, there was commitment. That was just the mutual agreement to see things through. Love was always a shared choice, a story you write together. Rachel Cusk was right about that.

Tara thought that if the three Cs were there, that a great love simply happens when two people just decide together, "This is a great love." Her sense was that most people did want that. They want someone who thought they were really special, and for that feeling to be mutual. They want to feel at home—to be comforted, understood, valued, and *loved* by each other.

That had been there with Michael when they'd gotten married, but it seemed to have been lost in all of the time they spent apart. Love wasn't always everything they wanted it to be! Things always change in nature.

One book Tara read was called *Divorce Among the Gulls*. Birds have personalities and one way that they express them is that some of them like to sit on a nest longer than others. Gulls usually mated for life, and usually split nest-sitting obligations roughly equally between male and female. When both the male and the female wanted to sit on the nest seventy percent of the time, they'd spend forty percent of their time squabbling.

But they would part the next season rather than continuing to quarrel—the gulls would somehow know to sort themselves out to get the balance right. That happened in about a quarter of all the mate-for-life birds. The author concluded that those gull couples just weren't right for each other.

For humans, circumstances changed. Tara might have been against having kids when she was young, but she was reconsidering carefully. What was she willing to give up to save her marriage? That sounded more martyr-like than she would have liked. Tara knew she was no martyr.

If anything, she was sometimes reckless and greedy. Her heart wanted what it wanted, emphatically and often. For the past few months, it had wanted nothing so much as to be with Jason. She'd been bruised and damaged trying to "thread the needle," as the two of them called it. That was code for maintaining an intimate friendship without straying into an affair. It was exhausting, but she'd kept to her limits.

When Tara thought about what was missing in her marriage, it was this: a shared interest in the environment, in literature and the arts. Shared ethics and ideas. And maybe (just maybe) a baby?

Chapter Eleven

~~~~~~~~~~~

SHOULD I STAY OR SHOULD I GO?

J ason settled himself in at the Blue Lake Café to wait for Tara. It
was an old-fashioned greasy spoon, full of noisy bantering and
the smell of bacon and fried eggs. He loved the view. There was a
comforting green stand of black spruce and white pines above the royal
blue of the lake and the softer blue sky.

He'd been coming to Blue Lake since he was a kid. Many happy
memories involved those visits and the four of them singing on the
drive up from Milwaukee when his father was still alive. Something
about the place calmed him, which Jason needed today. He hadn't slept
well since the bizarre conversation with Earl Franks in Lake Joseph.

"More coffee, Judge?" the waitress asked in her gravelly smoker's
voice.

"Please," Jason replied. Lots of people in Blue Lake knew who he
was after the Christmas tree case. A mixed blessing, to be sure.

"Your writer friend still coming?"

"I was a little early, and she's always late." It was nearly one hundred miles away for each of them, but Jason and Tara had come here the last three Sundays.

"A sign of being passive-aggressive, I've heard," the waitress cracked.

Jason smiled. Maybe there was something to that, but Tara wasn't so much passively aggressive as passively seductive. They flirted discreetly in their private emails, and Tara sent him suggestive snail-mail cards and letters too.

Last weekend, during their latest walk around Blue Lake, Jason had even confessed that he'd had a dream about her.

"What kind of dream?"

"Just a boring dream that you were in."

Though Tara pressed him, he wouldn't give her any details. There weren't many to give. He didn't let himself think about her sexually, but in the dream, he was lying on his side in a green field facing her. They were kissing and were both conspicuously aroused. Before he'd become aware of this good fortune, he was touching and then entering her—with her blue underwear on one leg and her black skirt still on.

Why was he here, meeting a married woman in Blue Lake, rather than back in Madison—safely away from the direction things seemed to be heading? And what exactly did Tara want from him?

As though it would offer him a clue, he took out the most recent card she had sent him, lingering over it happily. On the front, there was a simple but elegant line drawing of two intertwined human figures, a male and a female. Inside, she'd copied out a quote from Ralph Waldo Emerson:

"Why should we fear
To be crushed by savage elements,
We who are made up
Of the same elements?"

Since last Halloween, the two of them had read mostly the same books. Now, it was mid-June and they were intimate friends and reading buddies. Tara's husband knew all about it, she said. Michael worked long work hours. He had soccer and then beers and dinner with his teammates on Sundays and didn't pay close attention to Tara's whereabouts. They'd picked their books on a walk here a couple of weeks after the Christmas tree trial.

They were sitting on a red rock that was more or less their spot in Blue Lake. The sun was starting to set. They each tossed out a couple of names of books and authors they'd like to read next.

"How about Tessa Hadley or Richard Powers?" Jason asked.

"I was thinking of something more classic," Tara countered. "Someone like Emerson?"

"Emerson? That Unitarian windbag?"

She looked pained. "He's my favorite writer, my anchor."

"I'm so sorry." He felt like such an ass. Maybe Emerson was her way of keeping her own ideals in place. "Prove me wrong. What do you want to read?"

"There's this biography called *Mind on Fire* that I've been wanting to read."

"Okay. Deal," Jason replied. "And I'll try to keep an open mind."

Dear Jason:

The last time in Blue Lake, as we were saying our good-byes, the snarky waitress asked me if I wanted the coffee to stay or to go . . . That was the dilemma for me then, and it still is.

Nothing has changed there, either. I'm still married and still can't wait to see you again. But you make me happy to be confused.

I'm worried about what Earl Franks said to you at the Water Law Conference. I've been doing some digging

on his client, Tommy Calandro. People have used the
word Mafia. I'll tell you more in person.
   Please be careful!
   Sunday at noon at the Blue Lake Café?

                                        Love,
                                        Tara

Just then Tara arrived, out of breath, and smiling radiantly. She blushed slightly and then avoided his eyes. She was wearing a faded, short brown skirt and a tannish-green jacket. Her thick black hair was pulled back, showing off her thin white neck and fine features.

"Sorry I'm late," Tara said.

"I'd be more worried if you weren't."

"Coffee for the lady?" The waitress took in Tara's enormous diamond wedding ring suspiciously.

"I'll have a cup to stay. Thanks," Tara said. There was that strangely charming, bird-like way of cocking her head.

"So, you're staying, I guess," said Jason. "I loved your card."

"Now that you've finished the biography, do you still think Emerson is a windbag?"

"Emerson already?"

"Isn't our book club why we're meeting here?" This tone was new. She looked a little out of sorts.

"Okay. No, he's not a windbag." Just hopelessly out of date for Jason. "But something about his brand of spirit and all that still puts me off. He's too sure of himself and his ideas."

"That's what I like about him."

"That's what people always like about people who have simple answers to things," Jason said.

"His answers aren't simple." For the first time in all of their months of playful banter, Tara seemed genuinely offended. "Self-reliance, doing your best to live up to your ideals—you think that's easy?"

"No, but the world is a little more complicated than that."

"But what if it's not?" she insisted.

Jason's tone softened and he took her hand. "I liked the quote you sent. That's exactly how I feel about seeing you sometimes, like I'm driven by some irresistible force."

"Me, too," said Tara, still looking agitated.

Across from them, a couple of fishermen were heatedly debating Governor Walker.

"We can't even escape all this wretched politics here," Tara said. "Let's go out for a walk." Tara made eye contact with the waitress, who promptly came over. "Sorry, but can I please get that coffee to go?"

When they were outside, she took Jason's hand as they made their way toward the lakefront path. They'd silently seemed to have decided that holding hands was okay a few weeks ago—at least in Blue Lake.

"It's a beautiful day." She sipped her coffee, a little distracted.

"Seventy-four and sunny."

"How are you doing with the whole Earl Franks thing?"

"One good thing is that I now think of Earl instead of you when I wake up at four in the morning," Jason replied.

"Tell me about it!" There was her smile and earthy laugh. "Guilt kills sleep. But this bribe thing is way scarier."

"Did Earl and Tommy Calandro really expect me to just come back with a number—say, forty or fifty thousand—and then just take a dive? To be in their clutches for this the rest of my career? It just doesn't make economic sense for me to do it even if I was so inclined, which I'm not. I came through my divorce okay."

Tara winced and looked out toward the lake.

"Is everything all right with you?" Jason asked. "You seem a little down."

"Just that word: divorce. Things are bad with Mike and me." Tara smiled. "I spend all of my time thinking about you. About us. And, now, worrying about your safety."

Jason let go of her hand. "Would it help if we didn't see each other for a while?"

"No," she said firmly. "On Thursday, Mike called me again to say that he would be working late. Nothing new about that, really. Or about me eating dinner alone. But our conversation felt so strained, so stilted, after all our years together. Our marriage is in deep trouble."

"I'm sorry."

"And I've talked to you about all of the changes at my job way more than I've talked to Michael. Believe me, I've tried."

"I'm sorry," Jason said again. "It's hard when your partner doesn't listen."

Madeline had taken so little interest in Jason's career. She was brilliant but not an intellectual. Her parents had ruined that for her. "Push me into shallow waters before I get too deep," Maddie would cry, singing a late '80s pop song. Following folk and blue grass bands suited her. A legacy, she admitted, from being raised by two egghead Brown professors.

"My ex had no interest in environmental concerns," Jason offered.

"Michael doesn't even feign interest anymore."

"What about your personal writing, your poems and essays?"

"He just comments on the magazine cover," Tara said.

There was nothing for Jason to say. It was awkward to talk so frankly about her problems with her husband. He was trying hard to encourage her, to be her friend. But part of him also wanted to make love to her, with her underwear wrapped around one leg and her earth-toned skirt still on.

Her husband was a jerk. But so was Jason, just for being here. Again.

"Maybe it's just a bad patch?" he asked.

"Maybe, but it's been this way for a couple of years."

"Have you guys tried counseling?"

"He won't."

They sat quietly in the high June grass. The spring-fed lake was its reliable royal blue. Beautifully austere. The afternoon sky had already begun mixing up the pastel pinks and rich yellows, readying the canvas for the colorful Blue Lake sunset.

"It's lovely here. Thanks for meeting me." Tara gripped his hand tightly. "It's strange, but I always feel this odd sense of belonging in Blue Lake. I feel aware of some presence here."

Did Jason believe in such things? Certainly not officially. His years as a lawyer and his interest in biology had left him firmly in the rationalist camp. But he felt something like the same thing about Blue Lake. It had always been his refuge.

"What are you thinking?" she asked.

"I was just thinking that I suppose a place could have some kind of energy. Or atmosphere, at least. I've always loved Blue Lake, since I was ten years old." He gestured out at the lake. "Before that, I was feeling kind of shitty about my role in your marriage. I heard this term I'd never heard before this week: *emotional affair*."

"I saw that same article. That's us, an emotional affair with hand-holding benefits." Tara grinned at her own joke. "It started off as more of an intellectual thing with us, though. I mean, we're both nerds, sitting around arguing about our books and Emerson." She punched his arm in a sisterly way and laughed.

"You've got that right!"

"By the way, I've done a little digging on this Calandro guy, and he's a real thug," Tara said.

"How so?" Jason stood up and then offered his hand to pull her up. "Mind if we walk a bit? This conversation is making me nervous."

"Sure. Trying to get my step count up anyway." Tara put her arm around his shoulder. "Anyway, everyone calls him Tommy C., and no one messes with Tommy C. Be careful. I told you about the landfill site."

"Yeah, thanks. Did you find anything about this whole mafia idea?"

"It's just talk, from what I can tell. Prejudice, even. Even if he was in the mafia, the mafia isn't what it used to be. It's more like they can pick off a town or city official now and then. They don't have the same political influence anymore." They'd come to a fork in the path.

"You decide," Jason said.

Tara led them down closer to the shore.

"Not even in Chicago?" Jason resumed their conversation.

"Not even in Sicily, for that matter," Tara said. "I read one piece that said they've been moving to Germany and the UK. The family leaders don't encourage their sons to go into the crime business anymore. Of course, there still are remnants in New York, Jersey, Philly, and, yes, Chicago, but it's not like it used to be."

"Hard times for gangsters, huh?" Jason joked. "I guess that's good news for me."

It was all hard to make sense of, and it didn't seem completely real, walking along the lake path next to Tara.

"I'm not saying Tommy C. isn't dangerous—just don't get too spooked by the mafia whispers."

"I keep going over it. Could I have misunderstood Earl Franks? Was it just one of his tactless jokes?"

"Did he laugh when he said it?" Tara asked.

"Well, sort of, but he was also pretty serious. Threatening, really."

"What exactly did he say again?"

A wave of nausea passed through Jason. "He said something like, 'There's plenty of money to go around,' and, 'The money and the merits are two different things, Jay, *think* about it.'"

"That's right. He called you Jay. A bit odd, isn't it?"

"Yes, that was unusually personal. He always calls me Judge, or Your Honor, even off the record, trying to ingratiate himself. So, the 'Jay' was a bit weird."

Tara grimaced. "Tell me again exactly what happened."

He'd been over it in his mind so many times, there was an air of unreality about the whole thing. They sat down on a bench under a white pine. A young bunny hopped out from Tara's side and into the brush.

"Cute," Jason observed, before launching into every detail of his encounter with Earl Franks.

Tara listened intently, nodding occasionally. "I don't think you misunderstood him," she said when he was done. "I think he left things purposefully vague to be able to deny it. Earl Franks is not stupid."

"Yeah, that's what I think, too—going over it for the hundredth time."

Tara put her arm around him. "So, what are you going to do about it?"

"I don't know. For now, I just keep hoping that if I ignore it, it will somehow go away."

"That's been my strategy about the problems in our marriage." She paused. "I can tell you, it doesn't work."

"I guess I'm just waiting for him to bring it up again. Then I'll have to do something."

"What about telling your boss?" Tara turned to face him. "I know he's a political hack obsessed with his retirement."

"Yes, precisely," Jason replied.

"But he might have some idea of what to do."

"I don't have a lot of confidence in his judgment. And I'm afraid he might just use it as an excuse to take me off any case that matters. The administration is not thrilled with me, as you know."

In theory, Jason was an independent administrative law judge with civil service protection, but Steve Hayman could always make his life miserable in any number of ways, including making up bogus disciplinary actions or taking him off environmental cases altogether. Jason knew that he wouldn't stick around in either case. He'd had other offers.

"That makes sense," Tara said. "I'll try to keep poking around into both Franks and Calandro, but if it comes up again, promise me you'll go to the police."

"I will. What do you want to do right now?"

"I think we should finish our hike," Tara replied. "And then go out to an early dinner." Jason found himself staring at Tara's lips as she spoke, marveling at the words that came out and longing to kiss her.

"Perfect. Thanks for talking about that Lake Joseph stuff; I feel a little better about it."

"I'm glad. Where's your hearing tomorrow?" Tara asked.

"Not far from here. In fact, I took a room just up the path at the Lake of the Pines." Jason heard an unnatural nonchalance in his own voice, like he'd made an awkward pass at someone at an office party.

"How about that Randall's, or whatever they call it now. That old place on Pigeon Cove," Tara said.

"Sounds great," Jason replied, still sounding unnaturally chipper.

Chapter Twelve

~~~~~~~~~~~~~~~~~~

THE VIEW FROM THE COVE

Tara was feeling lousy as she drove to the restaurant. A hotel room? What was up with that? She couldn't blame him for thinking that that was where they were heading, but his voice had sounded weird when he said it. There was some calculation in it, at the very least. Tara pulled into the lot of Randall's, or Chandler's, as it was now known. Jason was already standing outside waiting.

"I beat you!" he exclaimed in his normal, slightly goofy voice. "Hard to think of this as anything but Randall's."

"I know. It was Randall's for over a hundred years. I made the mistake of staying here one night before a big conference," Tara said, as they approached the bright red door. "Ms. Chandler was hurt that I didn't eat any of her lemon-poppy seed muffins. It felt a little claustrophobic, the way they hovered over me."

"I've had that experience at other B&Bs."

"We have, too, and that's why I tend to avoid them." The "we" felt awkward, even hurtful on her tongue. How had she put herself in this position, gotten in so deeply with Jason that it wasn't hard to imagine the two of them in his hotel room?

There was a cloakroom and then a hallway that led down to a lower-level bar, and the upper dining room, which looked out over an impressive view of Pigeon Cove. They had phoned in a reservation, but when they arrived there was only one other silent, glaring old couple in the candlelit dining room.

"Welcome," said Sarah Chandler. "I'll be right back to take your order."

"So, Tara, how are things at your office?" asked Jason.

"Stressful. It's hard being told you're an anachronism. I can't wait to start writing about new ways to make blueberry muffins."

"Blueberry muffins that will have your friends green with envy!" Jason teased. "By the way, thanks for coming today. I know how busy you are."

"I wouldn't be anywhere else."

"Really, I appreciate all of it." He looked directly into her eyes. His were sky blue and steady. "All of it, your digging on Tommy Calandro, the letters, all the time you make for me."

"I confess," she began, distracted by his eyes. "It's the most exciting thing in my life." For all her useless guilt, she couldn't look into those eyes and lie.

"Me, too, Tara." Jason looked away and then back at her. This seemed a bit calculated too. It was something she'd seen Jason do with witnesses.

Ms. Chandler brought their wine and took their order.

"Do you mind if we check out the view?" She led Jason out to the deck on the balcony overlooking the lake.

"Cheers!" offered Jason, clinking glasses.

The sunset was in full bloom. The sky awash with pink and orange.

"The sky here is always pink," Tara said quietly. She had a sudden desire to flee. Her heart was pounding. They were in danger.

"I was just thinking that every halfway-decent-sized lake has its own sky," Jason said. "What's the matter, Tara? You look worried."

"I just had a feeling, a premonition—"

Just then Sarah Chandler stuck her head in the doorway.

"Excuse me. Your salads are here."

They went back into the main dining room and their dinners were served. The lemon-buttery walleye smelled and tasted like summer itself, like fishing trips to the Boundary Waters Tara had taken as a girl. The terrible feeling went away. Her father would love Jason, if it ever came to that.

"So, what are you hearing tomorrow?" Tara asked Jason.

"A large marina project, but it may be a little political. There's lots of letters in the file from the governor's office. What are you doing tomorrow?"

"Tomorrow night, I'm covering a city council meeting. I'm not sure what's up tomorrow morning."

She'd been too focused on coming to Blue Lake to meet him to think that far ahead. The piano player, a young man with a braided black ponytail, approached their table.

"Any requests?"

"The Beatles," Jason said, giving the young man a five-dollar bill. "How about, 'I Should Have Known Better'?"

Damn it. She loved that song. She was starting to love him, too. To her great confusion. His eyes. Sharing so damn much. How she enjoyed his company and conversation. That voice, once again back in its authentic, calming register.

How familiar they'd become, holding hands on their way back to her car. How natural it was for him to be seated next to her while she was driving. Michael always insisted on driving. She pulled into the Lake of the Pines Motel parking lot and got out with him.

They were standing outside under the red glow of the No Vacancy sign. She would've been content with his mind, his voice, his presence—but now here he was in her arms, kissing her good night. On the lips, for the first time. That taste of summer again. That taste of him.

"What a nice day," Tara said.

"Yes, but you should go. Won't he wonder why you're getting home so late?"

"Maybe. If he's home himself."

"Can you really have a day like today without him even noticing?" Jason asked.

"Sure. He probably won't be home when I get in." Her voice trailed off. "Do you think I could use your bathroom?"

Tara took his hand again, exhilarated and a little guilty. They walked up the path toward the sleepy little two-story motel and climbed the white metal stairs up to his room on the second floor.

There was a long, wrought-iron balcony and big cedar chairs in front of every room, perfect for lounging around, reading, and looking out over the lake. All along the balcony there were bright pink geraniums blooming in the seemingly endless summer evening sun. The effect was cheerful and picturesque, and helped Tara overcome the awkwardness of entering his motel room together. She made straight for the bathroom.

What was she going to do? She had no idea. For once, she had no plan.

"My turn," Jason said when she came out. Tara heard him singing the Beatles' song as he made his own utilitarian music.

She wasn't going to fight it anymore. Their feelings for each other were deep and sincere. Her marriage was a disaster. She was lonely and unhappy and ready to quit rationalizing these trips to Blue Lake and to accept her responsibility if her marriage didn't survive.

Tara stood in front of the window looking out at the sunset. There was a man standing under the motel sign, staring up at her. She turned her back to him. The last traces of sunlight were streaming in. The summer breeze blew the sheer white curtains all around her. The effect was otherworldly. Jason drew up to Tara and put his arms around her waist.

"Yes, hold me." She sank into his embrace.

"My pleasure."

"Mine too."

They stood there together holding each other, back in a delightful trance. Jason's desire for her was soon another throbbing presence.

"I told you I live in the real world," Jason said. "Now you know what you do to me."

"And this is what you do to me," she replied, guiding his hand under her skirt and over her underwear. They stood like that for an intimate, blissful moment.

"I can feel your pulse, and your desire," Jason said.

The spell was broken. "You're right. I'm blooming." She laughed and pulled away. "We should probably get out of this room and get me in the car."

The pink sun had already fallen down a notch below the lake horizon. The breeze blew gently through the white curtains, now more of a ghostly presence. They held each other again.

"Tara, you should know I'm falling in love with you. Hard as I've been trying not to."

"Well, I must be a little in love with you too or this never would have happened."

Tara walked back to her car, holding his hand. They kissed goodnight again. That same guy who she'd seen lingering under the sign got into his car and drove slowly away.

"That's strange; I think that guy may have been watching us upstairs," Tara said.

"The Peeper couldn't have seen much, but it's still kind of creepy."

"Yeah, maybe I'm just being paranoid. Good night," she said.

And with that she drove in the late-night darkness back to her husband, ninety-seven miles away.

Chapter Thirteen

~~~~~~~~~~~~~~~~

YOU JUST KNEW
WHAT IT WAS

G race was a little anxious waiting for the big telephone conference relating to the groundwater case, mainly because Jason Erickson was the presiding administrative law judge. They were contemporaries, and perhaps she'd always be measuring herself against her law school classmates. Even, unconsciously, all the way back to her high school class.

She took pride in never having to take a case she found ethically unsavory, and in her consistent sense of being on the right side of the issues she litigated. But there was another part of her that felt like a small-town, small-time mediocrity. One thing she was sure of: she was no environmental specialist.

"Hello, is this Grace Clarkson?" There was a Star Trek-like beep as the operator connected them.

"Yes, speaking. Hello."

"Hello, it's Judge Erickson for our Douglas/Tollefson conference call. How'd you like the Water Law Conference?"

"It was pretty helpful, but I'm new to this whole environmental hearing process."

"Well, you'll be fine, Grace."

She liked the confidence in his voice and in her.

"By the way, even though I think we may have been in a study group together in law school—I don't think that's something that comes close to rising to a conflict or even something that we need to disclose," Jason said.

"Yes, I had the same thought."

"Great. There are three more attorneys and two unrepresented people to put on as well."

Just then, Tom led Irene into her office.

"And I've got one of my clients, Irene Douglas, here with me," Grace said.

The conference went well. Erickson explained the procedure, and it turned out another local environmental group was also appearing with another female attorney, Diane Riccardi, whom Grace knew. Diane had even done a similar case in the past. They compared notes and promised to work together against the Milwaukee firm that was representing the dairy. The oddest part was that the attorney for the state EPA appeared to be pretty much openly supporting the dairy's position and was dismissive of the farmers whose wells were contaminated.

"Is that common?" Grace asked.

"Yes," Diane replied. "The agency has seemingly been captured by the dairy industry. Never mind that half the wells in that county are contaminated, by their own count, with nitrates and even E. coli. We tried to sample a well in another case and showed that it was bovine manure in the well, but they said we needed to do DNA testing on the individual cow to prove that it came from the dairy farm with ten thousand cows a quarter mile away."

"Yes, my clients had that experience as well. What did I get myself into?" Grace was feeling both challenged and overwhelmed.

"We can share some of those costs and pick our wells carefully. And the judge is not a tool," Diane paused before adding, "unlike the EPA attorney."

They both laughed.

"Erickson was in my law school class and seemed like a pretty decent guy."

"Hang in there, Grace. You've done plenty of trials. I know you've kicked my ass in court. It's just another trial. Just about the details of proving our case."

~~~~~~~

The next morning, Grace was excited to be out of the office and out in the field. The plan was to drive to Stevens Point, pick up the ground-water expert, Dr. Ken Walter, and then meet to take water samples with two of Grace's farmer clients with contaminated wells and two women who ran a B&B on a dead zone in Lake Michigan. It was a three-and-a-half-hour drive just to get there, but much of it would be productive in talking things over with Dr. Walter.

Grace arrived in Stevens Point ahead of schedule, but Dr. Walter was already outside sitting on a bench, going through his notes on his laptop. She recognized him from his website and rolled down her window.

"Dr. Walter, I presume?"

He smiled. "At your service, Ms. Clarkson."

Dr. Walter was a youthful and lean man in his forties. His website said he ran marathons, and he seemed to have boundless energy. He carried a large bag of the testing vessels and gizmos.

"Thank you so much for giving us this whole day pro bono," Grace said. It was so rare in litigation, where experts were often expensive parasites—willing to say anything for a price. "It's really appreciated."

Dr. Walter made a gesture, as though to brush away her gratitude with his hands.

"Well, some of us still believe that the waters are held in the public trust and that it's on us to be its guardians. I love talking about water and being where the action is as far as what's happening to it. I've seen plenty of groundwater contamination, but I've never actually seen a Great Lakes dead zone firsthand before."

"What's a quick lay definition of a dead zone?" Grace asked.

"Water that lacks the oxygen to support life."

Summer was peaking and even breaking down a bit already in late July—the lower scrubby brush was already starting to yellow. The drive north brought back memories of going to visit her uncle in Door County back in the 1970s. She'd seen her first play at a summer theatre there as a child. It would never have occurred to her then that the massive waters of either Green Bay or Lake Michigan could be at risk from farms, which were just small family operations that blended into the picturesque countryside. There were rustic old barns of numerous colors that contributed to the charm of the landscape.

But the CAFO farms were massive structures that raised dairy cows on an industrial scale. Some housed as many as twelve thousand cows, and they consumed enormous quantities of water and produced truly epic amounts of manure. She'd recently learned that the average dairy cow was thought to produce twenty tons of it in a year! That led to contracts to spread the manure, sought-after organic waste, to literally every farm field in the areas with numerous large dairy operations.

Grace and Dr. Walter spent the next hour and a half detailing the specific tests he intended to do, which included DNA testing that might identify the source of contamination down to an individual cow's poop.

She would have to try to get Judge Erickson to allow her to gain access to the cows to try to find a match, but it was like having ten thousand suspects in a lineup, and it would likely be too expensive to get DNA samples of them all. It was a problem for down the road, though. They would for sure be able to say that it was bovine-sourced fecal matter rather than human—in which case, every reasonable inference would be that it came from land spreading dairy manure.

By the time they arrived at the Douglas Farm, Grace and Dr. Walter were very comfortable with each other and ready to do their work and take the samples. Irene Douglas greeted them warmly. She looked more relaxed and confident without the funeral bouffant.

"Thanks for doing this with no fee," Irene said.

"No problem at all," Dr. Walter said. "Where is that well?"

Once they arrived on-site, the jocular Dr. Walter got serious. After he quickly took the well samples, they walked out to a creek that crossed the farm property and took samples from the water there. Then the three of them boarded Irene's three-seater ATV and crossed the fields to the neighboring Henson farm, where they were to take samples from both their well and the abutting river. Irene Douglas, looking very much in command, not only drove but also called Bart Henson on the way over.

Bart was the humble and taciturn man who'd raised his hand to speak in her office. "I don't need any fancy water test to tell me it's their cow shit in my well. I was eating Imodium AD like they were candy until I got on the bottled water."

Bart had used the same candy metaphor in her office. How many people had he told that sad story to?

"It nearly killed me, I swear," Bart continued. "But I got on the bottled water when it rained hard after they'd spread and the water came out of my tap dark brown. Smelled just like cow manure. You knew what it was. The same is true of the river. I took pictures of the fish kills."

"I'd like a copy of those," Grace said.

"Sounds good." Irene got back aboard the ATV. "We don't want to waste anyone's time, and we're paying Grace here by the hour."

Grace shook both Ron's and Irene's hands.

"I'm not planning on following you out to the two ladies' hotel," Irene said. "Got so much to do out here at this time of year."

Back in the car, Dr. Walter spoke first. "I really like your client! Is she the definition of no-nonsense or what?"

"Yes! And people like Irene and Henson aren't exactly whiners, so if they are willing to fight this, it must be just horrible." Grace shivered. "I'm thinking of the way he said he had brown tap water out of his kitchen faucet."

"That was chilling," Dr. Walter agreed absent-mindedly. He was already engaged with his iPad. "If you don't mind, I am going to write up my field notes on our drive."

He was still in work mode when they reached the Artful Lodger B&B on Lake Michigan. Two women, Rachel and Leslie, who looked to be a couple, ran the place, and they were thrilled to see them.

"We both put our life's savings into this place, and things were going like gangbusters a few years ago," said Rachel.

She was as tall and thin as Leslie was short and round, and they both spoke rapidly and finished each other's sentences.

"Show them the *Midwest Living* piece," Rachel said to her partner.

Leslie brought down the blue-framed cover. "We had it framed."

"Artful Lodging, Indeed!" the headline read.

Leslie was an accomplished sculptor and they had a sculpture garden with benches and tables for afternoon tea.

"But in the last three years, with the dead zone, our bookings are down seventy-five percent," Leslie said.

"Can we head down that way?" Dr. Walter asked.

"Of course, let's do it," said Rachel, leading them out the back door. "I swear, some days you can smell the cow shit from the sculpture garden."

"That's the gospel truth." Leslie shook her head. "I'm from Cleveland and remember the Cuyahoga River catching on fire when I was in first grade. But, almost fifty years later, it's okay to turn Lake Michigan into a manure pit?"

Grace felt the adrenaline rush through her blood. She was ready to fight for them with all she had, and she had wonderful Dr. Walter on her side.

Chapter Fourteen

~~~~~~~~~~

YOU JUST LOVE MY ASS

Earl Franks and Stan Simpson went back to the days when Earl was trying personal injury cases and Simpson was beating insurance companies to statements in accident cases. They weren't close, but there was mutual respect.

Stan had a kind of working-class distrust for lawyers—for anyone in a suit—even someone as unpretentious as Earl Franks thought himself to be. But Simpson relished finding the dirt on someone, and within the week he was in Earl's office with a slim folder on Jason Erickson.

Stan was bald and wiry, a little older than Franks, and reeked of cigarette smoke. He had a big red birthmark on his forehead, which he sometimes tried to cover with makeup during investigations.

"What did you find out about him, Stan?"

"Plenty. I think he's banging that reporter, Tara Highsmith, who's covering the case you all are doing in Lake Joseph." Stan looked pleased with himself.

"Oh, good for the good judge, and good for us."

"They have secret meetings up in Blue Lake."

"Well done!" Earl was at least equally pleased. "Got pictures?"

"Nothing too exciting, but yes, a few," Stan said. "She went up to his hotel room for what must have been a world-record quickie!"

"Hah! Or maybe she just went up there to use the head?"

"Have you ever invited someone up to your hotel room to have a pee?" Stan asked.

"Nope."

"Me neither."

"Either of them married?" Earl asked.

"She is. Jason's recently divorced, really took it on the chin. Moved from a place right on one of the lakes in Madison, down to a two-bed-room bungalow." Simpson smirked. "Wife left him for some loser in a bluegrass band. A banjo player, for Christ's sake." Stan couldn't help letting out a disgusted little laugh. "I'm not making this stuff up, Earl."

"That's great. Glad he's got some money trouble, too," Earl replied. "What about family?"

"Not much there. Parents are dead. He's got a younger brother, Justin, who lives in Minneapolis. The judge and his brother are both squeaky clean online too."

"Anything else?"

"That's all for now. Still digging, though."

"Great work. Keep it up."

Stan leaned in close. "So, Earl, is this a case where I should send a bill or what?"

Simpson had very flexible ethics, especially if money was involved.

"No, no bill. Talk to Tommy C. about it—I'll tell him you were helpful."

"Always glad to be of help to you or Tommy C."

Stan was just leaving when Courtney Sharpe came into Earl's office.

"Was that Stan Simpson, the illiterate PI?" Courtney asked.

Earl nodded. Stan was a great investigator, but he couldn't write. Earl tried not to use Stan for anything that required a written report, but when he had to, Earl's secretary would usually retype it and have Stan sign it.

"What's he up to?"

"Just doing some digging on another case," Earl replied. "Hey, could you help me with something?"

"Sure. What do you need?"

"Can you pull up Judge Erickson's calendar for me?"

Earl enjoyed seeing Courtney in the same long, blue-flowered dress she'd worn a couple of weeks before to the depositions in Indianapolis. What a night that had been. The way she'd looked in that blue dress as he'd yanked off her black nylons—he shouldn't think about it—so, of course, he thought of nothing else. Damn, that woman was wild.

"Nice dress."

She smiled a little blankly. "Glad you like it."

Did she even remember that night in Indianapolis? Earl had the constant sense that it all meant more to him than it did to her, as Maggie used to say to him. Now, he knew what she'd meant.

Just the way Courtney stood, the casual way she carried herself, drove him crazy. She was matter-of-fact and self-serving, but she was also more than that.

She'd put herself through both undergrad and law school and was something like $125,000 in debt as a result. What self-confidence it must have taken to keep signing those promissory notes. Earl, too, was still irrationally fearless about money. But for all her drive and strength, Courtney could be very tender, too.

When he'd had a chest cold a couple of weeks ago, she'd come over with chicken noodle soup and some kind of special herbal tea. She'd actually stuck a thermometer in his mouth to see what his temperature was. No one had done that since his mother when he was ten years old.

The next weekend, he gave her the expensive Swiss watch with the little diamond studs that he noticed on her wrist now, even though he was already in debt up to his ass. Bought on his credit card.

Earl's own tastes were relatively simple. He'd lived in the same nice-enough condo in Skokie since his divorce. But the one thing he really enjoyed was the giving of extravagant gifts, surprising someone with the brute force of his buying power.

Courtney had pulled up the Environmental Unit calendar and they looked at it together. He'd promised Tommy C. that he'd take another crack at Erickson if Simpson found out anything interesting. Like a secret affair with a married woman. That was promising. Maybe Erickson would play to protect her.

"What's Erickson up to next Tuesday?" Earl tried to sound casual.

"He has a hearing in Black River Falls. With me, as a matter of fact."

"Oh, right. That marina thing. I guess I'll have to try another date for a conference call. Just little housekeeping issues, but it might save us all time. Thanks, Courtney."

"I should thank you for the performance review." She smiled the fake smile he loved. "Want to come over for lunch?" Courtney asked.

"Sure thing, Toots."

They both called each other *Toots*. They'd already settled into a comfortable, almost domestic routine. Their evenings together consisted mostly of eating ethnic takeout food, which small-town Courtney still found exotic, making love every which way, and then talking for hours, lying around naked with a glass of wine. She wanted details about every partner in the firm, about judges and procedure and how to handle clients and situations of all kinds. As she said one night: "First, he pumped her, and then she pumped him."

Later, after lunch, shagging her furiously from behind, he blurted out, "I love you!"

But afterward she made a joke of it. "Aw, Toots, you don't love me. You just love my ass."

Chapter Fifteen

~~~~~~~~~~

CONFLICTED

For the first half hour on the drive home, Tara was full of the happiness of her day with Jason in Blue Lake. She'd boldly made him aware of her desire, and she was now fully aware of his. They couldn't pretend that this was just a friendship or a book club anymore. They'd both acknowledged that they were tempted and falling in love. Now what? Unfamiliar ground. Married and falling in love.

Yes, she wanted to read Emerson to help her get back to some terra firma, back to living what she believed. She needed to talk to someone. As always, she called her sister.

"Catherine?"

"Tara, how are you? You sound a bit upset."

"I'm sort of upset and sort of exhilarated at the same time." How much should Tara disclose? "I'm confused because I have a sort of a crush on someone I work with a lot."

"Another journalist?" her sister asked.

"No, an environmental judge. He's divorced and also pretty smitten with me. We haven't really acted on it yet, but we're getting perilously close."

Catherine listened without judgment. It felt good.

"Are you in love with him?"

"Yes, a little." Tara had started to drift into the other lane of traffic, and pulled the car sharply back. "And you know that things have been distant with Mike. We rarely even see each other."

"Well, maybe give it your best shot with Michael, go to counseling, and see where that leaves you?"

"Yes," Tara replied. Would Mike even agree to go unless she told him?

"You deserve to be happy, that's all I know," Catherine said. "But just try to make sure you have no regrets with Michael."

"Thanks, Catherine, I'm driving but I will call you again. Everything okay with you guys?"

"Yes, but we sure are boring compared to you." Was that a passive-aggressive dig?

"Boring is good," Tara replied. Or maybe not. Wasn't that part of why people had affairs—because things got boring? But Tara had never wanted to be like that.

When Tara arrived home, Mike wasn't even there. She'd been imagining, almost hoping for, some kind of scene. Instead, there was just their neglected dog, Shelby, who very much wanted to go outside. More reason for guilt.

But when she came back in, Shelby covered her with affectionate, forgiving licks. Then she lapped up some fresh water and settled in happily next to Tara on the sofa in the great room. Tara played back the blinking answering machine message. Mike.

"Hi, Tara," Mike said on the message. "It's about nine thirty. I assume you're taking Shelby out for a walk. Things are crazy here; we won our division! Don't expect me until late."

Why had he called their landline instead of her cell? Where was he? Could he be with someone else too? Susan?

So much went on that the other one knew nothing about! One

thing was true: Tara could get away with murder in this marriage. But she wasn't a murderer or even a natural adulteress. That sexist old word still had power over her. Why?

Mike had always been a little uncommunicative, secretive almost, since they'd met in college. It was almost the stereotype of being more comfortable with computers than with people. She'd thought it was a charming quirk then.

Shelby snuggled with her as she sat at the kitchen table. Then Tara got up, gave her sweet, non-judgmental dog a couple of her favorite treats, and poured herself a glass of chardonnay.

Jason had come along at just the wrong moment, a sort of vision of what was missing. Intelligent and stimulating conversation. Sharing so many concerns. Time together. But was Jason really what he appeared to be?

His ethics were sometimes flexible too. One time he'd even left the draft of a decision in his unlocked car, saying, "Who knows what an enterprising reporter might find in there?" She beat the Milwaukee paper by a mile when the final decision came out.

They both went blithely ahead to the very brink of an affair, knowing it was wrong. Tara knew she had to rein herself in. The guilt would eat her up. She wasn't cut out to have an affair. What would happen if she started sleeping with him? As things were, her conscience wouldn't leave her alone. She needed to cool things down, to get control of her feelings, her life, again. To have things out with Mike.

She started composing an email to Jason in her mind. She'd tell him everything. Maybe if she was totally honest she could explain herself to him, and to herself.

Today was as close as she'd ever come. Her underwear was still damp. Not that Michael would notice. Mike would come home late, raid the refrigerator, and then walk right past her, barely pausing to say hello, on his way to the shower.

They would sit watching ESPN or MSNBC, until Mike dozed off. Maybe one night a week he would feel obligated to make a pass at her.

He would seem relieved when, as was happening more and more frequently, she told him she wasn't in the mood.

But she was! She was! She and Jason had had that boldly intimate moment.

Tara undressed, put on her oversize sleeping T-shirt and got in bed to work on her email. She'd just begun when she heard a car door slam. Mike had finally arrived home. It was almost midnight.

Mike approached quietly, afraid of waking her. "Oh great, you're up!"

"Long day?" she asked him quietly.

He gave her a kiss on the cheek. She noticed his body odor, a sweaty, musky scent.

"Crazy." His eyes looked everywhere but into hers. Was she smelling sex? "How was yours?"

"A little hectic too. I had an interview."

"I see you're still working—anything interesting?"

"Yes, it is interesting. It's a story about what happens if we try to deny nature too long." Part of her still wanted a confrontation with him.

"I'd like to read it when you're done. Sorry I called so late. I thought you must have taken Shelby out for a walk." No, she hadn't given Shelby a proper walk all week.

"Right, I was." Was there no end to her lies, to the guilt she could feel?

"Well, I won't keep you from it. I think I'm going to watch TV a bit to unwind." He went back toward the door to leave.

"Mike?" she called, her tone bringing him back into the bedroom. "There's something I want to talk about. We should go to a marriage counselor." It wasn't as hard to say as she had feared it would be. "Things haven't gotten better since our fight after the birthday party."

"I'm just so busy—" he interjected rapidly, biting his right index finger.

"No, it's more than that."

"Is there someone else?"

"No." She paused. "Not yet, Michael. Is there for you?"

"No!"

"Good. Let's go before it's too late."

"Call my secretary and make the appointment."

Not what she wanted to hear. She couldn't imagine Jason Erickson saying, "Call my secretary."

But she said, "Okay. I'm worried, Mike."

"Don't worry, Tara." He came back over to their bed and gave her a hug. "We can make things better."

The next morning, Tara wrote Jason an email. It was very different from the brutally honest one she'd planned to send.

Chapter Sixteen

~~~~~~~~~~~~~~~~

FREUDIAN PIER SLIPS

As he entered the courtroom buzzing with people and excitement, Jason was in a buoyant mood. Could yesterday mean that Tara was making her move away from Michael? He had to give her space, but something like that might be going on. It was up to her. But he felt less—rather than more—guilty after yesterday.

They weren't messing around; they were falling in love.

Another day, another lake. Yesterday had been their eventful day in Blue Lake and today was a trial about a proposed marina on Pine Lake, a couple of hours north. Jason settled himself in his heavy brown leather chair that was the judge's seat.

He sometimes still loved his job. Across Wisconsin, wherever he went, people turned out to be heard. Environmental issues were one area of public life where apathy didn't seem to exist. How many times had he walked into similarly noisy and crowded rooms, or seen working people sit through hours of tedious technical testimony because they loved some small stretch of land or lake? Minnesota called itself the Land of Ten Thousand Lakes, but Wisconsin had fifteen thousand. Jason had been to many hundreds as judge, and had listened to the concerns of thousands of people.

At the counsel table there was Marcia Reimer, an old acquaintance from his undergraduate days, representing the state. Courtney Sharpe, Earl Franks's young associate, was there too, industriously marking exhibits and whispering to an engineer in a blue suit. Behind the engineer were the biologists and fisheries experts, people who'd quietly devoted their lives to preserving the fish and weeds and bugs that had once thrived together in intricate abundance.

In the back of the room sat the usual gray-headed group of couples: local history with legs. These folks knew every square inch of the lake, every tree stump and bog and fishing hot spot. Jason liked all of these people, even the much-maligned real estate developers. They were just the well-dressed predators of the environmental law habitat.

On the whole, they were people of energy and vision who seized the opportunities of their lifetime to transform land into highly valued real estate. Nothing sinister about that, just sometimes shortsighted. Lake property became more valuable every year—there was thirty-five percent appreciation *a year* on some North Woods lakes. Truly pristine shorelines were becoming harder and harder to find. Blue Lake was one of the last few.

A woman was trying to get his attention.

"I'm Janice Thorton from the *North Woods Weekly*," she said, taking Jason out of his reverie. A northern local with stringy gray hair. A bit unkempt. "Could I have your card?"

"Sure," replied Jason, wondering whether Janice lived in a small town in the North Woods just so she didn't have to shower every day.

Tara would call that thought cynical or even cruel. He couldn't always help himself. He had his mother's sharp tongue, but that didn't make him cynical.

Over the years, he'd received several offers to go over to the dark side with a big firm to double or triple his salary. If he were truly cynical, he wouldn't still be living in his little two-bedroom bungalow. Jason was in this crowded room, like most everyone else, because he loved lakes.

It was time for his opening spiel. He spoke, as always, for ten minutes and laid down the ground rules and governing statutes. When he'd started the job back in the late 1990s, he used to say, "This is a formal proceeding and not *The Jerry Springer Show*." But no one knew who that was anymore.

The parties were all agreed on the issues, but the case had one of those nasty sub-issues about whether the state EPA had delayed the marina project purposefully, to allow environmental opposition to take hold. Because it was framed as whether the statutory standards had been followed, it was very hard to keep it out of the case—though it would have little to do with Jason's eventual decision.

Courtney Sharpe was going to try to milk it for all it was worth. Maurice Abbot was handling the file for the state EPA.

"Did you complain about Maurice Abbott's handling of your permit application?" Courtney asked.

"Yes," replied John Logan, the marina's engineer.

"To whom did you complain?"

"The Secretary, Representative Lucke, Senator Klein; I think Lucke wrote the governor's office."

"He did indeed," Courtney stated. "Let me show you what's been marked as exhibit thirteen; is that the letter you were referring to?"

"Yes, that's it," John replied.

"Does Representative Lucke say he has been shown a stack of documents three inches thick about how Mr. Abbott was sitting on your application and quote 'stirring up environmentalists?'"

"That's what the letter says." John's lack of enthusiasm betrayed that he knew it was total BS.

Maurice Abbott? Mo was a decent but overworked career EPA employee nearing retirement. The idea of him stirring up anything other than a Bloody Mary on a Packer Sunday—least of all the local environmental community, which needed no shaking— was hard for Jason to imagine.

"Would those documents have come from you?" Courtney asked.

"Well, I guess," the witness stuttered. "I mean my partners didn't meet with Representative Lucke. I did."

"Do you have those documents with you now?"

"Forget about it. There are no documents." An expert witness with scruples. Inspiring. "He's a politician. What can I say? He exaggerated a little."

Jason was trying to bite his tongue, but he couldn't, not after a paid expert had blown the political backstory out of the water. "Of course we all remember *another* famous Wisconsin politician who went around smearing people's reputations with phony stacks of documents," Jason observed, knowing that it might cause a stir. "Redirect?"

"Did you ever get a promise from anyone, politician or otherwise, that your application would be judged by something other than the appropriate legal standards?" asked Courtney, fuming.

"No," John answered.

"No further questions."

"Okay. Let's take a break," said Jason.

"Thanks, Judge," Janice Thorton said to him on her way out of the room. "You've given me my headline."

Just what he needed. Jason could see it now—JUDGE COMPARES REP. LUCKE TO JOE McCARTHY. So be it.

Representative Lucke was the new chairperson of the Natural Resources Committee in the state legislature. Courtney would make sure Lucke and the whole world heard about it. Jason was making powerful enemies everywhere.

In the afternoon, things went from drama to comedy, but it was not much easier to bear. One of the older fishermen was quizzing a biologist about the impacts of putting pier slips in the near-shore area, the so-called littoral zone.

"What will be the impact on the clitoral zone, especially what with the clitoral drift, of building yet more piers?"

"You mean the—the littoral zone?" The biologist tried, not entirely successfully, to keep from smirking.

"Yes, yes, that's what I said, doesn't all of this ultimately have an impact on the *clitoral* zone?"

His wife, her face flushed, looked on in horror. Courtney was grinning like a Cheshire cat.

"Sir," Jason inserted at last. "It's littoral zone, with an *L*."

"Well, I'm just a humble fisherman, Your Honor."

"Of course, of course," Jason said. This time, he resisted a strong urge to comment out of sympathy for the fisherman's clearly embarrassed wife.

The poor woman came up to Jason at the next break. "Thanks for your discretion." She shook her head. "Talk about your Freudian pier slips!"

On his drive down to La Crosse after the hearing, Jason turned on public radio. Sure enough, he'd made the state news summary. Rep. Lucke was asked to respond to his comments.

"Judge Erickson seemed to compare you to Joe McCarthy. What's your response?"

"That statement is false and defamatory."

"But it came from an administrative judge in open court. No response?" the interviewer goaded.

"He is *grossly* misinformed," Lucke replied. "And is he a real judge? I mean, they even have judges at dog shows."

Chapter Seventeen

~~~~~~~~~~~~~~~~

DRINKING ALES WITH THE JUDGE

After the long day in the field with Dr. Walter, Grace stopped at the Bodega bar in downtown La Crosse for a quick beer. As she made her way toward the bar to order, Grace noticed Jason Erickson waiting patiently to order just ahead of her. The place was packed and they really had no choice but to stand next to each other in the little alcove in the back.

"Hi, Judge." Grace offered her hand. "How are you?" Awkward. She wasn't sure what was proper and what wasn't.

"Rough day. I'm afraid I put my foot in my mouth today at a hearing an hour north of here. I decided to stay over in La Crosse and hit the Bodega to compensate."

"To be honest, I heard about it on public radio."

"I'm always pissing off somebody in this job. But 'they even have judges at dog shows' will probably be in my obit now." Jason smiled.

"But don't worry, Judge. Lots of people in this state think it's a compliment to compare someone to Joe McCarthy!"

"Please call me Jason. Cheers!" He laughed and they clinked glasses. "Hopefully, there aren't any people from White Dairy here tonight," Jason joked.

"Yeah, it looks like we're hatching up a secret plan," Grace replied. "Is it okay? Are we allowed to have a beer with a case pending?"

"Funny. Fifteen years ago, I would have said no, but I'm not so sure anymore. It's not like we're going to talk about your case. DAs and judges have beers every night in lots of places." They noticed a couple leaving a small table.

"Let's grab it," Grace said, seizing the opportunity.

"Honestly, your case is the last thing in the world I want to talk about right now," Jason said.

"Same here," she said, taking a big sip of the foamy ale.

Her mom would be proud that she'd vainly taken off her glasses. Jason was animated and seemed to be very glad to be with her. When they'd finished, it was her turn to buy. But without her glasses, she couldn't even read the menu of available choices. Vanity was futile. She asked the bearded bartender for two more of the same.

"The same of what? We have hundreds of ales."

Grace looked over toward Jason and pointed him out.

"Oh, the dude with the suit?" the bartender asked. "He ordered One Barrel Penguins."

"Thanks." She caught Jason watching her walk back from the bar.

"The bartender remembered. Two Penguins, right?" She set them on the table.

"Yes, a great Madison brew. Cheers."

Grace clinked mugs again and put her glasses back on. "I'm basically blind without these."

"They suit you anyway." Jason grinned. "So, Grace, have you remarried?"

"No, it's been hard. In the first years, I was too full of grief, and then for the past bunch I've just been working so many hours. How about you after your divorce?"

"Kind of the same story, and all of the good ones seem to be married by now. One has to stay clear of them too."

"Oh, yes! I know all about that one." Grace heard herself laugh, with an almost carnal candor. "They're unhappy in their marriage, and because you're not married, it's your job to either buck them up or console them."

Jason shook his head. "Or to give them what's missing in their marriage." He took a long sip of his ale.

"Ding, ding, ding! Bingo!"

"You make me laugh. I almost wish we hadn't met trying this case," Jason said.

"What's your married person like? Mine is with an old college-era friend. He says his wife is kind of a cold person, but she's a very caring scientist. They work together on environmental issues out on the Hudson River."

"My married person has drifted away from her husband. She's an avid reader and he's an engineer who barely reads the paper. We're in a book club together."

"I'm in a book club too. But it's all women and I'm regrettably straight."

"Quite honestly, I don't have anything else going romantically, not even a single female friend to have a beer with." Jason looked a little silly, with a bit of the ale lace painted above his upper lip.

"You will when our case together is over!" Grace said.

They clinked glasses.

"That's nice. How about you?"

"I had a minor crush on my new office manager, but he just got married to his boyfriend," Grace said.

"Have you gone online? Personally, there's something about that that just turns me off a little. And it's hard to make plans with my schedule."

"Yes, I have. And I don't know about Madison, but here in La Crosse you have a pretty good idea of who the professional single men are."

"Well, here's to us then," Jason said. "Friends of the future, but ever so proper right now. Truthfully, I've got some bigger ethical concerns right now than having a drink with an old law school classmate. Want another?"

"Sure, if you'll tell me about it." She leaned toward him.

"Yes, but first, I need to hit the men's room."

Grace sat there, enjoying the hum of her favorite bar around her. When she was growing up, it was an actual bodega that had white tablecloths and matching napkins. It was the family place to celebrate, including her confirmation.

When he returned, the judge tried to change the subject, but Grace came back to it.

"So, what's your ethical problem? I used to be on the State Bar Committee that reviewed complaints, so maybe I have some idea of an answer."

"It's not really an ethical problem." Jason paused. "It's more like a threat that's been made against me." It was clear he didn't want to say more. "Things can be said in ambiguous ways that make it hard to tell and even harder to prove. You know lawyers and wiggle room."

"If someone threatens you, you should err on the side of reporting it," Grace said.

"Thanks, that's good advice, Counselor."

Grace wasn't sure if he was being patronizing or not. He looked a little nervous. A threat to a judge was no joke.

"One judge in Seattle had more than a thousand threats over one case," Grace said.

"Yikes. I guess I should feel lucky then." Jason seemed to pull away.

But when he got up to leave, Jason kissed her on her cheek. Then there was a soft glance at her lips. Who had done that, Jason or her? It didn't matter. She was happy and walked out the door with him.

"I'm so glad I ran into you, Grace."

"Me, too, Jason." This time, she gave him a lingering kiss on the mouth. Delightful as it was inappropriate.

He pulled away, but not immediately. "That's amazing. But we shouldn't. I mean, we can't."

"I know."

He gave her a quick hug. "That was some strong ale, wasn't it? Have a great night."

Chapter Eighteen

~~~~~~~~

TEMPORARY
FEELINGS

S tanding on the porch outside his little white bungalow, Jason felt a surge of joy. There was a long email from Tara waiting on their private account. Even her name gave him a thrill. Seeing it made him feel guilty about his night in La Crosse with Grace. It was all so damn confusing.

He went inside, grabbed a beer, and fired up his iMac. Oh man, Tara had attached Emerson's essays on *Love* and *Friendship*. A bad sign.

As he began to read Tara's letter, laying out why they could only be friends, he became angry. Angry with Tara for dumping him in a letter, and with himself for getting into the absurd, hackneyed predicament of being in love with a married woman. He'd always thought he was above that kind of thing. But he was just another Cusk character. Deluding himself.

He paced around his living room a little manically. He read through it again. Actually, it wasn't that bad.

Dear Jason:

Sunday in Blue Lake was exhilarating, mysterious, and wonderful. I am so glad to have you as my friend. I want to keep you as my friend and fear that we are headed down a path that might lead us somewhere beyond friendship. This is hard for me to write. I'm struggling, and when I struggle, I often turn to that old "Puritan windbag" Emerson.

I hadn't read his essays on "Friendship" or "Love" for a while, and you had me wondering whether my views on these relationships are skewed, impossible, or flat-out wrong.

As usual, Ralph Waldo and I are on the same page. Fortunately, he is far more eloquent than I could ever be. And just how closely and consistently my own intuition mirrors his thought is a constant source of wonder—and comfort—for me. He is one of the few ideals of mine that hasn't been trashed yet.

Do I sound guilty? Well, yes, there is some of that in all this. I guess I'm telling you that I'm pulling back. I'm offering you up my friendship as a sort of challenge. To find out how much you are prepared to give, really.

Anyway, you'll probably read these passages of Emerson and write us both off as earnest Puritans, hopelessly misguided. But if you don't respect my ideals, how can you really respect me?

I'm not saying that you haven't, Jason—you've been very patient. I'm more afraid, after today.

The thing about journalism is that my geography, my whole habitat, keeps changing! I have so few anchors in my life! We've moved around so much—my friends and acquaintances keep changing. I've distanced myself from my family and, increasingly, from Mike. He has been one of the few constants, one of the only anchors that have kept my restless spirit from going out to sea! I need him. And I need you, as my friend, to understand.

To understand so much. Things I can say and things I can't. What I'm saying is, of course, that I want to take the last flight back to friendship. Anything else scares me too much. And you want me to arrive whole, my best self, if my destination should ever be your arms.

I loved being there, however briefly.

Yours,
Tara

Jason impulsively picked up the phone and dialed Tara's number. He knew it wasn't a great idea. They rarely called each other at home, and it was getting pretty late. But he was wired. He didn't even say hello.

"Is this a good time to talk?" he asked as soon as she answered.

"No. Not really," Tara replied, her voice unusually brittle.

"Well, I'd like to talk. I just got that spineless Emerson friendship letter." He sounded more bitter than he would have liked. "You didn't have to hide behind him. I told you that I wanted your marriage to work out."

"Yes, I know. But no, we really don't need any more credit cards," Tara said abruptly, hanging up the phone.

Damn! She'd never been so cruel to him before. Stunning. An anguished few minutes passed.

Of course, it was time for Jason to simply back off. He was in the wrong, feeling the way he did about a married woman. Nothing he could do or say would change that. But he still felt righteously indignant that he couldn't even feel righteously indignant.

He decided to take himself out for a walk. That strategy had worked, intermittently, during his tumultuous divorce.

It was a cool summer night. The sky was clear and bright with star constellations and a blood-orange moon. He walked a couple blocks to Lake Wingra Park and found a bench. It was already a little wet with dew. The vivid moonlight set off sparks above the shining black water of the lake. There was even a whistling breeze. It was a perfect night, yet none of it could reach him.

Jason felt the buzz of a text message on his phone. A contrite Tara? No, it was his good friend Ben.

Hanging at Gates if you're up and want to come down for a nightcap.

On my way, on foot. Five minutes! Jason replied immediately.

He and Ben had gone from running buddies to best buds as Ben had gone through his divorce and the heartache of not seeing his two daughters every day over the past couple of years. They still ran the arboretum loop 10K most Saturdays.

The crowd had already thinned out at Gates and Brovi, the cozy neighborhood bar and restaurant that frequently fed Jason after a night out of town. Ben, athletic and tall, greeted him with a nod and a smile.

"I took the liberty of ordering you a gin and tonic."

"Thanks, man. Good timing. I was just out for an agitated stroll."

"Walker's people?" Ben asked.

"No, not this time." How much should Jason share? "How are the girls doing?"

"Great. It's my weekend and we're going camping at Devil's Lake."

"Hey, Jason." Lonnie, the bartender, set down the cucumber-and-lime gin and tonic. "Cheers," all three said in unison. Lonnie went to serve the group at the opposite end of the bar.

"You look troubled, what's up?" Ben asked.

"I've kind of got this thing with a woman who is married. Not sexual. Yet."

"Are you in love with her?"

Jason nodded. "I keep thinking about having a kid with her," he confessed. He hadn't even admitted that to himself, but it was part of his love for Tara since their second book club email. Funny, that thought had never once crossed his mind with Madeline.

"Heavy," Ben said. "Is that mutual?"

"In theory, but not tonight," Jason replied. "Tonight, I've got the Other Man Blues."

They both laughed and clinked glasses.

"Dude, that is heavy."

"Thanks for that perspective," Jason said. "When I called tonight, she pretended that I was trying to sell her a credit card."

"Ouch."

Lonnie approached. "Last call, guys."

"Let me buy you one, Ben."

"Sure. So, what are you going to do?"

"Probably nothing," Jason replied. "Being passive is my fatal flaw."

"The only remedy for that is action," Ben said.

"I know, but what?"

Ben shook his head and took a big swig of the gin and tonic.

When the bar closed, Ben offered to drive Jason home but he declined. Jason walked home, muttering to himself. When he finally checked his watch, it was almost 1:00 a.m.

When he got home, he reread all of the cards and emails Tara had sent him. In their letters, he noticed now, they'd done a kind of dance. They seemed to take turns leading, one of them offering some bold step forward, just as the other brought them a cautious step back.

Jason had been such a fool. Tara had led him to this island and then deserted him, treating him cavalierly in the name of her long-lost Emersonian ideals. To hell with Emerson, and his pompous essay on friendship! Wasn't respect an essential element of friendship?

Only an ethical narcissist could be so callous in the name of self-serving ideals. So there, Tara! He chuckled, catching himself doing it again.

He'd long had the habit of intellectualizing his deepest feelings. Was this just another way of not dealing with things—another legacy of his father's death when he was fourteen? Madeline would have said so, and Justin, too. His brother said losing both parents so young had messed them both up royally.

Then they'd held each other intimately at the Lake of the Pines. Their deep feelings and their desire could no longer be ignored. So, of course, Tara was taking a huge step back. He decided to write her a letter rather than an email.

> *Dear Tara:*
>
> *I want things to work out for you and Mike. But the fall from Sunday in Blue Lake to Tuesday night on the phone was pretty stark. I went out for a walk, but even the most beautiful moon, lake, and sky couldn't console me. Maybe it's for the best. I'm not sure that I can relate to your Emersonian spiritual idealism.*
>
> *At times, yes, but not always. To me, it often seems like putting the cart of ideas before the living, breathing horse of reality. I'm good at that—I can turn all of my feelings into ideas, but it just doesn't work. It seems like a way to pretend that the world is the way we want it to be rather than the way it really is.*
>
> *A while ago, I found a quote from Herman Melville, a specific response to Emerson. Since you hide behind Emerson, I guess I can do the same with Melville.*
>
> *"This 'all' feeling," Melville wrote to Hawthorne in 1851, "there is some truth in it. You must often have felt it, lying on the grass on a warm summer's day. Your legs seem to send out shoots into the earth. Your hair feels like leaves upon your head. This is the all feeling. But what plays the mischief with the truth is that men*

will insist upon the universal application of a tempo-
rary feeling or opinion."

What has played mischief with my heart, Tara, is
giving far too much weight to the "temporary feeling" of
being close to you. It won't happen again.

Yours,
Jason

He slept fitfully that night, dreaming about nasty scenes with Tara at a trial. In one, first Franks cross-examined her and then Jason did himself. Then it shifted to endless conversations about Emerson and Thoreau and how the whole damn world was organized. He woke up exhausted, but managed to get himself into work more or less on time.

Around 9:30 a.m., Tara called. He didn't pick up the first time but finally did after she left a voicemail apologizing.

"Hey, Jason. How are you?" She sounded guilty when Jason finally answered.

"I'm a little tired."

"I didn't sleep much either."

Jason made a dismissive grunt. "A lot of that going around."

"Well, I'm calling to say I'm sorry about last night."

He remained silent, waiting to hear her explanation.

"It was just too much to talk to you, with Mike right there."

"Then say, 'I've got to go,' not 'We don't need any more credit cards.'"

"That was pretty lame." Tara laughed.

Despite himself, Jason laughed too.

"How are you doing?"

"I sent you a letter late last night."

"Oh, no."

"It's not too bad. I was really more pissed at Emerson."

"Damn, that old windbag." Tara laughed again. How he loved her intelligent, sympathetic laugh.

"Of course, I was hurt, but I want you to keep working with Michael. If not, you'll never know for sure if things could have worked," Jason said. "So, yes, I'm officially backing off."

"I just have to cling to something. To my ideals, to Mike," Tara said. "He's really my main family. My parents are so weird, and my sister is in California. We've moved around so much. He's my anchor."

"Well, until you figure it out with your anchor, please leave me alone," Jason said.

"Don't mock me."

"I'm not. I mean it. I can be patient. But I just can't deal with yo-yo-ing from 'I'm falling in love with you' to, 'No, we don't need any more credit cards.'"

"I hear you," Tara said. "Mike and I are doing marriage counseling—starting Thursday."

"Great. I mean that. But this is hard for me. I know you think I'm so skeptical, so tough, but I'm not." Jason paused, looking for the right words. "I'm just another hopeful romantic, like you."

Tara let out a laugh—or was it a sniffle? "I like that."

"Then that's a good place to end it."

"I'll see you next week at Lake Joseph," Tara said. "Have you heard any more from Earl Franks?"

"No, maybe I was making too much of that, too. Seems to be a habit of mine," Jason replied.

"Stop it. We'll talk."

Chapter Nineteen

WHERE DOES THIS LEAVE YOU?

Tara pulled into the counselor's tree-lined parking lot at the side of the house that was the marriage counselor's office. It was a three-story Victorian, painted dark green with off-white-and-red trim. She looked but didn't see Michael's blue Acura anywhere. Late, as usual. He'd better show!

She'd been lucky to get this appointment. They were doing back-to-back sessions over the next two days. On her website, Dr. Reesa bragged that if she couldn't fix your marriage in a couple of back-to-back sessions, it was probably not salvageable. The focus on rapid progress made both the HMOs and her patients happy.

Was Tara going to recommit, or was she going to leave her husband? Today and tomorrow would make it clear.

After waiting in her car until almost nine, Tara decided to go in first anyway.

Dr. Reesa Hanson, tall and chic, greeted Tara with a welcoming handshake. She ushered Tara into the waiting room. She was surprisingly young, in her early-to-mid-thirties. She was wearing a sort of floral silk jacket and a black T-shirt that said, *Just…*

"I'm Dr. Reesa. Is your husband here?"

"Not yet."

Dr. Reesa gave Tara a look of pity. Tara had made the appointment, and Michael was late. Bad signs for a counselor, no doubt.

"I'll leave my door open," Dr. Reesa said softly. Her voice made Tara think of a guided meditation tape that she couldn't stand.

Michael arrived, apologetic and out of breath.

"Sorry, it took me a while to find this place," Mike said.

He had a new, very short haircut this summer that he thought gave him the look of a 1960s Olympic athlete or a well-heeled European playboy. He was lean and athletic. The haircut did suit him. Mike's fine features could pull it off.

"That's okay. You're just five minutes late now," Tara said.

Dr. Reesa was quickly back in the waiting room. Maybe she didn't want to miss their interaction? She introduced herself to Michael and led them into her office. Her walls were full of colorful art gathered from her travels around the world—mostly South American rugs and a few Japanese drawings.

Tara felt a little jealous. Michael only wanted to travel in the States. She hadn't been out of the US since they were married.

"Please, have a seat." They sat next to each other, on a plush green sofa. She told them to call her Dr. Reesa, gave them a long spiel about the process and a little notebook to work on that night. Then there were more getting to know you questions. At last, she asked them each to define what they saw as the two biggest problems in their marriage.

"Tara, you go first, since you're the one who set up the appointment."

Tara took a breath, nodding. She didn't want to go first. She didn't want to go at all.

"We're not talking to each other much anymore." Tara watched them both anxiously watching her. "We rarely see each other, and when we do, we are so distant."

Dr. Reesa smiled professionally. "Good. Mike, what about you?"

"Well, I agree with that." He looked down at his shoes. "Our schedules are both very erratic and don't lend themselves to regular habits."

"Now, I want you to think about not these problems," Dr. Reesa said slowly. "But focus instead on how they make you feel. Mike, you go first."

"Umm, sad, I guess." He shrugged. "And a little guilty."

"Excellent," Dr. Reesa purred, trying to draw him in. "Guilt about what?"

"That I've neglected Tara and our marriage. I know I'm too wrapped up in my work." Michael smiled. Pleased with his answer. Tara was, too. She suddenly felt hopeful.

"What kind of work do you do, Michael?" asked Dr. Reesa.

"Software engineering." He looked relieved to be back in his comfort zone. "Lots of crisis situations and long hours."

"I see. That explains the work piece." Dr. Reesa paused. "And Tara, what do you feel when Michael is gone so much?"

"Separation, loneliness. So much loneliness, sometimes even when we're together." Tara closed her eyes and let herself feel. There was guilt about the way things had progressed between her and Jason. "I guess I feel some guilt too."

"And what's the source of your guilt?" asked Dr. Reesa.

Her searching look almost made Tara flinch. That night at the Lake of the Pines motel. She was glad she'd stopped things with Jason when she had. What had she been thinking?

"Just that I've pursued my own interests instead of trying to make things better," Tara said at last.

Dr. Reesa nodded with that empty, well-trained smile again and then looked to her husband. "Michael, you look like you're about to say something."

"The word that just came to mind for me is emptiness." His voice trailed off. He was always censoring himself, or at least his feelings. But he went on. "I feel regret, too, that I've spent so much more time on my career and neglected Tara."

"Tell me about the emptiness for you, Michael."

"Sometimes, I find myself avoiding her." He looked directly into Dr. Reesa's eyes. "It's just so empty when we're together. We seem to have less and less to talk about. And I almost fear the demands she'll make on me."

"What demands?" Tara fumed.

"Not now, Tara. I want to hear from Michael first," said Dr. Reesa.

Tara had the sense that Reesa was following a script—"Not now, *fill in name here*. I want to hear from . . . "

"Michael, when you feel this emptiness, is part of it a sense of loss about how things used to be between you?"

"Maybe. But it's mostly this kind of numbness." He looked both bitter and slightly relieved. Or was Tara projecting? "I feel so far from her."

"Okay, now, before we finish today, I want you to tell me why you are here, and why it's worth the effort to work things out together," Dr. Reesa said. "Tara, do you want to go first?"

"Sure." It was a little hard to focus through her irritation. "I'm here to try to make things right, because I still care about Mike. I'm afraid that if we do nothing, we'll lose each other." Tara's voice was suddenly full of emotion. "I need more from you, Mike." Now, she was crying openly. However messed up it had become, she *was* trying to save her marriage. "When we met, there was so much hope for us, for our future."

"Good, Tara." Dr. Reesa nodded. "Your turn, Mike."

"Well, I guess I'm more practical. But my first thought was that if we split up, we would lose the house that we both love."

His words went through Tara. The house?

"And Tara's right. There was a time when we were such good friends." Michael Highsmith, the stranger she'd been married to for ten years, paused, straining for words.

"Anything else, Michael?"

He had that blank, stupid look that Tara hated. "I do miss our friendship." He was all the more ridiculous with his macho new haircut.

"Well, that's something positive to build on." Dr. Reesa's voice was bright, but her knowing smile was nowhere to be seen.

The look on Tara's face must have shown her devastation. The house. "We used to be such good friends." That's what ten years together had meant to him?

"How does that leave you feeling, Tara?"

"I don't know." Like shit, like roadkill. "A little betrayed, abandoned."

"Michael?" Dr. Reesa prompted.

"I don't know. This is all new to me . . . I'm here. I'm trying. I can't be expected to perform on command."

"I understand. Think about that last question: why it's worth the effort, for tomorrow. I'm sorry but our time is up for today."

Dr. Reesa stood up, ready for the next bad marriage. Michael got up quickly, relieved the hour was over.

He was so uncomfortable talking about his feelings. He was always hiding—what was he so afraid of exposing? There really never seemed to be that much to him, other than his job and those fears of exposure. Did she even care anymore? For the first time, the possibility of divorce seemed real. Imminent, even.

"There's more, of course, Tara. Be patient with me." Mike touched her shoulder. "I'm trying."

"Okay." How long could he expect credit for just showing up?

He looked briefly at his phone to check the time. "Did you remember that I'm going to Boston tomorrow night?"

"Yes. Do you need a ride to the airport?"

"No. Ted's flying out too. We're sharing a taxi."

"You seem to have given up," Tara said. Was she talking to him or herself?

"Be patient."

"I've been patient, Michael." Tara had the familiar urge to shake him, to wake him up to the possibilities in their life together. To have him acknowledge her presence in his life. "I've been too damn patient!"

"Don't take things so hard. This is just the first session. I'll see you later tonight." And with that, he was gone.

Tara was in bed by the time he came home, and he slept in the guest bedroom, as was becoming his habit. Would he even do the little couple inventory questionnaire?

The next morning, though they both left from home, they took separate cars again. Tara was feeling slightly optimistic by the time she arrived at Dr. Reesa's office. Why? Michael had always been a little remote emotionally, but maybe he could grow. He kept so much to himself: his feelings, his motivation, his hopes. Did he even explore or know those things about himself?

Michael arrived a little later, on time for once. "How you doing?" Her handsome husband planted a kiss on her cheek in greeting.

"Okay. You?"

"Tired. Didn't sleep too well last night."

"Me either. Reesa's running a little late, I think." Tara sat there awkwardly, looking for the right words. "I feel optimistic, Mike."

He looked away and gave a half nod.

Dr. Reesa, looking distracted, came in to get them.

"Yesterday we were talking about reasons to keep working at your marriage. And my notes say that Tara was a little upset that Michael had mentioned the house first. Michael, have you thought of other reasons?"

"Well, I think I said we were once good friends. We're really not anymore. We seem to have so little in common these days."

"Now, that's positive," Tara chimed in. Where was all of that optimism she'd just been selling herself?

"Tara, how does that leave you feeling—"

"—I don't know. I'm getting close to giving up, Michael. Don't you see that, or do you just not care?"

"Tara, I think *I have* given up." For the first time in years, she saw tears in Michael's eyes. "This seems like a spineless way to tell you, but I've been seeing someone else. A woman at work."

"Susan?"

He nodded.

"Are you in love with her?"

"Yes, I think I am. I didn't mean for that to happen. She's a software engineer too, and we spent so many hours together before anything—"

"—I don't want to hear any more," Tara interrupted. Despite everything, it was devastating. "For over a year! I hope that you and Elisabeth Moss will be happy," was what came out of her mouth. Lame, but it made her chortle out a mean little laugh.

"Elisabeth? I thought her name was Susan?" Dr. Reesa asked. "Anyway, where does this leave you, Michael? Are you still committed to trying to work this through with Tara?"

"I don't think so," Michael answered immediately. Then, he tried to soften the blow. "I mean, I was at first, but I think it's too late. I think our differences are just too deep to ever conquer them."

"Okay," Tara said quietly. "Are you saying that you want a divorce?"

He nodded. "I'm so sorry, Tara. So sorry. But don't act so surprised; I've heard you on the phone with your friend the judge, and you weren't talking about books or any cases. I think we both knew our marriage was over."

"The judge and I are just friends. And I wouldn't have come here if I'd thought that," Tara said. She stood up and looked at Dr. Reesa coldly. "And we even did it in two sessions!"

Tara went into her car and put on her favorite Solange CD. She sat there for a bit, laughing and crying.

Chapter Twenty

~~~~~~~~~~

THE ONLY THING
THAT MATTERS

Grace was even more pumped up than usual, getting ready for a multiday trial. That was always nerve-racking, but this was the White Farms Dairy case, with a presiding judge that she'd had a drink with and kissed on the lips a few weeks back. She wasn't really sure who kissed whom first. It was confusing, unprofessional, and just added to her stress.

But she wasn't thinking so much about Jason as her Uncle Ray, who'd taught her how to prepare for a trial. She always thought of Ray, the would-be actor and trial master, whenever she got ready to try a case. Ray had taken her to numerous trials, where she saw him in his theatrical element. Her uncle had a rich, compelling voice and a shrewd but down-to-earth mind that could cut right to the heart of any dispute. He understood what motivated people and invited juries to feel good about themselves by doing justice for his clients.

He was full of old tricks and folksy lawyer adages that his clients loved.

"You know the difference between *I don't know* and *I don't remember*, don't you?" Ray would ask.

The client would nod dubiously.

Ray would say, "If I asked you what I had for breakfast this morning, your answer would be what?"

"I don't know," the client would reply.

"Exactly, but if I asked you what you had for breakfast one year ago today, what would you say?" Ray would ask.

As often as not, the client would repeat, "I don't know" before Ray would gently remind them that they'd once known but no longer remembered the details. If the person was especially thick, Ray would sometimes say it all over again two or three times. Eventually even the dimmest bulbs would light up, as Ray had put it.

"But don't forget, Gracie, that not everybody is quick as we Clarksons."

Grace made notes and document files with the names of every witness on it—hers and from all the other parties—something she hadn't done since her first trial with Uncle Ray.

Tom was in working on Saturday too and had done a lot of the paralegal work—including helping her decide what to put in the folders. Tom made her all the more confident that she was ready. She did her opening statement for him.

It was a precise roadmap to the statutes and what her experts would opine, but she also wanted it to be funny and moving. She ended by mentioning that she'd met her late husband working on a water project when they were both in the Peace Corps. They'd worked hard and saw the project through. She could drink water today from those wells in West Africa, but not from the wells ninety miles from her hometown in western Wisconsin.

As she finished, she could tell it hit home.

"I loved it." Tom wiped his eyes.

Grace changed into her running clothes and ran the trail along the river that was only a block and a half from her office. Her late uncle had championed the trail he rarely used himself. Ray's walks were far more likely to lead to the Popcorn Tavern, the Casino Lounge, or one of his many favorite bars on Third Street. But he'd understood the value of walkability and would have been thrilled with thriving downtown La Crosse, with its chic hotels and restaurants with Beard-nominated chefs.

She was feeling excited about the trial and not nervous at all. A nice, Ray-like thought occurred to her. No matter what time the trial was over tomorrow, no matter how it went, she would run this same path and be glad to be there. With Ray it would have been the Popcorn Tavern or the credibly retro Casino Cocktail Lounge.

The next morning, Grace made her way to the courtroom, thirty minutes early. Tom helped her load and unload the suitcases and set up her PowerPoint and posterboard exhibits.

But first they all had to do the site inspection for the judge. She'd already seen the site, but still had to go along to keep the other side honest. Grace had won a motion to view the site with her expert a couple of months back, and had pored over the building plans and aerial photos for the past four weeks.

Now, she recoiled a bit as she watched the judge and his journalist friend exchange flirting glances. There was no doubt they were both paying attention when it counted, though. Jason had given Grace almost every pretrial ruling and made a terrific record that would aid any appeals.

The bus bounced to a stop. Confident of getting a permit, they were already adding row after row of white buildings, with green roofs and a crude little gully for the waste of these hundreds of cows who shared this crowded factory floor as their home. They entered one state-of-the-art building already operating on the old permit that allowed five thousand cows. The brown-and-white Guernsey herd members had big yellow ear tags with numbers on them—these were number 891 and 893. Cow number 5985 was around in one of these buildings, and White Farms was hoping to double that number.

After the quick tour, they were on the bus, and soon they were back in court. During her Opening the judge looked into her eyes thoughtfully, with almost a boy-meets-girl intensity. She looked back. Briefly. But only because she was trying to speak to him in a directly personal manner.

He had the power as judge to help right a wrong, the harms the dairy farm had imposed on its neighbors. He had the power—so he had to do something. It was that simple. Uncle Ray had taught her well.

The next day, Grace noticed again how close Jason seemed to Tara Highsmith. Was there something between them? Maybe she was the married person Jason was entangled with? Grace fought off a mild pang of sadness.

But it didn't matter now.

The only thing that mattered was Irene Douglas and her neighbors and their water. What mattered was Mrs. Tollefson's granddaughter Emma, taking a bath in water contaminated with cow feces. That wasn't right, and it had to change. Now.

Chapter Twenty-One

THE QUESTIONS
OF THE HOUR

Tara let Shelby out and found all three of her daily newspapers. As she crouched down to gather them, Tara had the same thought she'd had yesterday when she saw the sign. What was Sheila thinking when she posed in that hat? The colorful For Sale sign with her friend's picture in an absurdly frilly purple hat was now a daily reminder that Tara's life would never be the same.

Within two weeks of Michael's confession, they'd listed their house with Tara's realtor friend. Sheila had already scheduled five showings and an open house. It was all moving so quickly.

The day he got back from Boston, Michael moved some things (including most of his clothes) and himself from their house. Was he moving right in with Susan? Who knew? Frankly, Tara didn't care.

She sat on their screen porch, glancing at *The New York Times*. She'd known all along something wasn't right. One consolation was that her instinct to get close to Jason had been healthy. She could still trust her instincts. That was good to know, with so many changes coming.

Tara had decided to wait three full weeks before calling Jason. She wanted to take it all in herself first. Finally, she was ready.

She refilled her coffee and called him. She told him all about the fatal counseling session and laughing and crying in her car.

"So now there's a big For Sale sign in front of our house," she told him.

"I'm very sorry, Tara." Jason paused. "But I can't say I'm surprised. I've thought all along that—well, you know." He was trying to sound neutral but his tone still kind of bugged her.

"Yes." Many times. Tara would disagree that her husband was cheating and say that she *knew* Michael. "You did. More than once."

"I'm sorry." He was trying to hold back, but she felt judged. Wasn't that what judges did?

"I know."

During their long conversation he told her about his White Farms Dairy hearing in La Crosse the next week.

"You should follow it," Jason said. "It might be big news."

"You're right. CAFO groundwater contamination is a big story nationwide," Tara replied. "I'll ask my editor."

~~~~~~

Much to her surprise, Tara's boss signed off on both her going to cover the trial and spending the night. She'd played that national syndication angle. That made the corporate people happy.

She was more focused on their rendezvous than she was on doing her job. It was barely a month after the counseling session, and yet here she was, entering into a whole new phase of her life. Was she going to sleep with Jason tonight?

Suddenly, that was the new question of the hour. Things had changed so fast. It felt almost like a date. Both she and Jason were staying at the Charmant, a posh new hotel above the scenic park on the river.

Could she sleep with another man so soon? Even Jason, whom she'd been getting to know and flirting with for more than a year?

Tara just made it to the soulless nineties era courthouse and found the courtroom just as Jason called the case and began describing the process for public testimony. He nodded to her and smiled and Tara did likewise, hoping that she hadn't blushed in front of her media colleagues.

The White Farms Dairy case didn't lack for newsworthiness— both the local NPR and the local public television reporters were there, as well as Jay Carney from the other statewide newspaper chain. Tara nodded at him, too, and sat on the other side of the courtroom. It was a good thing she'd come.

The inside of the courthouse was much nicer than the outside, lined with a warm, honey-colored maple. A line of people who wanted to testify had signed in on a yellow legal pad and were jostling for a position. Tara took a picture of their names for the spellings. She'd already written her background paragraphs the night before and found out the names of the lawyers so that she could just fill in some quotes, file her story immediately, and get on to their date.

An obnoxious bearded guy about Tara's age was cutting in line and insisting on going first. Men could be so damn pushy and entitled. Tara was sick of them all after learning of Mike's year-long infidelity. As usual, this one got his way. The bearded dude was an area director from Fish Unlimited, and angry about a recent fish kill sourced to an accident at the dairy.

"More than one hundred brook and another eight hundred brown trout were lost just two weeks ago. It literally breaks my heart that White Farms Dairy can keep having these so-called accidents that threaten all our years of hard work and millions of dollars to upgrade these streams, which have made them some of the best in the country." His voice was strident and self-righteous, but he was also dead right.

"They keep having predictable problems, not accidents, and yet the state still keeps letting them add in more cows," he continued.

"The trout stream is a tributary to the Kickapoo River, which brings in hundreds of thousands of people for canoeing and other recreational uses. The economic argument is not on the side of the dairy, just the politics."

"I object," said Rick Wilson on behalf of the dairy. "This is not about economics; this is about the permit."

"This is public testimony," said Grace Clarkson, attorney for the objectors. "The judge can give it the weight it deserves."

"Your Honor," the bearded guy insisted. "I want to put in a list of political contributions made by the dairy industry to top Republicans, including the governor."

"That's not relevant to your decision, Your Honor," said Wilson, shaking his head.

"Well, in the past I've taken that kind of thing into the record," Jason said. "But I usually withhold ruling on it until the final decision to see if there is some proof that the proper legal standards were not followed because of political pressure. It will come in only if someone provides a nexus linking some political pressure to a failure to follow the proper legal standards. Who's next? Ms. Mueller."

A red-haired nurse in blue scrubs came forward and was sworn in. "My name is Lisa Mueller, I'm a registered nurse, and I live with my husband and children about four miles from the site. Our property is on low ground near a swamp and our well water is contaminated with E. coli. Our family doesn't have a septic system with a drain field, so that couldn't be the source of the contamination. White Farms Dairy is the only likely source of the cloudy and contaminated water that comes through our tap and which has made my family sick with diarrhea and stomach cramps."

The nurse had been calm and deliberate but now her voice began to crack. "Even though we invested in an expensive holding tank to treat our own waste, our family suffers the daily stress, embarrassment, and financial cost of E. coli contamination in our well."

The day continued for hour after unsettling hour, with similar stories.

Sylvia Anderson lived just fifty feet from the proposed expansion and was concerned that she would be forced to conduct regular, expensive testing of her well water to ensure her family's safety.

Similarly, Tom Stevens lived just three-quarters of a mile from the White Farms Dairy farm and had regularly inspected and kept his septic system in good repair. However, his well water had tested with both E. coli and high nitrate concentrations. Stevens feared for his family's safety and had been testing his water recently on an almost daily basis. He testified about his concerns for the safety of his three-year-old daughter, who sometimes swallowed small amounts of bathwater.

After a dozen or so residents had told their moving tales of woe, one of the state EPA witnesses was back up on the stand and the objector's attorney, Grace Clarkson, kept asking him probing questions.

"How long has the department known of these conditions?"

"What specific conditions?" replied the witness.

"Let's start with this." Grace paused for effect. "Let's start with the undisputed fact that over half the wells in the county are contaminated with E. coli or other bacteria?"

"I think that study came out six months or so ago."

Jason intervened to ask his own question. "And how did the department respond to this massive regulatory failure?"

The reporters in the room, Tara included, all exchanged looks. They would all feast upon that phrase.

"Well, I am just the permit writer, and so I looked to see if this permit met the standards," the witness replied.

"Isn't one of the standards to take into account the local geology?" Jason asked.

"Yes."

"Counsel," the judge said, turning it back to Grace.

"And the karst cracks are part of that?" she probed.

"Yes, that is one consideration, but only as to whether or not to install monitoring wells."

"Yet the permit you wrote doesn't require any monitoring wells, does it?"

"There's one on-site."

"But none that would give the residents we heard about any more information about the effect of another eight thousand cows on their drinking water?" Grace questioned.

"That's right."

"The judge just used the phrase 'massive regulatory failure,'" Grace began. "Do you agree with that assessment?"

"Yes."

"I object!" Rick Wilson was on his feet and a vein in his neck was bulging. "With all due respect, the comments of the judge are not evidence, they are just editorial comment, and in my view inappropriate."

Jason wasn't having it. "First, your objection came in after the answer. But it's not a valid objection to Counsel's question in any event. The objection is overruled.

"With respect to my comments being inappropriate, I just want to note that that's how we've always approached public hearings. When I was first hired, my boss, former Chief Judge Goldman, told me that one of the functions of the public hearing process was to bring important issues to the attention of the leadership of the state EPA and especially with issues relating to public health and safety.

"I've been doing this job for nearly seventeen years, and I've never heard about residents of this state being worried about their children's bathwater or wondering if their father's death was caused by their well water. As I was listening to this testimony, I thought of the public officials in Flint, Michigan, who were charged criminally for not doing what they could to protect that city's residents. So, I think my comments were in fact very appropriate and much needed. Now, let's finish up with this witness and call it a day."

That whole exchange was broadcast as the leading state news segment on public radio, and it made every statewide newspaper as well. Jason had listened to the evidence and stuck his neck out for people. Tara filed her story, which her editor put live online within fifteen minutes.

Then she made her way to meet Jason up on the roof of the Charmant Hotel. It was a red-brick masterpiece, a former candy factory, with high ceilings and a sophisticated clientele. From the roof, she could see the wide Mississippi, the blue bridge over it, and even the sandstone bluffs across the river in Minnesota. She ordered a half bottle of chardonnay and met Jason with a wineglass in hand. She poured him one too.

"A toast to the man of the hour!"

"Cheers!" said Jason. "I'm surprised you're up here already! Story filed?"

"Yes, filed and live online! Cheers! It's such a beautiful spot. I've always loved La Crosse, and this hotel is really gorgeous." Tara was aware that she was chattering nervously. "How are you doing?"

"As though I didn't have enough enemies, now I have the dairy industry, which means the governor will be after me too. Sometimes, I feel like that graduate student who stood in front of the tanks at Tiananmen Square."

"That's good. I wish this was on the record."

"Thanks." Jason took a big swig of his wine. "Do you think it's cool for us to have dinner together?"

"Up here?"

"I meant at the restaurant, but I'm sure we could order room service. I'm staying here. Room 314."

"Me too. Room 322," Tara said. "We can go down to the restaurant, but let's finish our wine first."

The sun was starting to set over the blue bridge. Jason took her hand. They sat there silently for a few minutes, taking it all in.

Tara made her decision. "Maybe we should just have dinner in one of our rooms?"

"Your room or mine?" Jason asked.

"Mine."

She kissed him and then led him by the hand across the roof toward the elevator.

"Deal," said Jason. "I need to run down to my car and I'll be right back up. 322?"

"Yes. Should I come with you?"

"No, just order more of that delicious chardonnay and I'll be right back up."

When they got to the elevator, there was an older man already in it, though the roof was the very top floor. He had a distinctive red birthmark on his forehead.

"I accidentally hit Roof," he explained. "What floor for you two?"

"Three and the lobby. Thanks," Jason replied.

"Sounds great."

The old guy got off at five, so they kissed as Tara left. When Tara approached Room 332, a young man was coming out of what turned out to be her room.

"Turndown service," the guy explained. "The chocolates are homemade. This building used to be a chocolate factory."

"I know. Well, thanks."

Her hands were trembling as she ordered the wine.

Chapter Twenty-Two

~~~~~~~~~

A PRETTY SWEET OFFER?

Grace had made it through the White Farms Dairy trial and had the whole day to start getting caught up. But her morning run was kind of unsettling. Down near Myrick Park, she'd watched a man pacing back and forth near his black Lexus. It had Illinois plates and the guy looked familiar.

She stopped and got a drink of water. Where had she seen him before? Then it hit her. It was Earl Franks, who'd presented at the Water Law Conference. What the hell was he doing in La Crosse, pacing back and forth in the parking lot at Myrick Park?

She decided she should tell Jason Erickson.

After her run, Grace came back into her office and the phone was ringing. And ringing. Where was everyone? She was paying Tom, Louisa, and Jenny in part so that she would never have to answer the phone. Nevertheless, she answered.

"Is this Grace Clarkson?"

"Yes, it is." *Irritably yours.*

"Hi, Grace. It's Doug Barstow over at Harper Realty. We've met a couple of times."

"I remember." She remembered the name at least. "I'm not looking for anything right now. I love my house.

He laughed. "Glad to hear that, but I'm not looking to sell you anything. Grace, I represent the Wilson Brothers, and they want to make an offer on your office building downtown."

"It's not for sale. Been in my family for years, as you probably know."

"Of course, but you have to at least listen to this offer. They're pretty serious. They're willing to go pretty close to seven figures."

"A million dollars?" Grace exclaimed. "It's assessed at $675,000 and I probably still owe $250,000 on it at least."

"They love the historic character of it and the location and want to make it sort of the showpiece of their whole operation."

"What kind of time frame are they talking about?"

"They can be flexible." Doug paused and cleared his throat. "I know we're just talking here, but can I tell them that you might be receptive to something like that?"

"I'd have to seriously consider it. That's for sure."

It was actually a fantasy of hers to sell the building and move somewhere bigger. Different. A warmer, bluer state. A million dollars would give her plenty of time to take a bar exam somewhere else.

"I'll try to get you a formal written offer in the next couple of weeks, okay?" Dan said.

"Can you do me a favor and give me at least ten days to accept or counter?" Grace said. The standard two or three days wouldn't cut it. "I've just finished up this big CAFO trial, and there's so much to do to get any time to really think this through."

"Of course. Look forward to working with you; it's a pretty sweet offer."

"I know." But her uncle had left her the building only three years ago. "I've got to balance our family history and the needs of my practice." And, mostly, the guilt. Her family legacy.

Grace got up and stared at the photo of her uncle above her desk.

She'd spoken at Ray's funeral and finished with lines from his favorite W.H. Auden poem. She had the lines printed up and framed with a photo of Ray and his partner, Christopher, on a hike in the sandstone bluffs between La Crosse and Winona. It had watched over her in her office in this old Romanesque Revival building, with its limestone belt course, since he'd passed.

> When I try to imagine a faultless love
> Or the life to come, what I hear is the murmur
> Of underground streams, what I see is a limestone
> landscape.

Tom popped his head in. "Hey, boss. Louisa and I made a run to the Breakfast Club if you're hungry."

"Thanks, but I ate already."

"I see that you're consulting your Uncle Ray again."

"No, W.H. Auden this time." If Grace sold the building, she'd probably have to let Tom and Louisa go. More guilt. "You guys are the best."

Late that night, well after nine, Grace's phone rang. It was Dr. Walter.

"I reran those final results their expert challenged, and they're the same as we put in the record. Off the charts with fecal coliform. The young mothers are right to worry about kids in the bath."

"It's just so gross to think of showering in that, too." It made Grace's skin crawl to think about it. "Well, thanks for doing all of this. I wasn't worried about their challenges."

"Me either. Of course not. Umm . . ." This was followed by a long and slightly awkward pause. "Grace, umm . . . can I ask you something personal?"

"Of course, sure."

"Are you seeing anyone? I mean, I hope this is not inappropriate, but maybe we could go out sometime if you're not."

Grace took a minute to think, hoping the pause wasn't too long. She hadn't thought of Dr. Walter in that way.

"Maybe, sure. It's flattering but unexpected, Ken." Awkward as hell, too.

"I know I'm not too good at this kind of thing, but I couldn't stop thinking about you after the trial. You were sensational."

"Thanks for saying that. It's a nice surprise at the end of a long day. Ask me again when I get my posttrial brief done."

"Oh, I will!" Dr. Walter laughed. "I'm not smooth, but I'm persistent!"

Strange dude, seemingly so absorbed in his work and yet asking her out that same night. Men were all alien creatures these days. Lots of them seemed oblivious to everything important—until something important hit them. Ken wasn't like that.

But he was definitely lacking social skills.

Nonetheless, two sweet offers in one day? Who knew? Grace was feeling strangely fine.

Chapter Twenty-Three

~~~~~~~~~~

BRUTE ECONOMICS

J ason and Tara spent the night huddled together happily. After being thwarted for so long, it felt like a homecoming. Jason's life suddenly made sense. He was in love with Tara, and she was in love with him. It was finally that simple.

Tara got up and put on that blue skirt he liked. Jason called her over for a kiss, and they wound up back in each other's arms. Later, she got dressed again and smiled.

"This time I really have to go. I have to cover that meeting."

"I know," Jason said. "But I miss you already."

"I could definitely get used to waking up next to you." Tara gave him a farewell kiss.

"Drive safely."

"Good luck with your boss, my dear."

Jason had received three calls from Steve Hayman, but in the throes of his first night with Tara, he hadn't returned them. Now, he was dreading the call and especially returning to his office on Monday. He knew what was coming.

The governor's people would be angry. The way it would happen, the way it always happened, would be a call from them that would require closed doors in Hayman's office. That call had probably already occurred.

When Jason returned, Hayman would gather up his courage, and the governor's talking points, and stand outside Jason's office. A bit of sports talk would precede Hayman coming in and closing the door behind him. The desired outcome would be conveyed as the only reasonable way to rule, to think, to be. Jason would listen and nod. He might offer a counterargument or two. Not always. All of his decisions were subject to the chief judge's review.

If Jason's decision was not the desired outcome, there would be handwringing, disbelief, and head shaking from Hayman. Edits would be demanded. Some, not impacting the ultimate decision, Jason would offer willingly. But he would not change an outcome. Through two Republican and one Democratic administrations, no one had ever requested that he do so.

Until now. The rule of law meant nothing to the new team. It was the rule of big donors for this bunch.

Hoping to avoid that whole charade, he went down to the lobby and finally called his boss back.

"You've pissed off a lot of people, Jason." Jason could picture Steve, standing, shifting his weight from foot to foot. More was coming. "For the record, that's not part of your job description. I got a call from the governor's office, and they're wondering why you can't seem to get along with anyone and are always running your mouth."

"You have to look at each event, each case separately. What are they most upset about?" Jason asked.

"Everything. Senator Lucke was livid that you compared him to Joe McCarthy. Understandably," Steve said. "And White Farms Dairy, too. They thought you were editorializing from the bench."

"Editorializing must mean dealing with reality and not just parroting the industry's line. When I was first hired, before you came over, my old chief told me that the department wanted to know about any issue that impacted human health," Jason said. "They actually wanted the heads-up so that they could stay on top of what was coming along."

They cared. Unlike this new crew, they gave a shit about things other than donor-economics.

"That was a different time," Steve countered.

"Do you realize that over half the wells in that area are contaminated? It's close to a Flint-type situation," Jason continued. "I'm sure you know that the government people who hushed it up in Flint were all charged with felonies. The governor should appreciate my heads-up!"

"Well, he doesn't. And neither the governor nor I expect to hear you calling his administration a massive failure again. Nor disparaging the largest industry in the state. That's not in your job description either." A pause. Steve still wasn't finished. "You are getting a private reprimand to your file. If it happens again, you will be Publicly Disciplined."

"On what grounds?"

"Making personal observations from the bench."

"I'll appeal it," Jason replied.

"Consider this your verbal warning. Public Discipline is next."

Jason fumed for a while and then went out for a run. It was a path he knew that led along the river from his hotel to the marshes and bluffs near the UW-L campus. To hell with Spineless Steve, anyway; he was still in a great mood.

Were his feet even hitting the ground? Tara! After their night and morning together, he even found himself thinking about their prospects of being together longer term. Why not?

The day ahead was looking like an easy one, just a drive-back day and a single scheduling conference that afternoon. It was good to get that inevitable conversation with the chief judge out of the way too. Now he could start mentally writing an appeal.

How would Jason explain himself for speaking out? As each person had spoken of their hardships and pain, he'd simply become more and more ticked off. He'd never heard anything like it before in all his years on the job. What had happened to the US that its citizens could no longer even count on government to ensure clean drinking and bathwater for its children?

Jason thought of Flint and the series of negligent acts by public officials that had led to that crisis. Some of those people were charged criminally. He would play that angle in his appeal—that he was just trying to avoid any liability.

Spineless Steve hadn't had an answer for it—maybe because the Governor's Office hadn't yet given him his reply talking points? The federal laws gave administrative judges sweeping powers, and great deference from the courts. But behind the scenes, Jason was just another state employee subject to political pressure from the governor.

He was running well, all of the pressures of the hour fading into the rhythms of his movement and the soothing background of the green water and wetlands. He went by the bench dedicated to Grace Clarkson's uncle. She was an interesting person, a fine lawyer and very persuasive too. But it wasn't meant to be.

As he approached the parking lot at Myrick Park, Jason thought he saw big Earl Franks standing up ahead in a light blue jacket and tan shorts.

It couldn't be. La Crosse was almost a five-hour drive from Chicago, and at least three hours northwest of Lake Joseph. It couldn't be, but it was.

"Well, look who's here," called Earl Franks.

The jacket made him look like he had breasts, but his hairy legs were powerful and thick.

"What the heck are you doing up here, Earl?"

"Oh, my practice gets me around. Did you know that I was raised on a farm near here?" Earl was in good form, trying hard to turn up the high beams of his Irish charm. "A lot like you, Jason—smart kid from a humble background."

"What?" How did Earl Franks know anything about his childhood? "I'm from the east side of Milwaukee."

"Just saying that you and I have a lot in common."

"Well, thanks, I guess."

"Know when to seize a rare opportunity."

"Just what the hell are you talking about, Franks?" Jason was hot and sweating. He took his baseball cap off and wiped his brow. "I'm getting sick of all this cryptic threatening crap."

Franks, a bit taken aback by the reply, looked Jason sharply in the eye. "Power has its own opportunities, Judge." Franks looked away, out toward the marsh.

"And?" Jason hated the melodramatic son of a bitch.

"Right now, for example, you have the power to do something that my client wants to have happen very much. Whether you like it or not, a lot of people express that in economic terms."

"Are you trying to corrupt the hearing process, Franks? Because that's—"

"*Corrupt* is harsh. I would call this an opportunity. Don't you get sick of dealing with these people, these lake property owners, year after year, and never owning a place like that yourself? I know I did. Now, I have a nice place on Blue Lake."

"Look, I want this conversation to be over. We have a system of law that regulates brute economics—" Jason struggled for the right words.

"Divorce." Franks shook his head. "Another thing we have in common."

"Have you been prying into my personal life? What the fuck is going on here?"

Franks moved closer. "Calm down, Judge."

"What are we talking about?"

"Call it an opportunity—"

"To accept a bribe?"

"Your word, not mine." Franks had lowered his voice to a near whisper.

"Just tell them no, if that's what this is about. Tell them *no*. This conversation never happened. Basta."

"If only it were that simple, Jason. Some people won't take no for an answer—"

"If that's a threat, then maybe we did have this conversation."

"Don't mess with them, Judge," Franks said slowly, emphasizing each word. He was formidable, with his linebacker arms and barrel-breasted chest.

"The answer is no."

"These people don't play. I don't want to be having this conversation any more than you do."

"Tell them *no*. We never had this conversation," Jason said. "But if I hear even the slightest hint of any of this again, the whole thing goes on the record in open court with a sheriff's deputy in the room."

"You're smart enough not to do that." Beneath his bushy gray brows, Earl's eyes were bright and mocking. He looked away again and added, "You love your brother, your reporter friend, too much."

"You're pathetic, Franks. And I'm disgusted with myself for having voted for you to be on the supreme court."

"Watch out, kid," Franks said softly. "I do like you. You and Don Quixote. But you see, that's not the way the world really works. They find your weak spot and then milk it for all it's worth. That's what they've done with me." Franks turned and bolted to his car.

"Fuck you, Franks!" Jason screamed.

He stood there stunned, not knowing what to do. Should he immediately go to the police? Would anyone believe that the well-connected Franks was trying to bribe Jason, a lowly administrative judge?

The police would want him to record Franks. And Franks was not stupid—he would be on his guard. Franks had talked so freely today only because they were in the middle of nowhere and he had the advantage of surprise. Recording Franks would be dangerous, too. And not just for him. Now, he would have to warn both Tara and Justin. Jason could see the parking lot past the end of the trail, and Franks just about to get into his black Lexus. Something made him call out to him one more time.

"Franks, tell them I won't do it, and to just let it drop. I don't even have a clue how I'm going to rule yet."

Franks smiled, seemingly so sincere. "These things are not really in my control. I don't like this any more than you do, but it's a rough world out there."

"Tell them I said no, or I go to the police. Period."

"Your call, Judge. You've got three weeks to decide."

Franks got in his car. Jason started to run again, but Franks drove up next to him and rolled down his window.

"By the way, Judge, how was your hotel turndown service last night?"

"What?"

"Are reporters allowed to bone the people they're covering?"

"Fuck you!" Jason yelled. He impulsively gave Franks the finger. "You crude piece of shit!"

"Very mature, Judge. Wouldn't sleeping with a source be against journalistic ethics too?"

Jason's head was spinning as he walked back toward the hotel. The whole sky seemed to be swirling, the fading morning sun already slanting helplessly across the cloudy horizon. He had to warn Tara and his little brother, Justin, and then he had to deal with his idiot boss about the White Farms Dairy case. But most of all he had to figure out a way out of this mess with Earl Franks and Tommy Calandro.

Later that same afternoon, Jason got a copy of a private disciplinary letter to his file for making personal observations during the course of the White Farms trial. It was outrageously slanted and bogus. Livid, he started dashing off a formal Appeal of Discipline letter himself later that afternoon.

His observations had been accurate and anything but personal. They went to the heart of the case he was presiding over. Wisconsin residents were living with toxic water quality. He even attached an article about public officials in Flint, Michigan, being charged criminally for covering up a drinking water problem. Screw them.

If he let them privately discipline him, the hacks would soon step up the process with some other perceived wrongdoing, say, speaking out against a corrupt state senator. One thing the discipline letter had clarified was that his boss was not on his side.

PART TWO

DELIGHTS AND ENDS

"These violent delights have violent ends."

—WILLIAM SHAKESPEARE,
Romeo and Juliet

Chapter Twenty-Four

~~~~~~~~~~~~

IT'S HARD TO
BEAT THE HOUSE

Earl Franks had to take a leak, and he needed a beer. But he made himself drive for forty-five minutes. He loved this car, his black Lexus hybrid, which he'd won the money for on a bet for his underdog New York Giants in the 2012 Super Bowl. He pulled Black Beauty into the parking lot of the Drop On Inn and made his way straight to the men's room.

He was still in the throes of the adrenaline rush associated with his conversation with Jason Erickson. There was a special rush of fear and energy that he'd learned to recognize as the thrill of consciously doing the wrong thing. His juice.

The tavern was the sort of downscale backwoods trailer-trash hangout that would have been his lot in life if he hadn't made his way to Michigan on a football scholarship. The men's room in the hallway was a disgrace to the human race.

The place was crowded for a weeknight, but there was a poker machine open and they had Surly Axe Man Ale on draft. He ordered a large mug of it and put ten bucks into the machine.

Fuck Jason Erickson. Fuck Tommy Calandro, too. Earl was getting sick of doing Tommy's dirty work. If he could just make a couple of things happen, maybe he could retire in a year or two. Maybe he'd bail sooner. Who knew? Some of his stocks were riding higher again.

He'd retire in Blue Lake. By deeding it to Laurie, he'd managed to hang on to the family cabin there through the divorce. He'd just sit on his ass, pass gas, and fish for walleye on Blue Lake.

There was a nice, plump, little, late-fifty-something blonde woman seated appealingly at the machine next to him. Earl had her pegged as a barfly divorcee—his specialty. He pretended not to notice her, but made sure she would see him, calling out, "Yeah, yeah, come home to Daddy," as his cards came up. She smiled.

"How's it going?" he asked, pretending to have just noticed her.

"All right, but it's hard to beat the house," she replied. Her voice had a surprisingly genteel quality to it.

"That's the story in life, isn't it?"

She laughed and gave him a different—more interested?—look. She was really kind of pretty, in a forlorn, dyed-blonde sort of a way.

"Say, what are you drinking?" Earl asked heartily. "I'm going up for another beer."

"That's all right." She focused on her machine. "I buy my own drinks."

It looked like rum and coke. As he passed her, he thought he smelled the sickeningly sweet smell of Planter's Punch in the air around her.

"Another Axe Man, better make it a small one this time, and a Planter's Punch or whatever she's drinking for my friend over there."

The bartender looked a little skeptical but brought him the two drinks.

When he came back from the bar, Earl put the rum drink down beside the blonde woman and slid back in behind his machine. She half-smiled and shook her head but didn't say a word. A couple minutes later, when he saw her drinking it, he thought of it as a little victory.

But this triumph was short-lived when the blonde picked up the disputed drink and headed back to the bar, away from him. What did he care anyway? Was he really so hot for this country barfly?

She did present herself well, in her ass-hugging white shorts and the low-cut blue blouse. Trashy, but a nice kind of it. Despite himself, those white shorts called out to him. Earl made his way to the barstool beside her. She'd finished his drink and was now drinking a big glass of ice water.

"You're right. It is hard to beat the house."

The blonde gave him a dismissive little laugh and shook her head.

"Do you have a name?" Earl asked.

"You could just call me 'unavailable' and leave it at that." She didn't even look up.

For some reason, that pissed him off.

"What makes you think you're so hot, Blondie?"

She seemed unnerved by this more aggressive tone. She called to the bartender, an old guy in wire-rims. "Karl, this Harvey Weinstein wannabe over here is bugging me."

"Wannabe," Earl said. "Who are you calling a wannabe? I used to be on the state supreme court!"

She looked him up and down coldly. "Yeah, right."

Everyone seated along the bar laughed.

The old bartender came over and said firmly, "Leave Jenny alone, Your Honor. It's her birthday."

The guys along the bar laughed again.

Earl stood up and drained his beer. "It's the truth, whether any of you hicks know it or not."

But it was apparent that none of them believed him. At that moment, it was hard for him to remember it himself.

Chapter Twenty-Five

~~~~~~~~~

ABOUT LAST NIGHT

"Tara?" Jason called her from the lobby of the Charmant Hotel in La Crosse. Ten minutes after his conversation with Earl Franks. "Hey, it's me. Where are you?"

"About halfway back to Green Bay. I was just thinking about you," she answered. "About last night, and this morning!"

"Oh, me too! But I'm calling about something that may have also happened last night." She sounded so happy. He was having a hard time getting it out. "Remember the chocolates that showed up out of nowhere at five o'clock?"

"How could I forget? Very romantic. That whole night was so much fun."

"Of course, it was. But I think maybe we were being set up. I just had another bizarre conversation with Earl Franks. He seemed to know about the early turndown service, and he implied that he knew what we were doing in the hotel."

"Maybe he saw us go into my room?" Tara didn't seem to believe her own words. "Maybe, you misunderstood him?"

"I wish it was just that, but he drove slowly toward me to make sure

I got his point. He also threatened both you and my brother, Justin. And he specifically asked me if reporters are allowed to sleep with someone they are covering in a story. I think he has us on video, probably from the guy who brought the chocolates."

"Oh shit! That's all I need." Tara paused. "Mike is also being a real ass about the terms of our divorce."

"I'm so sorry."

"Neither one is your fault! What did he say about your brother?"

"Earl said that I love you and my brother too much—"

Damn. Jason just noticed a woman in the lobby who looked like Grace Clarkson. Yes, it was her.

"Too much not to go along with him," Jason finished.

Grace appeared to be milling around, waiting for him.

"You should warn your brother right away, and call your friend Skip the prosecutor," Tara said. "And I mean soon."

"Franks said I had three weeks to decide. That's like the second or third day of the Lake Joseph hearing, if I'm remembering right. I'll call Justin tonight and Skip on Monday morning."

"I miss you!"

"Same here." He was free for the day and had already put in over sixty hours this week. "What would you think about going up to visit Justin in Minneapolis this weekend? I could even pick you up in Green Bay this afternoon. It's just a little over three hours from the Charmant to your door."

"You checked?" Tara laughed lustily. "But don't you want to go home first?"

"No, I'd love to see you. But can I maybe do a load of laundry at your house?"

"I know what we can do while we wait for it to dry."

"I was hoping you'd say that," Jason said before ending the call.

Grace pounced on him as soon as he hung up. "Hi, Judge. How's it going?"

"I've had better days." How much could he share with her? "That ethical problem seems to have gotten more urgent."

Grace gave him a quizzical look. "Does it have anything to do with Earl Franks?"

"Yes. How did you know?" Yes, he trusted her.

"It was bizarre, but I ran into him on my morning run. Here in La Crosse."

"I saw him there too. It was bizarre and more." Jason awkwardly shook her hand. "Thanks for telling me, Grace."

Jason went upstairs and packed, loaded up his car, and started driving to Green Bay. Driving for multiple hours was something he'd become used to.

He turned on NPR and let the familiar voices soothe him. They'd traveled thousands of miles together over many years. His mind was lost in Tara's arms, in their joyous time together, when the state news came on.

"Dairy industry spokeswoman Barbara Currie is speaking out about a judge's comments about what he called a massive regulatory failure to protect groundwater. Tom Curtis has her response."

"We think it's just outrageous that he would disparage the state's signature industry and its family farmers," Barbara Currie began.

Blah, blah. She was talking shit, literal shit. Jason turned the radio off. So much easier to talk it than bathe in it every day.

He took a couple of deep, meditative breaths. Meditation could make one feel attached as well as detached. Soon, he was back in Tara's arms again. Yes, all of that had happened.

When he arrived at Tara's house, she was on the phone.

"Come in," she called, then whispered, "My lawyer."

Jason snooped around her nearly empty house. Mike had moved out much of their living room furniture, with the exception of a beautiful green leather chair. Tara's style and taste favored large abstract paintings and bright colors. The wall between the entrance and the kitchen where she was talking on the phone was painted bright red and had a black-and-white photo of an old chestnut tree.

Her bag was packed and sitting neatly in the hallway. She was looking forward to their trip! The conversation seemed to be winding down.

"Just so they know, I'm not going to give an inch on those brokerage accounts. Those are mine, from my money and my good sense in buying things low. Okay, then, Liz. Is there anything else you need?" There was. But Tara, still on her cell, bounded from the kitchen to embrace him.

Then, still on the phone, she began unbuttoning her blouse. She looked so luxurious in her lacy blue bra. Confident, too. Jason took off his own shirt. He'd been running thirty miles a week from all the stress and was feeling good about himself too.

Charming, that was the word for Tara. Sexy, too.

"I should be able to get those to you early next week," she said to her lawyer.

Jason took off his jeans and kissed Tara's neck and shoulders. She stepped out of her own khaki shorts and, still talking on the phone, walked over to her packed bag sitting neatly in the hallway. He watched her waltz across the floor in her bra and her matching blue underwear, so comfortable in her own skin. Her nonchalance was thrilling. They were lovers now.

She located what she'd been looking for—a new box of condoms. She handed them to Jason, making hand signals that she would try to wrap up the conversation. She sat down on the green leather chair in the living room and, pulling off her underwear, motioned for him to join her. He stepped out of his boxers and made his way to her.

"Yes, Liz. Okay, well, I've got to go." She clicked off the phone.

"I missed you so much."

"Put one of those things on, Jason." She kissed him. "I'm ready."

"Really? I couldn't tell."

She laughed, which turned into a groan of pleasure. This led to another, more urgent moan, which he answered in equal measure. The leather chair squeaked a little obscenely.

"I've wanted you all day long," she said.

"Me too. I almost drove off the road a couple of times thinking about making love to you."

"That's what we're doing." Tara touched herself lightly. He put his hand over hers to feel her rhythm before they traded places. "Make love to me, Jason."

Lost somewhere wonderful, he didn't answer. She closed her eyes and got lost too.

~~~~~

They were still savoring their happiness the next morning, heading out of town listening to Tara's favorite radio station. Finally, twenty miles down the road, she turned it off. They talked, about their families, mostly. Hours later, as they approached Minneapolis, they drove through St. Louis Park, the suburb where Tara had grown up.

"I feel kind of bad about not going to see my parents," she said.

"Are we going to see the house you grew up in?"

"They don't live there, but we can drive by it."

"Tell me more about your parents," Jason said.

"As you know, my father's a trial attorney. A big firm downtown. Tall, dark, and handsome in an old-fashioned, suit-wearing, church-choir-baritone kind of way. My mother is more high-strung. She was a high school teacher for twenty years. Strong-willed. Her nervous energy dominated the house and my more laidback father. But she had another side. Her seeming need to charm any and every one she met. My father was oddly passive socially. He preferred to sit and read. So, it was all very complicated."

"Which one were you closer to growing up?"

"I was pretty much under my mother's spell until late adolescence. I idolized her charm, her style, the way she carried herself with people.

But then in college I moved too far to the left for my mom's country club golf-and-martini set. She thought I was a little too crunchy."

"That sounds kind of hard."

"She was hard to please, that much I know," Tara said. "The one thing I'd ever done right was marry Michael, and now I've managed to blow that, too. I would take you to meet them, but it's too soon. My mother adored Michael. She pressured me to take his name, for the kids we never had. Mom always wanted me to quit my job, with its insane hours, and have a kid with him."

"My mother never quite understood Madeline, but my father said she was a 'good egg'—his highest compliment."

"That's it, the blue one." Tara pointed to one of the houses ahead of them. The house was a sprawling Midwestern Gothic, now painted bright blue with yellow trim.

"The neighborhood is great, too," she added. "There's a trail right down there at the dead end."

"I can see you riding your bike there," Jason said.

"And climbing the trees? I loved climbing trees. So much peace and quiet up in a tree, away from my parents and their endless bickering. After a fight one night, I found myself literally wrapping my arms around that tree." She smiled and bobbed her head happily. "Like an old friend."

"So, you were literally a tree-hugger?"

Tara nodded.

"That's so sweet."

When they arrived at Justin's, Jason's sister-in-law, Sunny, opened the door of their little red bungalow. Sunny was tall and thin, with long blonde hair and a mischievous smile. She hugged Jason fiercely.

"How are you?"

"Hanging in there, great to see you!" Sunny let him go and hugged Tara. "And you must be Tara Highsmith."

They all talked a bit, waiting for Justin to come back with tonic and beer. Their walls were filled with an eclectic mix of nature scenes, computer graphics, and touchingly personal artifacts: cards they'd given each other, a menu from a Japanese restaurant in San Francisco, and photos from their numerous camping trips. A little personal history gallery.

Justin came sauntering in. He was a little thinner and shorter than his older brother and had shoulder-length black hair parted down the middle. Sunny put one arm around each of them and led them to the living room. They huddled around the antique oak coffee table. Justin poured them each a gin and tonic and then addressed the elephant that had brought them all to this room.

"Do you think they would do anything to harm you?" Justin asked. "Wouldn't it just be too obvious?"

"If they hurt him, they're finished," Tara answered. She paused before asking, "But what if they, um, kill him?"

"It wouldn't do much good!" Jason laughed nervously. "But just so it's clear, if anything happens to me, it's Tommy Calandro and Earl Franks!"

"Earl Franks, the former supreme court justice?" asked Justin incredulously.

"The same."

"I voted for that jerk when I was in college!" said Justin. "Typical fake liberal."

"He said I should go along with them because 'You love your brother and your reporter friend too much' to do otherwise."

Tara laughed. "It just occurred to me that it makes no sense to threaten someone who could put it on the front page."

"They're counting on the fact that you won't," Jason replied. "They may have filmed us at a hotel in La Crosse."

"It was our first time together," Tara put in. "So, it was probably pretty good viewing."

"Does it impact your divorce?" Sunny asked. "Been there, done that."

"My husband was already having an affair, so that doesn't concern me as far as our divorce." Tara took a sip of her drink. "But as far as that covert film, for me, the answer is simple: I just told my boss that I can no longer cover cases involving Jason as the judge because we've started seeing each other."

"That will suck, but, you're right!" Jason exclaimed. "And as for me, I don't know that there is any ethical prohibition for courting the media."

"Literally courting the corporate media!" Justin smirked. "That's hilarious."

"Tara's not corporate, Justy," Sunny said. "They mentioned your brother as well, right? Do you think there's any chance they're going to come here tonight and just kill all of us?"

"Here, tonight?" asked Jason in reply. "No, I doubt that they followed us from Green Bay across that weird little Highway 29. We are safe here. I think we are, anyway. They gave me a couple of weeks to decide, but we should all be really careful from now on."

"Do you think I should warn Mike, too?" Tara asked.

"Your ex?" Justin asked. "I think you should."

"I agree," Jason put in, feeling bummed. "You're all in danger because of me."

"Not because of you," Tara said interrupted. "Because of Tommy C.! Don't worry, I'll just text Mike. I've got some other, financial issues I've got to touch base with him on."

"Anybody want another G&T?" Justin tried to change the subject.

They all did. And at some point, they all became aware that, despite everything, they were having a really nice time together. That they hit it off.

Madeline had always been slightly disapproving, holding something back, when she was with Jason's brother and sister-in-law. They were a little too out there for her. But wasn't Madeline always disapproving, holding back from everyone? Certainly, she had been in their marriage. Maybe not with her new guy. Maybe that was the whole point.

"Okay. Let's say the tape is embarrassing but nothing we need to be that concerned about," Jason began. "What about you and Sunny, Justin? Is your number listed in a phone directory?"

"No! I haven't had a landline for, like, ten years."

"Me either," said Sunny. "They'd have a hard time finding us, since we rent this place and are pretty cautious about our online footprint."

"Please be careful anyway," Jason said. "They have access to really sleazy private investigators."

"I'm sorry that you have all of this shit on you," Justin mused. "Is it totally out of the question to tell your boss or go to the cops?"

"My boss is such a tool and so incompetent that I'm pretty sure no good would come of that. And I will go to the police at some point but, so far, I'm not sure that any crime has been committed. I was thinking of calling an old friend of mine, Skip. He's a public corruption prosecutor. I want to explore my options with him."

"Yes!" Justin insisted. "That's perfect."

"Promise us that you will do that first thing when we get back?" Tara asked. "It'll be great to hear another perspective, and you'll have someone more official to corroborate your story if anything goes wrong."

"I have to go to a seminar in Milwaukee on Monday, but I will call that night. I promise."

They drank a couple of gin and tonics. Justin put on music, and they all danced around their apartment. Sunny suggested going out dancing, but they were all too scared to go out anywhere. It got late.

Jason and Tara went to their room and danced around to his phone in each other's arms. Half undressed. He put on Chet Baker's "Let's Get Lost." Nude.

"You're very romantic," observed Tara.

"Oh, hell yeah." He held her close. "I told you, I'm a hopeful romantic."

Chapter Twenty-Six

CASH OR CHECKMATE?

As many times as he'd been there, entering the Pfister Hotel lobby was always a shock to Jason. Here was a grand European hotel on Wisconsin Avenue in downtown Milwaukee. The impressive lobby had a hand-painted fresco of cherubs playing in puffy clouds on the high ceiling and gaudy Victorian paintings in gold frames everywhere the eye rested. When the new owners took over the slightly beaten-up hotel, they soon discovered that the value of the art collection exceeded what they'd paid for the place.

In Jason's years away from it, Milwaukee had changed even more than Madison. The Historic Third and now Fourth Ward districts were full of trendy shops, avant-garde theater companies, and high-end restaurants. There was also a meandering river walk downtown that led to the more established theaters. The NBA Bucks were said to be planning a new arena set to be announced any day now. But for all its progressive new style, it remained a very segregated and troubled city. And, for Jason, one full of sad memories.

Would he have time to take his trip down the appropriately named Downer Avenue and swing by the gloomy house he'd grown up in, where his father had suffered his heart attack on the basement steps? Maybe. Maybe not. Too soon to say.

Jason took the elevator up and registered for the continuing education credits, grabbing the materials binder from the same table. Amazingly, he was only five minutes late. Traffic had been fairly light on the freeway from Madison.

What was this seminar about, anyway? Oh yeah, state and US Environmental Protection Agency relations in the era of bitterly divided government. In the era when Republican governors didn't want any regulation, but the second-term Obama administration wanted plenty.

People regularly took their grievances to the USEPA these days, only to be told a year or two later that those complaints were legitimate and that the states should vaguely do more. USEPA was able to set new goals and policies but had little ability to see that the states would carry them out. Its only real recourse was to take away the delegation that allowed the states to write permits and enforce the Clean Air and Water Acts. But there was little chance of that.

Jason helped himself to a cup of Colectivo coffee, grabbed a yogurt and spoon, and found a seat in the back. There were maybe a couple hundred lawyers and regulators assembled from the whole Chicago EPA region.

Ten rows up, he spotted someone who looked like it could be Earl Franks.

Yes, dammit. There was the unmistakable back of his enormous, dyed-brown melon. And that rush of adrenaline that Jason felt whenever they were in the same room. Maybe it was an opportunity?

Jason gathered his materials and found a seat up past Franks on the other side of the room. Franks would see him for sure but would likely think that Jason hadn't seen him. He'd get up and go to the bathroom in an hour and see if Franks would follow him. Maybe he could record the bastard and have something concrete to take to Skip Munson?

Meanwhile, Jason's mind was spinning. He was full of a gripping fear of Earl Franks that came with his hopes to get him on tape. And memories of Justin and Sunny celebrating their wedding under the crystal chandeliers of the grand Imperial Ballroom. He and Maddie, part of the wedding party, dressed to the nines and slow dancing. Jason's mother was still alive then and so happy in her flowing yellow gown. Dancing with that grocery store guy she was dating at the time.

The occasional sentence from the podium got through to him. Republican obstruction to Obama, to regulation, was complete. Was there any hope of reasonable compromise anywhere?

Not for Jason. What would Earl do to Jason if he caught him trying to record him? Something horrible, no doubt. But it was worth the risk. He had to take some action to get out of this mess.

Had an hour passed? No, only forty-five minutes, but Jason's nerves had made the trip to the bathroom more of a necessity than a ruse.

He rose, conspicuously keeping his eyes forward. Out in the hall he noticed a slightly naughty painting of a Victorian gentleman making an unwelcomed pass at a formidable young maid. Boys being bastard boys.

He found the men's room, went into the stall and used the facility, and then turned his phone on record and waited. His heart was racing. Would Franks follow him in? Would Jason stroke out from the stress of waiting for him?

He waited for five full minutes and then lingered a bit, washing his hands. He checked his reflection and noted he needed a haircut. Damn. Still no Franks.

But when he started down the hall, there was Earl Franks, bluffly heading toward him. Jason extended a slightly sweaty hand.

"There's my good friend, Earl Franks."

"Hiya, Judge. Boring speakers, no?"

"Johnson's always kind of monotone, but his outlines are good. I'm actually glad to run into you."

"Oh, yeah?" Franks looked a little leery.

"One thing that's puzzled me is that in all of our previous conversations, you've never given me a number."

"A number?"

"Your client wants the permits guaranteed, but you haven't told me what it's worth to him. Are we talking about 50K, or are we talking about something more like one percent? It makes a difference."

"Of course it would."

"So?" Jason urged.

"I don't have any authority from my client. But what's one percent, two-fifty? I would think somewhere between the last two numbers."

"Say 200K?"

Franks nodded, but Jason pretended to be looking over his shoulder.

"Roughly," Earl answered. "No meeting of the minds on that one. Like I said, I'd have to talk to my client. Would that do it for you?"

"Let's just say you're starting to persuade me. Cash?"

"Of course. What do you think I'm going to do? Write you a fucking check?" Franks snarled.

Jason nodded. "I can use it."

"Can't we all, Jay. Can't we all."

"And, mainly, I don't want to lose Tara. Get that?"

"Of course I get that. And the two of you could start a nice little new life together somewhere." He put his hand on Jason's shoulder.

"Just so you know, this is a one-off." Jason got right in Earl's sweaty face. "I'd quit a few months later."

"Smart. That was my mistake with these guys," Earl said. He seemed sincere. "Look, I gotta go use the john. We'll talk."

If the recording turned out okay, Jason had him. Cash or checkmate, fucker! But for the first time, Jason was kind of half-considering playing ball with Franks. A new life with Tara sounded grand.

Franks turned around. "Hey, Judge, do you know that bar up on the twenty-fifth floor?"

"Yeah, sure. Nice view."

"I'm going up there for a quick drink," Earl said. "Come and join me if you get a chance."

Chapter Twenty-Seven

~~~~~~~~~~~~~~~~~~~

OLD MILWAUKEE

Earl rode the elevator up to Blu, the bar on what turned out to be the twenty-third floor. He was trying to take in his conversation with Erickson. Jason had surprised Earl coming out of the john, and surprised Earl again by being open to the money conversation. There was something almost desperate about Jason just now.

He must really need the dough. The greedy bastard had wanted 250K! Tommy had given him authority up to a hundred, so there was probably some more there. But 250K wasn't going to fly! If it did, Earl's fee would have to be drastically reduced.

It was probably the woman, not the money, that had reached the target. When Earl had talked about Jason making a life together with his new girlfriend, Jason's eyes had a faraway, pained look that said he was at least considering it seriously. Maybe the lovesick fool just couldn't bear to share her chubby little body with the whole internet? Tara was one of those pear-shaped women who was thin on top and round on the bottom.

Earl sat down at the bar with the stunning views of the city and the lake all around him. "Do you guys still have Old Milwaukee?"

The waiter shook his head disdainfully, like Earl was asking for a glass of warm spit. Old Mil was a perfectly fine malted-barley beer. He sometimes bought it at home—sentimentally, not ironically.

"Then give me the Lakefront IPA."

Earl remembered coming to this bar with Maggie on a romantic New Year's Eve, years ago. The truth was, he'd loved Milwaukee and his first litigation job. Laurie was born at Froedtert Hospital here. Earl was making bets then too but had it under control. He somehow seemed to have more winners then. When it started to go a little south, he'd even tried to Twelve Step his way out. Maggie had twisted his arm to try.

The problem for Earl was that his higher power was always something he could touch or feel. His juice. First, it'd been football, then sex, and then litigation. The horses, too. How could he give up the horses if they were his higher power, if they were what made his life vital and uniquely his?

He'd said all of that to Courtney and she'd said, "Earl, you just were never meant to be a choirboy. And that's fine with me."

Ah, Courtney. She'd been cooling off for days, so it wasn't a big shock when she came into his office last week and asked to be taken off the slipominium case. It wasn't a great surprise, but it still didn't make Earl's day, either.

"So, what's this all about, Courtney? The case or you and me?"

"Both. Earl, I've started seeing someone else, a doctor more my own age."

"Ouch. Out with the old . . . paging Dr. Young."

"The old dog has had his day." She smiled faintly and looked into his eyes. "And frankly, I don't know what the whole story is with you and Tommy Calandro, but something about it smells bad. And I know it's not my stink. Never heard of putting a corrupt private eye all over a sitting judge. Not even at Higgins and Clark."

"You're one smart woman," Earl had replied. "Smart and tough. Still admire that."

Earl wanted to be gracious at the end. He'd come to think of that as being his style. And he genuinely liked Courtney. She just went for what she wanted in the same way that he did.

"Steve Olson, a third-year associate, is hot to get into the environmental unit. Could work out well for you. His father owns a big metal plating company. I'm sure he'd be willing to step in."

"All right, all right. You can bring him up to speed, Toots."

Courtney winced. "Better lay off the *Toots*, too."

"Sure thing, and whatever you smelled, you keep to your—"

"—Of course! Haven't I shown that I'm discreet?" She put on her trademark little pout.

"Yeah, yeah, you have."

"Hey, don't be sad, Earl; you've still got it. In spades."

"I think I'll live, babe."

Like she really gave a shit. She was always just a touch patronizing. Courtney would eat alive any man her own age. For some reason, this thought gave him comfort.

"Got to run, big guy."

"Okay, then. Good luck with Dr. Young."

Earl watched her walk away, with her Cheshire cat grin, pleased with how he'd taken the news. With that, the Courtney Sharpe era of his life was over. She'd blown in and out of it before he'd even gotten used to her mug. And, for once, Earl hadn't even lined up any replacement prospects.

He was already halfway into his ale when Jason sat down with him.

"Glad you could make it, Judge." It was true and a surprise, too. "Please show me that your phone is turned off and I will do you the same courtesy." They laid them, like cards, on the bar. Earl pointed to the building that towered above them. "I love it up here; I used to work in that building right over there."

"At Schwartz and Benson?" Jason asked.

Earl nodded. "Yep, know 'em?"

"Sure. Work with them a lot. I like it up here, too. My brother had his wedding reception here." Jason ordered a bourbon on the rocks. "Like I said, this is my hometown. I didn't know that you'd lived here."

"About five or six years until I let them talk me into politics and we moved to Madison. What a mistake that was."

"I hear that. But the law seems to be about eighty percent politics these days. My God, you had one state supreme court justice literally trying to strangle another one in chambers."

"They're both assholes!" Earl laughed and they clinked glasses. "Look, for the record, I'm just following orders."

"Isn't that what Eichmann said?"

"Touché!" Earl replied. "I'm not saying it gets me off the hook. I'm telling you man to man."

"I get it, but still, I feel your hands around my neck just the same as that justice strangling his colleague."

"What do you think of this place?" Earl asked, turning back to the safer subject.

"I like it up here."

"Me too. Celebrated the New Year up here a couple of times. But that lobby is a trip. Chubby pink fauns and fairies floating around in gilded frames on all the walls, like some rich Midwesterner's wet dream of Victorian London. It kind of gives me the creeps."

Jason smiled. "Thanks for this invite. I needed a drink."

"Thanks for coming up. None of this has to be a big deal; this is how it's always been done for years."

"Let's not talk about all of that. This place always makes me miss my mom—she loved the Pfister especially. Could see her dancing in that ballroom."

"Let's toast your mother," Earl said.

Jason frowned but their glasses touched.

Earl looked out at Lake Michigan in the distance, remembering his own happy old Milwaukee days.

Chapter Twenty-Eight

LAKE JOSEPH EXCURSIONS

J ason put in a couple of loads of laundry—socks and underwear for the upcoming week of hearing—and tried to work up the guts to call his old prosecutor friend. He was procrastinating. Skip Munson was an old work friend, but it wasn't like they were best buds.

Jason poured himself a glass of Maker's Mark on the rocks for courage. No, courage wasn't quite right. It felt far wimpier to be going to the cops than it did to try to deal with Earl Franks on his own.

It was like that time in Milwaukee when he'd lost control at a trial and had to call in a bailiff. Two court deputies threatened to remove the disruptive guy, and he did settle down. But it felt more like a failure than a success. And there was something else.

Sitting in the bar at Blu, Jason had started playing around with numbers in his head. He had about five hundred in his pension, a couple hundred or so in deferred comp, maybe $80,000 in cash savings and at least $250,000 in his house. Another $200,000 in cash would give him some time and some freedom to pack up and move.

A new life, with Tara and without all this other shit—a completely different life in a solidly blue state with better weather. Shouldn't he at least consider it? What would Tara say if he asked her? Would she lose all respect for him? His calling card had always been his integrity.

He called Tara.

"Hey, how are you?" she said. "Did you call your friend yet?"

"No, I wanted to tell you about today first." He told her about getting Earl on tape and the one percent idea. "It was weird, but for a second I just sort of felt like you and I could just ride into the sunset and live happily ever after somewhere else. We could take a few months to get your divorce settled. I could get my cases out, and then we could just get the hell out of Dodge."

"That part sounds good." Tara paused. "But you're not seriously considering it, are you?"

Was he? "No, I don't think so." He sighed. No, he wasn't. "Just a passing fantasy." He laughed. A fantasy of being selfish for just once in his life.

"Good, I didn't think you could be bought that cheap. There's a couple of things I need to tell you, too. The first is that I have some money. Quite a bit, actually. Whenever I heard of something good, I bought stocks. And for years. I started with some money my grandmother left me."

"I always said you were a genius, but I didn't know financially, too." Jason laughed, embarrassed. *Mid-level functionary* was about right.

"The other thing is that I told Michael about the threat from Earl Franks," Tara continued. "Sorry, but I just felt like I owed him that."

"I understand."

"It's terrific that you got Franks on tape." Tara changed the subject. "I'm so proud of you!"

"I'm not sure if the recording will be admissible, but at least the cops will know I'm telling the truth."

"The photos of us will be everywhere, won't they?" Tara asked.

"Probably."

"Good thing we make such a nice couple."

"You're so brave, honey," Jason said. "I guess I better call Skip before it gets late."

Jason finished the delicious bourbon and tried calling his friend. But Skip's landline was busy, and Jason didn't have his cell. He thought one more time about telling his boss first. That would probably be the proper protocol. But Jason trusted Skip's judgment more than Hayman's, which was invariably clouded by indecision and political considerations. The bogus disciplinary letter had been the last straw.

Skip was a veteran prosecutor who now advised both state and local cops and prosecutors, mostly on high-profile public corruption and white-collar-crime cases. Skip wouldn't overreact or underreact—he was experienced and politically savvy. He'd sent two members of the legislature, one from each party, packing for prison four or five years ago.

Once he'd met with Skip, Jason would take his friend's advice on what to tell Hayman and when. Jason was halfway into a second glass of bourbon and water when he finally got through.

"Skip, Jason Erickson here. How you doing, buddy?" He hoped that the sound of his ice cubes tinkling wasn't audible, not that Skip would judge.

"Pretty good, but a little preoccupied." There was a pointed pause. "I just now put my mother into a nursing home."

"Oh, sorry to hear that. That's tough."

"Life stinks, doesn't it?" Skip sounded like he may have had a beer or two himself. They'd drained a few green bottles together back in the day. "I'm sitting here with my sister, trying to sort things out. Is this a personal or professional call?"

"Professional. Sorry to call you at home, my friend."

"No sweat. What's up?"

"I'm still doing environmental cases, and I've got something of a problem that I thought you might be able to help me with."

"Smoke or coke out on the waters?" Skip asked.

"No, someone's trying to bribe and threaten me, and it's starting to get a little scary. Wasn't sure at first, but now I think they're serious. High-profile people involved." Damn. It felt good to tell someone who could do something about it. What had taken him so long?

"Jesus, that's not good," said Skip. "What do you need?"

"I guess to sit down with you, and with maybe one good, honest public corruption cop that you trust, to tell you both a story about Earl Franks."

"Earl Franks from the state supreme court?" asked Skip.

"The same. Kind of hard to believe, and that's why I might have waited too long to tell it."

"I'm in court all day tomorrow."

"Me too. With Earl Franks, no less."

"Good. Look, you were right to call me," Skip said. "This is the kind of stuff I do now. I'll bring my favorite late-shift detective. Come up to my office at seven tomorrow night. You didn't tell that twerp Steve Hayman about any of this, did you?"

Jason laughed. "No."

"Good. I don't trust him."

"Me neither. Thanks so much, Skip," Jason said warmly. "See you tomorrow night at seven."

After a celebratory third glass of bourbon, Jason crashed.

Soon, he was lying on a large purple rock in the sun. He had a sudden urge to stand up and skinny-dip. He threw off his shirt and shorts. Ah, Tara did the same from a neighboring black rock! She dove gracefully into the water. He swam out toward her with determination. His efforts won him a kiss from her, looking like an otter with her dark hair all wet and her head bobbing up and down.

"Look at the pine trees," she exclaimed. "Towering over us mere humans!"

She swam off into the deeper water, and he set off after her again.

Jason woke up feeling rested. He had to quickly shower, throw on his suit and tie, jump in his car, and head straight to the old courthouse in Lake Joseph.

He'd discovered a shortcut route on back highways that eventually took him downtown along Lakeshore Drive. He'd never liked highly developed Lake Joseph, just an hour and change from Chicago. Wealthy

Chicago families still owned most of the large estates and homes along the shore, but an aversion to local zoning or regulation had left most of the lakefront the unattractive hodgepodge that he drove by now.

The nearshore area was cluttered with piers, boathouses, jet skis, and all manner of brightly colored flotation devices. The overall effect was more that of an amusement park than of a natural lakeshore. The housing was random and chaotic as well: huge gated mansions loomed over next-door-neighbor ranch houses in need of paint and repair. It was a bizarre but democratic mix—maybe that was part of the appeal of the place?

Crowds of Chicago- and Milwaukee-area tourists created traffic jams downtown on the weekends. Weekdays were a little better, but it was still hectic. It took him fifteen minutes to find a parking spot near the Lake Joseph Excursion boat. At least he wouldn't have to move his car during the day at this spot, as he had last week.

The first tour boat was already heading out, full of tourists in shorts and T-shirts gawking at the big houses while their obnoxious tour guide blared out juicy if garbled tidbits about the moneyed mansion dwellers behind the gates. For once, he wished he were joining them.

Jason was sick of his job. Sick of sitting up in his judge's perch in the high-ceilinged old courtroom, looking down all day on the man who'd threatened him and trying to act like nothing had happened. It was exhausting.

He walked quickly and just made it into court by 8:20 a.m. That gave him ten minutes to write down questions to ask Skip Munson. He wrote them down on the yellow legal pad as though they were notes from the testimony.

He'd already written: *Disqualify myself immediately? How to protect Tara and Justin?* Jason knew he shouldn't do anything out of the ordinary before he'd given a complete accounting of Franks's statements and threats to the police.

The case was in Wisconsin, and Franks and Calandro were from Illinois. Justin was in Minnesota. Didn't that make it some kind of a federal crime or conspiracy? He wrote down, *Alert FBI?* Maybe Skip could arrange a meeting with both state and federal law enforcement agents, and, hopefully, then gain some kind of protection for Justin as well?

The morning flew by without incident, and Jason was able to follow the evidence with attention. They finished up the technical and lengthy cross-examination of a lawyer for the title company that had insured the slipominium transactions.

There were several times when Jason came close to making an announcement from the bench that, for reasons he'd explain later, he'd chosen to disqualify himself from the case. That would be something to talk to Skip about tonight. He was lost in making these notes—but a familiar voice called him back to the hearing.

"Judge? Judge!" Franks bellowed impatiently. "Do you want to take our lunch break now or after the next witness?"

"Sure, let's break for lunch until one this afternoon."

Jason went out to lunch at a quiet café on an obscure street with the young court reporter Jennifer Ritter, hoping to have time to call Tara. "Hopefully, none of the others know of this place," he said to her. "I could use a break from all of them." He would have preferred to be alone, but Jennifer was new to the area and didn't know where to go to eat and get back in an hour.

He'd just put in his order for split pea soup and a toasted bagel when Earl Franks, Courtney, the new associate, Steve Olson, and Tommy Calandro walked into the café. Fuck. What were the odds?

"Isn't this cozy?" Franks said. "Very cozy."

"Excuse me, folks," said Jason, heading to the men's room, hoping for a moment of calm.

But big Earl Franks came barreling in too, standing at the next urinal. Franks was always into power plays.

"Well, they keep sending you the hottest little lunch dates, don't they?" Franks unzipped his fly and proceeded to unleash a furious yellow stream at close range.

"If you say so," Jason replied. It figured that Franks was a pig with women, too.

"Thought any more about things?"

"Yes." Jason zipped up his own pants and moved toward the sink.

"And?" demanded Franks.

Jason slowly washed his hands. Two could play mind games. "Tell them I'm seriously thinking about it, but I need a number."

"They said 150K, and they want an answer by the end of Friday's hearing. After that, I can't guarantee anything."

"I'll give them an answer, Earl. Like I said, I'm thinking about it."

"Well, to aid you in your thinking, let me give you some legal advice." Earl stood with his back to the bathroom door, his thick arms crossed over his burly chest. Subtle. "I took a few minutes to look into the employment contracts of both you and the lovely Mrs. Highsmith, and there's no question that one of you could be terminated for consorting with each other without disclosing the potential conflict."

"It's not a conflict for me, and there's no statute or rule against a judge being friendly with a reporter." Jason's supervisors even encouraged it to get friendly coverage.

"Maybe there's not a formal statute, but you should look into the new management-friendly work rules that have replaced your old civil service protections. It's pretty clear that you're at risk, and it's a no-brainer for Tara. We used to represent her media company."

"Oh, I'm sure you did," was all Jason could muster. "Earl Franks, one-stop shopping for all your sleazy legal needs."

Franks sniffed purposefully. "Tell Tara to check out Section Fourteen on Journalistic Standards in her union contract."

"What makes you so sure we've slept together?"

"You make a striking couple." Franks had finished his business and, without washing his hands, he showed Jason a couple of photos from his phone. "These photos are really impressive."

"Yeah, right." The photos were grainy screenshots of Tara and him in her hotel room in La Crosse. Who the fuck did Earl Franks think he was? "You're never going to be able to get this kind of garbage into any court."

"I don't need a court. I can just mail them to both of your bosses."

"Feel free, Earl. These were taken in Wisconsin, and we still have a right-to-privacy action. I will be very happy to sue your ass off for the triple damages and attorney's fees that statute provides for."

Jason was bluffing but it sounded good. He wasn't even sure if the legislature and governor hadn't already gotten rid of the privacy action. They were hellbent on eliminating anything that got in their way.

"I wouldn't do that if I were you." Earl sounded slightly taken aback.

"Just try me. And one more thing, Earl."

"What's that, Judge?"

"You may think we're drinking buddies, but I think you're the biggest asshole I've ever met." He approached Earl and looked him directly in the eye. "I think people like you are responsible for ninety percent of the bad shit in this world."

"How's that, Your Honor?"

"Your limitless fucking greed! Your willingness to cozy up to any sleazebag who will pay you, to help them contaminate people's wells or let little kids drink water full of lead, or to make frogs end up with flippers instead of legs. It's all because your fragile little ego needs more. Needs a better bottle of wine or a finer luxury car that you trade for filling the whole world with the poison that's inside you—you lowlife piece of shit!"

"Oh, gee. That really breaks my heart! Mr. Boy Scout thinks I play too rough!"

"Fuck you, Franks!" Jason yelled, heading out the door. "Fuck you!" he repeated, just as Steve Olson entered the men's room.

"What'd I do, Judge?" the young associate asked, smiling.

"Nothing, Steve." Jason tried to regain his composure. Tried to smile. "Just letting off some steam."

Chapter Twenty-Nine

~~~~~~~~~~~~

A SWIMMING POOL
WITH FISH IN IT

Over his awkward group lunch with Tommy Calandro, Courtney, and clueless Steve Olson, Earl couldn't stop thinking about his conversation with Jason Erickson. Ninety percent? What a crock! Earl would take his share of blame for the world's shitstorm—what, maybe fifteen, twenty, twenty-five, even—sure, but ninety was fucking nonsense.

If he didn't represent the scumbags, someone else would. No doubt about that. And, like the woman lawyer says in *The Big Chill*, his clients only raped the earth. Ninety percent was nonsense. But Jason's idea of suing for a privacy violation was far more concerning. Tommy put a proprietary arm around him.

"Can I huddle alone with Earl for a minute?" he asked, knowing the only answer was yes.

When Courtney and Steve were gone, Tommy leaned over close to Earl, his breath heavy with the garlicy reek of the falafel he'd already half-consumed. "Does this Stevie kid know anything about our forthcoming arrangement with Judge Erickson?"

"Of course not."

"What about your little Ms. Courtney?"

"No," Earl replied. Though, as she put it, she could smell that something was off. "And Erickson said he was seriously thinking about the 150K. That's new. The pictures got to him a little, but he reminded me that there is a right-to-privacy law in Wisconsin that would make it hard for us to get them in."

"Well, all we have to do is leak them. They'll both be toast," Tommy said, without his usual bluff certainty. "Right?"

"I'm sure he's thinking about that, too," Earl said. "You should give the Associated Freedom Council a call to get rid of that privacy statute, too."

Tommy shook his head. "That's not my concern right now."

"I'm sure they'd be happy to help, though it may be too late here."

The liberals in Wisconsin—Earl's ex-wife, Maggie, included—had gone ballistic when the national lobbying group AFC had helped to eliminate civil service protections, screwed teachers, and cut environmental regulations. They called the Associated Freedom Council *Ass Fuck* for short.

Even prim Maggie. She grinned as she said it. He missed that grin. That whole life.

"But I think the pictures were still a good move."

"Yes, he's gonna play ball," said Tommy. He seemed to be trying to convince himself. "We've got him right where we want him. By him and his girlfriend's short hairs. His career will be over if those are splashed in the papers. Hers too."

Courtney and Steve had come back into the room but were keeping their distance. Courtney was smiling flirtatiously with Steve. Tommy waved them over.

"Like I said, Tommy, it's definitely progress that he's considering your offer."

When they got back to court, the next witness was a familiar face:

Marge Paulson, who was Earl's neighbor at his family place on Blue Lake. Marge had been friendly with Earl's Maggie back when they were married and raising their kids. Maggie and Marge this. Marge and Maggie that. They were a formidable team.

For several years the Blue Lake Arts Festival had been the Maggie-and-Marge show. Back when Earl was a respectable, rising attorney. How had he fucked up that productive and purposeful life with Maggie? He *would* take ninety percent of the blame with her.

Marge was now the president of the State Lakes Association. She was a beautiful woman, with her long gray hair and serious blue eyes. Still impressive in her mid-seventies.

"Your Honor," Earl noted, "I just want the record to reflect that I've had the pleasure of meeting Ms. Paulson up on beautiful Blue Lake."

"Yes, of course, and I have, too," replied the judge.

"I have an exhibit I'd like to mark, Your Honor," said Marge. All business, as per usual.

"Of course."

"I have a copy for you, too, Earl." It was a photograph of six small children in a beautiful old wooden canoe.

"May I proceed?" Marge asked.

"Yes, just let me swear you in," Jason replied.

"I grew up on Lake Joseph, and was here, in this canoe, back in the summer of 1956. I am the youngest one there, either nine or ten. I now reside in Blue Lake, north of here—and very happily, I must say."

"Yes," the judge replied. "I remember you from cases we've done in Blue Lake."

"At that time, Lake Joseph was much less developed, and showed no signs of the environmental degradation we see here today. We had none of the algae blooms and no slimy green beards on shoreline rocks. You never smelled the manure from all of the big dairy farms—no matter which way the wind was blowing."

This earned Marge a laugh from the objectors in the crowd.

"Yes, the air was pure, and the fishing was great! We used to listen to a Chicago radio station, WBBN, and old Chuck Monsoon would be talking with a local fishing guide about what was biting and where—"

"I object, Your Honor," Earl interrupted. "This is all as interesting as hell, but it's just not relevant."

"Overruled. This is relevant to historic use. And Ms. Paulson never wastes our time."

"In 1967, I had my honeymoon at Lake Joseph," Marge continued. "I remember my late husband and I dangled hot dog bits in the water and delighted as crayfish ambled over to nibble. I ask everyone in this room—when is the last time you saw a crayfish in Lake Joseph?" She paused and looked around.

Earl did, too, and he could tell that she was scoring some points.

"Of course, that's a rhetorical question, Your Honor, but the answer is a fact. There are no crayfish left. There were even freshwater shrimp back when I was in that canoe."

"Your Honor," Earl interposed. "The piers will be there if they are owned privately as a slipominium or leased out. Where are we going with this?"

"May I respond, Your Honor?" Marge asked.

"Of course, Ms. Paulson," Jason replied.

"If you allow this legal fiction to rule, our public waters will go to ruin. There will be too many people rushing to build massive piers, and then selling off the slips."

"The objection is overruled," the judge began. "This goes to the cumulative impact analysis."

"My family owns over one thousand feet on Blue Lake," said Marge. "I could chop it up and put ten slips on every hundred feet and sell them. If they fetch seventy-five thousand dollars here on Lake Joseph, I'm sure I could get at least thirty thousand dollars on Blue Lake. You do the math, but I think that's three million dollars, and all I have to do is build one hundred pier slips."

"I object," Earl said. "This is speculation."

Marge shot him a look of contempt.

"Overruled."

"Fishing has declined. The very life of the lake has declined," Marge said. "You see people tearing out the nearshore vegetation. What they want is a swimming pool with fish in it—not a living, breathing lake! Don't let this happen, Judge Erickson. Don't allow money to squeeze the last bits of life out of our precious inland lakes!"

"Thank you, Mrs. Paulson," said the judge. "Any cross-examination?"

"None." It was better not to. Marge Paulson was forbidding and very well informed. "Nice to see you, Marge."

She nodded stonily.

Tommy gave Earl a dirty look. He felt like Marge's fish in the swimming pool—there was nowhere for him to hide or take cover.

Chapter Thirty

~~~~~~~~~

INTEGRITY, SEX,
AND VIDEOTAPE

Jason shut down the hearing at six o'clock, grabbed a slice of pizza and a beer downtown, and just made it to Skip's office. Skip had brought not one but two cops to their meeting. A short, fat, white man and a tall, thin, black woman. The man was in uniform and the woman was in a stylish suit. They both greeted Jason with a nod. The man shook his hand and the woman gave him a thumbs-up.

"This is my former colleague Administrative Judge Jason Erickson," Skip said. "This is Detective Maya Rollins and Sergeant Ralph Gaebler. They're both from the Public Integrity Unit."

"Nice to meet you both."

"We've only got a few minutes," Skip interrupted. "Jason, can you please tell them what you told me?"

Jason took them through each interaction with Franks, right up to his conversation today.

"You told him you were thinking about it?" Sergeant Gaebler frowned. He was drinking a large Starbucks coffee, even though it was after seven o'clock in the evening.

"Yes, and he told me I had until Friday to decide. Franks cornered me in the men's room to have the conversation. And I've made a recording of him on my phone a few days ago, where I also played along like I was interested."

"Play it for us," Skip said.

It was a little garbled but audible. Jason sounded like a felon himself. Skip nodded.

"Jason called me and set up this meeting, so I know he was just playing along. Doubt if it will be admissible, as you probably know."

"Why do you think they're trying to bribe you?" Detective Rollins asked. "Did they have any reason to believe that you might go along with it?"

"It's twenty-five million dollars to Calandro, at least."

"What's your history with these players?"

"I've never dealt with Franks's client until now. Franks has always behaved himself in my prior dealings with him. I think I've done two prior cases with him. I have the recording of Franks, but they do have something on me. Or they think they do."

"What's that, Judge?" asked the detective.

"They apparently have a sex tape of myself and a journalist who covers some of my cases."

Three pairs of eyebrows went up simultaneously.

"A *sex* tape?" Skip asked. "This part you didn't tell me before."

"It's pretty new. Earl Franks gave me this today." Jason pulled out the photos, which Earl had put in his hands just as the hearing was winding down. Fortunately, they weren't that graphic. "I don't know of any ethical issues I'd have from having a consensual relationship with a journalist, though she may be in some hot water. I'm not sure it matters—and you probably won't believe it—but this was our first time sleeping together. I'm divorced, and Tara is going through one now."

They were all studying the photos. Their first time together. Fucking Franks!

"They went to some trouble," Detective Rollins said. She seemed to be trying to be sympathetic. "They must really, really want to sell those pier slips."

"Franks told me that Calandro said that he'd already spent the money from it and couldn't have any uncertainty about the outcome," Jason began. "There's plenty of uncertainty, but my decision gets a lot of deference from the appellate courts. So, they are in pretty good shape if they win at the trial level. I've never been overturned on appeal."

"So, you've just kept doing the trial as though nothing has happened?" Sergeant Gaebler asked. "That can't have been easy. You've got a lot going on right now, don't you?"

"Yes."

"Why did it take you so long to call Skip?" Sergeant Gaebler asked. They seemed to be doing a good cop, bad cop routine on him.

"I wasn't sure if Franks was serious, but he has been getting more aggressive. In the parking lot in La Crosse, he was menacing. So, in Milwaukee, I tried to get him on tape. And, like I said, Franks sought me out in the men's room just this afternoon. They gave me a final offer of 150K. What do you think I should do?"

"How much are you willing to do to help us?" asked Detective Rollins.

"Pretty much anything. Do you mean like wear a wire?"

"They'll be looking for that," said Sergeant Gaebler. "You'd probably be better off just using your phone. We have a way of making that undetectable."

"That would be hard. He made me turn off my phone the second time we talked at the Pfister."

"Let me back up a minute first," Skip interjected. "Jason is an old friend of mine. I have to ask you very directly—do you feel like your life is in danger with these people?"

"Oh, hell yes! My life, Tara's life, and possibly my brother, Justin's, are all in danger!" Jason said.

Skip nodded and ran his hand over his forehead. "Imminently?"

"He gave me a deadline of Friday, so the clock is definitely ticking somewhere near the imminent."

"I love the way you lawyers talk." Detective Rollins smiled. "So, is it fair to say that you feel like any violence would likely come after Friday's trial testimony?"

"I think so, but who the hell knows? If they catch me recording them with my phone, I can't imagine them being very pleased with me."

"You're right. It will be dangerous," said Skip. "You should go into it knowing that. We wouldn't use your phone now. But you can just bail right now if you want. You've given us probable cause of an effort to corrupt or blackmail a public official. I was also thinking that it's clear that Franks has already committed some ethical violations as an attorney."

"I probably have too," Jason said. "I told him I'd sue them for invasion of privacy; it's like treble damages and attorney's fees. But he could do the same with my tape, right?"

"I don't know about any of the civil stuff," Skip answered. "But other than any embarrassment, these photos harm him more than you. They corroborate the idea that they were threatening you and trying to get something over you. Did anyone see you with Franks?"

"Yes, I ran into Grace Clarkson, one of the lawyers in the case I was working on," Jason replied. "I ran into her in the hotel lobby, and she pointedly told me that she'd seen Earl Franks on the running path near the university in La Crosse."

"Okay. That's great," said the detective. "We'll try to get a statement from her."

"Knowing that there's some risk, do you still want to try to bust them?"

"Yes, of course," Jason said. "But is there any way you could have some kind of police protection for Tara and my brother?"

"No, sorry. We don't really have enough for that kind of resource allocation quite yet. Tell them to be careful." Skip looked at his watch. "Now let's talk about the details of how we get these guys."

Chapter Thirty-One

~~~~~~~~~~~~~~~

THE LAKE CAN'T HOLD

Tara poured herself another cup of her favorite coffee, grabbed a yogurt, and juggled these necessities and her laptop out to her sunny porch. Somehow, the morning sunlight always managed to dodge her big oak and pine trees, and today was no exception. There would be shade, too, when it got hot in the afternoon. A perfect screened porch, and one of the best things about their house.

The right setting for working on her nature poems and essays. She spent a peaceful hour or so finishing up her latest, *The Blue Smell of the Pines*. The essay *was* pretty good. Her main contribution was to take the idea of *terroir* from wine tasting and extend it to writing about place. In writing about nature, the terroir could include geography, history, the waters and winds, and the taste and smell of a particular soil and locale.

Her essay was also enlivened by a couple of public domain photos she'd found of almost exact contemporaries Paul Cezanne and John Muir. The great French painter and the Scottish-American naturalist looked very much alike, with their scruffy but scholarly beards and rustic rucksacks. Her essay found that their ideas about landscape had much in common as well.

She sent it out, electronically, to two journals she had a reasonable shot at, and then printed out a copy to send by mail to *The Sun*. They'd rejected all her stuff but urged her to keep submitting. This was her last try. Screw 'em if they didn't like this piece.

She showered and then headed out for the downtown Green Bay US Post Office. It was the lucky one for her writing. The day was Tara's. The blue sky beckoned.

From Green Bay, she could go north to beautiful Door County in a flash. Say, a hike up rocky Eagle Bluff or a stroll along the beach at Whitefish Dunes to catch some sun. But with her usual planned impulsivity, she decided now that she'd go south two hours, down to the John Muir park.

She loved the little lake there and, even better, the rare calcareous fen and all of the amazing wildflowers there. And she was feeling close to John Muir. She'd take a nice hike there instead.

Tara had taken the personal day impulsively, too, just after telling her boss about her relationship with Jason.

"You know, of course, that you can no longer cover any of his cases?" Simon had asked, using his most patronizing editor's voice.

"Of course I know that." She was stalling, still debating whether to tell him about the possible sex tape. "And I know that I may be in violation of the contract."

"Yes, I may have to discipline you." That came out sounding perverted. They'd never gotten along particularly well, but she sometimes noticed Simon staring at her in a creepy way. "Probably speeds up the food-and-health beat, too," he added.

Tara searched his face for any small bit of human sympathy. There was none.

"Well, I also know that under the contract, I'm entitled to about a month of unclaimed personal days and I'm taking one tomorrow."

She wasn't going to tell him about the possible sex tape. There was no reason to at this point. They weren't even sure that there was such a thing. If there was, pervy Simon would probably demand some editor's right to see it.

Jason had finally gone to the police about Earl Franks. What a relief! But Tara also worried about the plan to take Franks down that involved Jason recording them with his phone. She wanted to see Jason in person to talk things through, but she knew he would tell her it was too dangerous for her to go to Lake Joseph. Was that part of the reason she was heading south to the Muir Park State Natural Area? Yes, there was the rare fen and the prairie full of wildflowers, the Muir terroir, but it was closer to Jason, too. And it was only another hour from there to Lake Joseph.

So much change, so fast. Too fast for Tara, a creature of habit. The joy of sharing had become a regular part of her life. But so had fear and anxiety. Her legs had started twitching nervously again for the first time in years.

Chewing all this over made the drive go by fast. Soon, she was pulling into the parking lot, at the slightly obscure place where the great naturalist had lived as a child. Hers was the only car there. Strange because she thought she'd heard a car door slam. Tara made sure her pepper spray was in her backpack.

Her gloomy paranoia—but did she now have real *enemies?*—was a sharp contrast to the almost-perfect summer day. It couldn't have been sunnier or milder. She tried to shake off her fear of Earl Franks and that whole unsavory crowd and pulled out her plant identification books.

She knew to look for nodding lady's tresses orchids, bog birch, white lady's slipper, and Kalm's lobelia (like surreal purple houseflies), but to her great delight, she almost immediately stumbled upon one of her favorite wildflowers, the strangely named grass of Parnassus.

Of course, it wasn't a grass at all but a delightful little ground cover. Its small white-and-light-green-pinstriped flowers were in full veiny bloom. Its bean sprout-like little brown pistils stood femininely erect over its swollen ovary! It was so perfect that she took a photo and emailed it to Jason. *This is how you make me feel, lover!*

Would he get it? He knew a surprising amount of science, but it didn't really matter. He got her.

"Show me how you touch yourself," he'd asked her that first night at the Charmant.

Love. Lust. Honesty. Ideas. She finally could be herself—in bed and elsewhere.

Michael liked being in control, and he didn't like her taking the lead. Part of it had been that he was a couple of years older than her in college and had seemed to know what he was doing more than she had. Like some D.H. Lawrence hero, Mike's desire was something he thought was to be gallantly bestowed upon her. That pattern had become stale years ago.

Yes, she and Jason were in the initial throes of it, but part of the excitement was knowing that it wouldn't be like that anymore. When the moment came, she immediately asserted herself. He loved it. Was this rare intimacy—of mind, heart, and now body—really now hers to explore? She missed Jason.

She snapped a photo of a perfect stand of little orchid flowers, too. *Nature Heals! So does your love. These are called nodding lady's tresses orchids—isn't that perfect?*

It didn't matter whether Jason understood all of the details or not. They talked on the phone every night now, and his calm voice sometimes put her off to a dreamy sleep.

She sat down on a bench, pulled off her backpack, and took out the lunch she'd made for herself: a spinach-and-walnut salad, hippy peanut butter on homemade crackers, and a pear.

She thought of John Muir, who'd grown up here and was captivated by the wildflowers, too. Lake Ennis was named after some of his people. Muir had learned much of what he knew from his days at the University of Wisconsin. He'd famously taken his first botany class there, under a black elm tree outside North Hall on Bascom Hill. Abraham Lincoln, who now sat as a dignified green statue at the top of the hill, was president in Muir's strange student days.

Muir had taken only the courses that interested him, and had no interest in jumping through the hoops to get his degree. He had still been listed as a first-year student even after several years of study. But everything he'd learned was his from then on, as she'd written.

Tara had also called Muir out for his casual racism in her new essay. She loved its title, which came from Cezanne. *The Blue Smell of the Pines*. But what was the terroir here? She took a deep breath and then wrote in her green idea Moleskin.

The Lake Can't Hold

The odorless perfume
of the rare calcareous
fen fills the wildflowers
and varied ground cover
with a lusty late July
calm—the sweet and salty
alkaline soil drains
the rain and spring water
the lake can't hold.

A noise in the bushes gave Tara a start. But it was only a stoop-necked parade of wild turkeys wandering by, bobbing heads-down, scrounging for their dinner on the ridge above her. A sight to remember, even if she was too late to capture it with her cell. She looked at her phone and saw the time—almost three—and the spell was broken.

And Jason hadn't replied.

As she was packing up, she heard the message-alert noise from her iPhone. She had a text! Maybe Jason was on a break at the Lake Joseph trial? But it was some anonymous number she didn't know. An offer of health care she didn't need or an "important" message about her credit card rate?

No! Two nude photos from their intimate night in La Crosse were attached.

How would you like to see these on the Internet? How would your employer like it? Get real.

She looked briefly at the photos. They were unmistakably Jason and Tara. This brutal violation of their privacy was sickening. Fear. Palpable and ominous fear. She was going to go to the cops now too. Her hands were trembling as she forwarded the photos to Jason.

Those bastards! I'm on my way to Lake Joseph. We can go to the cops together, my love.

The highway to Lake Joseph was full of obnoxious trucks and even more obnoxious truck drivers. And some yahoo in an old blue Toyota truck seemed to have it in for her, or some vague passive-aggressive road rage. She passed him a couple of times and then he just kept following too close for comfort. She was grateful for her new hybrid SUV's blind spot beeper.

As she was driving, Tara remembered that Jason usually left his personal phone at home and used his government phone during hearings. He wouldn't get her messages until tonight after he drove home!

It was after four by the time she found a parking spot about halfway between the old courthouse and the sprawling new jail that housed the sheriff's department. The same was true in every town in the state—someday people would write about the decline in small-town America based upon the shift of resources from building beautiful courthouses to erecting enormous jails. What did it mean that people were so fearful?

And yet here she was, scared to death herself, looking over her shoulder in what she hoped was just paranoia, making her way toward the courthouse. She stopped near the bank to check her phone. Nothing from Jason yet.

She texted both of his phones: *SURPRISE, I'm here in Lake Joseph!*

We've got to get together. It's URGENT! Going to cops now. Call me as soon as you can. Love, Tara

The courthouse was in view a couple of blocks ahead. Was that Jason, hurrying down the street? She started running toward him. Damn, these heavy new hiking boots. Waterproof, but impossible to run in.

"Jason! Jason!"

He was still too far off. A man in a black baseball cap was running after him. Jason turned toward him.

Then shots rang out, and Jason went down.

"No, no!" she screamed too late.

And now someone was coming up behind her, too. Shit, the guy from the blue truck.

A bullet tore through her shoulder. She heard another shot.

Chapter Thirty-Two

~~~~~~~~~~~~~~~~~~~~

THE MESS HE'D
MADE OF THINGS

After about ten minutes, Earl started to worry. Where was Judge Erickson? Earl was sitting at the counsel table next to Tommy C., Courtney, and Steve Olson. Erickson was never late, but it was already 1:15 p.m. when he said they'd be back on the record at 1:00 p.m. Was that little prick going to walk back into this whole room full of people and put it all on the record like he'd warned? Was the judge off getting a bailiff right now?

Earl wasn't convinced that Erickson was really on board. Jason Erickson, whatever else he was, was a talented lawyer. He'd no doubt had plenty of offers to work for large firms and make more than Tommy C. was ever prepared to stick in an envelope. They should have offered two hundred like Earl had suggested. Earl was sweating and his heart was pounding. Calandro was giving him none-too-subtle looks, mostly with his eyebrows.

Tommy leaned over close. "For the record, it wasn't us!"

"I don't want to know," Franks whispered. "I still don't think any of this was really necessary. I could've won the fucking case."

"Earl, listen to me, it wasn't us!" Calandro raised his hands and shrugged. "But the timing stinks, because I gave Stan the okay to send the pictures."

"Shit."

Earl got up and paced the halls, like a nervous expectant father. Only waiting for a death instead. There he ran into the annoying mailman, Richard Borker.

"I wonder what's holding up the judge? He's usually so punctual," Borker observed. As always, stating the obvious. Two or three firecracker bursts were heard. "What the heck was that?"

"Who the hell knows?" Earl fired back. Did they shoot Judge Jason Erickson just like that? A group of three deputies dashed down the hallway.

"Damn," Borker said. "Something's wrong."

Franks stuck his head into the courtroom. "Sheriff's deputies running around out here," he said. "I hope the judge is all right."

Calandro shot him a look. A crowd from the case—experts, farmers, and spectators—had gathered, looking out the courtroom windows. The reporters ran out toward the stairs.

"There's two bodies down in the middle of the square!" one of them called. "An ambulance, too!"

"And here comes another one!" Borker said.

Two bodies? Earl rushed outside with most of the others from the courtroom. If Erickson had balked, Tommy C.'s people would no doubt put a bullet into his head. They'd taken out that landfill deal witness and who knew how many more. But two bodies? What the hell was up with that? Maybe it was all some freakishly random coincidence?

"Maybe the judge had a heart attack," said Borker. "So much stress."

"That's probably it," said Earl, knowing damn well it wasn't.

For the first time in his life, Earl Franks found himself wishing someone was dead. He caught himself before putting up one of his fucked-up gambler's prayers—*Please God, let him be dead.* No, that was beyond sacrilegious. That would be evil.

A crowd had already gathered in the main square in the street. A body had already been placed in the ambulance on a stretcher. There were two pools of blood in the center of the square. The deputies were keeping the crowd back. It was a woman in the first ambulance, probably that journalist, Tara. It was hard to tell with the oxygen mask over her face. A second ambulance was already there.

Damn it, Erickson was alive, thrashing around inside the second fire department ambulance.

"He was shot!" called Borker.

"The judge has been shot!" others clamored.

"Why? Why?" Marge Paulson asked, in tears.

It was a scene right out of the evening news. Earl put his arm around Marge. Calandro had made his way down to the courtyard. Marge broke free from him and walked off away from the crowd.

"What's up?" Tommy asked no one in particular.

"Judge Erickson and some woman have been shot," said Richard Borker. "And you better not have had anything to do with it."

"I'm sick of your slander, you little prick," Tommy snapped. "Just shut your fat fucking mouth."

"The judge was still alive," Earl said, trying to calm Marge Paulson and unnerve Tommy C. at the same time. "He was thrashing about like a madman." They were both fucked.

A court bailiff had come down, now that the coast was clear. It was just like one of those losers to be all brave and bossy now that the gunshots had stopped.

"The Lake Joseph Resort case is officially adjourned until further notice by mail or email," the bailiff said.

Chapter Thirty-Three

~~~~~~~~~~~~~~~

FLOODPLAIN MANAGEMENT

For a few hours that morning, the Floodplain Conference had been eye-opening for Grace. How were environmental professionals going to deal with the new reality of a changing climate? With the practical impacts of one-hundred-year floods once or twice a year and five-hundred-year floods every couple of years? The recent heavy rains had washed out state-of-the-art engineering. They'd put up endless photos of eviscerated banks and mangled concrete retaining walls.

But now Grace was listening to an old land surveyor drone on about the historic metes and bounds method of property boundaries at the State Floodplain Management conference in Madison. The surveyor was enjoying his moment in the sun, his captive audience.

The guy without a name tag sitting next to her had rolled his eyes at some of the surveyor's musty witticisms. She was expecting a snarky comment when Mr. No Name leaned toward her. "Did you hear about Judge Erickson?"

"No. What?"

"It's all over the net. He and some reporter were shot in Lake Joseph, and then med-flighted to University Hospital here maybe an hour or so ago."

"Shit," Grace replied.

"You know him?"

"Yes, and in all likelihood her, too, if it was a woman."

"I'm sorry. It was. First name was Tara, I think."

"Damn," Grace said. Poor Tara.

Feeling a little dizzy when she stood up, Grace packed up her things and left immediately for the hospital. She wasn't sure why or even that they would tell her anything. But when she arrived, there was just one friendly security guard, and the unit nurse greeted her kindly.

"Can I help you?" The nurse was in her early fifties, in purple scrubs.

"Yes, I want to see Judge Jason Erickson. I'm . . . I guess you could say, I'm his work friend."

"Come in. You can look in but you can't go into his room yet. He has been seriously injured. But so far, he seems to be stable. Let me look at his chart for you. Do you mind signing in, please?"

"I want you to know that I'm an attorney, but that I'm here as his friend. We were in law school and have done cases together. One of them may have put him here."

Was it really the creeps who owned all of the Big Dairy CAFOs? Or Tara's husband? Earl Franks and his sleazy clients? Judge Jason Erickson had plenty of enemies.

Unexpectedly, Grace started to tear up.

"I understand completely." The nurse looked at the sign-in sheet. "Grace, let me check his chart for you, dear."

Jason was lying helpless and pale, connected to numerous tubes and beeping machines. Grace tried to count the tubes. There was a large garden hose right in the middle of his chest that was connected to some kind of suction device with blue water in one chamber and what looked like blood in another. There was an IV in his right arm and a heart monitor on his left wrist, and a catheter appeared to be jammed into his groin under his gown. He had an oxygen mask over his face, but was still oddly some essence of himself, like certain corpses at a funeral.

This last thought went through her like a wave, and her eyes were clouding again when the nurse came back with his chart.

"All of the vitals have improved or at least stabilized. That's really all I can tell you without violating confidentiality."

"What are his chances?" Grace asked.

"You'll have to talk to the doctors."

"What does your gut say, woman to woman?"

"Things look better now than they did two hours ago." The nurse shrugged. "We don't know what the other effects could be. He has a chance, maybe even a good chance, but things can change fast." She stopped herself there.

"Thank you. I really appreciate your kindness."

The nurse put her arm around Grace's shoulder. "Do you know what I've found that helps?"

Grace shook her head.

"Meditation," said the nurse. "Meditation helps."

"Thanks," said Grace, giving her a hug. "Just one more question. What about Tara Highsmith? The police aren't releasing anything."

"I can't tell you anything about her. I've probably gone too far as it is."

"I understand. Thank you!"

Grace was relieved that she wouldn't have to tell Jason Erickson, if he came around, about whatever condition Tara was in. She wasn't the right person to do it, anyway.

As Grace was leaving, a woman came running after her. "Excuse me. Can I talk to you for a few minutes?" She showed her a badge. "I'm Detective Maya Rollins of the Lake Joseph Sheriff's Department. Will you please follow me?" She was a tall African American woman in her early forties.

She led Grace to the local county sheriff's little office in the hospital.

"What is your name, please, and what brought you here to visit Judge Erickson?"

"My name is Grace Clarkson, and I'm an attorney. Known Jason since law school. I was just now at a Floodplain Management Conference in Madison and heard a rumor that he and Tara Highsmith had been shot."

"Tell me exactly what you heard, and from whom."

"The man seated next to me at the conference told me that there had been a shooting in Lake Joseph and that Judge Erickson and a journalist named Tara had been med-flighted here. I came immediately. Those of us who practice environmental law or deal in the profession all know both Judge Erickson and Tara Highsmith."

Detective Rollins nodded, neutrally. "And tell me about your recent contacts with Judge Erickson."

"I've been doing this very controversial case involving a large dairy operation; my clients are opposing it, and Erickson is the judge. Before that, I saw him at the Midwest Water Law Conference, and I ran into him in a bar in La Crosse shortly after that." She didn't tell her that they'd kissed.

"Do you think the dairy case could have something to do with this shooting? He criticized the dairy and the state EPA, right?"

"Yes, but I have no reason to believe that they would shoot him for it. I mean, the corporate dairy industry controls the legislature and governor in this state, so it's hard to believe that they would need to kill Judge Erickson to get their way."

The detective gave a half-smile. "Can't say I'm a huge fan of our governor either. Do you know of any other enemies Judge Erickson had?"

"Well, he is doing controversial cases all the time. But one especially nasty one is the Lake Joseph Resort. The lead attorney from that case showed up in La Crosse unexpectedly to talk to Judge Erickson."

"Who was that?"

"Earl Franks. I saw Franks there, too. On my morning run down by the UW-L campus."

"That's very interesting. And he was shot just outside my office here in Lake Joseph. Anything else?" the detective asked, looking her right in the eyes.

"Well, I'm not sure how Tara's husband felt about the close friendship between the two of them."

"Do you know if they were an item?"

Grace nodded, feeling a little guilty. Was she ratting them out or helping to find their assailant? Detective Rollins searched her face carefully.

"You have to say yes or no."

"They appeared to be pretty close, but I have no idea how far it went."

"So, you and the judge were close friends?" the detective asked.

"No, we haven't kept in touch since law school, but we've been seeing each other regularly professionally this year."

"Did you ever have a romantic relationship with him?"

"No."

"Did either of you want to?"

"No, I was married, and we were just friends in law school," Grace replied. "Then we were on a case together recently. So, no, it was never a possibility."

"Thank you very much. Please let me get your telephone number and contact information. Here's my number." Detective Rollins handed Grace her card. "Please call me if you think of anything else that may be helpful."

Chapter Thirty-Four

WHAT GOOD WOULD
THAT DO HIM?

A t about eight o'clock on the night of the shooting, Earl Franks got a call from Courtney Sharpe. Really pissed. "So, Earl—Judge Erickson was just shot in Lake Joseph town square in broad fucking daylight?"

"Yes, apparently it was a bullet very near his heart."

"Did Tommy C. have something to do with this?"

"Do you think that they would tell me?" Earl paused. "I hope not. I don't think he'd go that far. Do you?"

"Maybe."

"But what good would that do him, as you would say." Franks chuckled. That had been her response when he had asked her if she had ever faked an orgasm.

"I can't believe you're laughing about this."

"Just a dumb joke. By the way, I had nothing to do with what happened to Jason Erickson." Earl tried to say this with all of his lawyerly authority, as though he were addressing a jury, but it came off as a little pompous.

"Yeah, right, Earl. But one of these days, you're going to see that this is not so damn funny! You don't know how much your ass is in my hands!" she yelled, slamming down the phone.

He tried calling her back, on the half hour, but her phone was off the hook. The last thing he needed was Courtney making any kind of veiled threats about what she might know. What the hell did she know, really? He hadn't told her much. But Courtney would love to get her name in the papers for being a righteous hero.

After brooding around his condo for a couple of hours and then knocking down three scotch and waters at Mike's Place downtown, Earl found himself at Courtney's apartment at about 11:30 p.m. Specifically, he found himself a little drunk, beating the hell out of her door.

"Open up, Courtney. I know you're home!"

There was no answer. So, he just kept banging—stopping only to repeatedly buzz her doorbell.

"Come on, open up," he pleaded. Then, more menacing, "Open the fucking door now!"

Finally, she came to the door in her red silk pajamas.

"What is it, Earl? It's late," she said. He'd never seen her look scared before.

"I need to talk to you."

"But I'm not alone."

"I don't care." Just then he remembered the young doctor she had said she was seeing. "Young Dr. Fuck can just share you for a minute."

He forced his way past her. "No, Earl, don't—"

In the split second that he entered Courtney's familiar apartment, Earl caught sight of old Jack Singleton, the seventy-plus managing partner of his law firm, hustling into Courtney's bedroom in his matching red silk boxers.

"Oh, color-fucking-coordinated, isn't this cozy!" said Earl. He was wild with glee and fear. He snapped a couple of pictures with his phone.

"Earl."

"I knew you were a sleaze, Courtney Sharpe, but I thought you were an honest sleaze!"

"Don't try to slut-shame me, Earl. You prick." She sounded a little wounded. "I didn't want to hurt you!"

"Like I'm just so fragile!"

Courtney, regaining her stride, got up in his face. "Oh yeah—so what are you doing here, then?" She gave him a stare worthy of his ex-wife. "What the hell do you want?"

"I was just hoping we could keep seeing each other," he said, a little louder so Singleton could hear it. "I miss you."

"Go home, Earl," said Courtney.

"It's okay. None of this happened," called Jack Singleton, getting into his pants.

"Hah!" Earl called out. "In your dreams, both of you."

He took a couple of snaps with his cell. Earl had them, cold. Singleton would lose his managing partnership for having an affair with an associate. Singleton was married, but, more importantly, managing partners, by the express terms of the partnership agreement, were not allowed to mess with the help. Particularly not the attorney associates help.

"Hello, Jack."

"Evening, Earl," said Singleton, offering his hand. His neck and chest were a wrinkled white and his puffy nipples were a hideous bright pink that reminded Earl of Pepto-Bismol. "Why don't you come in tomorrow and we'll sit down and figure out where you're at on this whole Jason Erickson affair. We've already thrown up the idea of some kind of leave of absence for you until things sort themselves out."

"I guess now there's just one more thing to sort out," said Earl, regaining his form. "Where is this going to leave you two at the firm? I think both of you are in big trouble at Higgins and Clark."

Courtney wouldn't want word of things with Singleton to be common knowledge at the firm. They would let her go. There were fifty more resumes just like hers coming in every month. Even if they didn't fire her, she would never make partner. Earl let this fact set in with both of them.

"I guess a paid leave of absence might be something to consider."

"We hadn't discussed your compensation during the whole investigation, but I must say, people are concerned about any perception that Higgins and Clark is a mafia firm."

"Well, I think we can come to some kind of a fair resolution, don't you, Jack?"

"Quite possibly."

"Now, go home and get some sleep, Earl," said Courtney. "Everything is going to be all right. My lips are sealed about all of this."

"Good night, babe. By the way, Jack—"

"Earl?"

"Nice boxers."

"Come in tomorrow and we'll talk."

The next morning, it was agreed that Earl Franks would be represented by an attorney to be paid for by the firm, and that he would be suspended until such time as he be either convicted or acquitted of a felony, assuming he was going to be charged with one. It was further agreed that he receive a salary in the amount of $5,000 a week until such time as he be convicted or reinstated at his full salary, if he was cleared of all charges.

Now, he had to find a good criminal defense lawyer.

Chapter Thirty-Five

~~~~~~~~~~~~~

A VISIT TO TARA

Jason woke up with a start. His mouth was dry and his tongue felt enormous. Some kind of steel pipe had been rammed up his penis. He felt a little out of breath. That was the most concerning. But his brother was there.

"Justin." He knew his voice was garbled. "How long you been sitting there, man?"

"Hey, look who's awake!" Justin stood up, leaned toward him, and grabbed his hand. "I got the tan in Santa Barbara, if that's what you asked me."

"No." Jason took a breath, struggling. One word at a time, he repeated. "How long you been there, man?"

"Just a couple of days. You're doing great." Justin sat back down beside him. "You're going to make it!"

"Lots of tubes."

"The big one," Justin pointed, "that garden hose thing, is just draining the crud out."

"Never mind that one." Jason paused, catching his breath. "Tell them to take that thing out of my dick!"

Justin's face lit up with his unmistakable smartass grin. "I've got to get the nurse," Justin said. "They wanted me to tell them. By the way, your friend Ben has been up here a lot too."

By the time Justin had summoned the gray-haired nurse, Jason had begun to drift back to sleep, but his brother's familiar loud voice revived him.

"He recognized me right away," Justin was saying. "And he asked how long I'd been here."

"That's wonderful," the nurse replied. She checked her watch and added it to Jason's chart.

"He also told me he wants the catheter out of his groin, though he used another word."

"They all do." The nurse smiled. "Definitely some pressure there."

"Hell, yes!" Jason said. He sounded old.

"Hah, your voice sounds better already!" Justin grinned.

"So, you are awake, after all," the nurse said. "Sorry about the pressure. Some guys say it's better sitting up. My name is Martha, and I've been taking care of you." She raised the back of his bed up a couple of inches. "Let me know if you want this back down."

Jason was in a small private room with a bathroom directly across from his bed. He saw his disturbing reflection in the bathroom mirror. He was pale and weak-looking with wildly disheveled hair. A crazy mad scientist caught up in his own web of tubes.

"Martha, am I paralyzed?"

"You have a collapsed lung and a hole in your upper back, but—" Martha was carefully choosing her words. "Based on where that was, your legs should have a pretty good chance of coming back." She paused. "But I'm an RN, and you should talk to your doctor. Those nerves in the back are pretty complicated."

"I think I moved my toes," Jason said. Or was that a dream?

"That would be a good sign." Martha made a note. "Do you remember when that was?"

"No. How long have I been here?"

"Three nights and this is your fourth day."

"Tell me what I've missed from that chart," Jason said. He pointed to Justin. "It's okay for him to hear."

"Your lawyer brain is working," Justin noted. "He's thinking about HIPAA already!"

"You're right," Martha replied. "That's complex thinking." She made another note.

"What a genius," Jason grumbled. Make a note, he still makes bad jokes. It was getting harder to speak again. "Where's Tara; is she okay?"

"How about this? You rest, and if you're up to it, I'll get Dr. Silvan to come over and she can fill you in."

"Sounds good." Jason started to drift.

Soon, he was back on Twisted-Something again. It must have been quite a ride, because the next time he saw nurse Martha again, it was early morning and they were serving him coffee and peach yogurt. Justin was still there, drinking a Starbucks.

"You sleep here again?"

"Yeah, it's the safest place in town," Justin replied. "They've got two deputies out there."

Martha came back in, looking cheerful. "Dr. Silvan's doing her rounds and will come in shortly to go over your chart if you want. She did your surgery and follow-up care," said Martha.

"Yes, and it's still okay for him to hear."

"I heard all of that too, and I'm here now. I'm Dr. Riya Silvan," said a tiny woman whose enormous glasses drowned her face. "I'm delighted to see my star patient sitting up and speaking!"

"Thank you for saving my life."

"You are very welcome," she replied, displaying no sign of either false modesty or a sense of humor. "You wanted us to review your chart with you and your partner here."

"Brother," Justin said.

"Brother. Sorry," Dr. Silvan said. "The gunshot entered the right middle of your chest and there is an exit wound just below the right scapula. Let's see, you were conscious most of the time and kept trying to fight off the mask because you couldn't breathe."

The word *gunshot* echoed through him. He'd been shot. *Gunshot, gunshot.* His heart raced.

"You want me to continue?" the doctor asked.

Jason nodded.

"You lost a lot of blood, two hundred to three hundred ccs at the scene. But we've already brought your blood back up. Oh, and there's been a steady improvement in vitals."

"That's important?" Justin asked.

"Yes, all of Jason's vitals have improved or at least stabilized." Dr. Silvan turned back to Jason. "You have what we call an open pneumothorax. The bullet tore a hole in your left lung, which allowed air to rush in, and the lung partially collapsed. Now there is blood, fluid, and air filling up the space left by the collapsed lung. Well, the fluid and blood are trapped and can't get out, and this makes it hard for the other lung to breathe and for the heart to pump blood. That's what the drainage tube in your chest is for, to pump out everything that's in that other lung."

"Am I going to make it?" Jason asked, with effort.

"It's a great sign that we're having this conversation," Dr. Silvan said calmly. The nurse nodded.

"And will I walk again?"

"I would think so, yes, based upon the exit path." Dr. Silvan looked at Martha. "Go and get Deandre or Dan and tell them to bring a walker."

Martha left. Dr. Silvan looked back at Jason, but seemed to be addressing his brother.

"We used to let patients lie around for weeks, but now we understand that it's better to get them up and going," she said. "ASAP."

The brisk way she said this made Justin laugh. Dr. Silvan cranked the bed all the way up and Martha returned with a large male aide.

"Any pain from sitting up?" the doctor inquired.

"No," Jason replied.

"We'll let you catch your breath for a moment or two and then we'll get you up."

"Can you please shut the bathroom door?" Jason asked. "I look fucking crazy."

Even no-nonsense Dr. Silvan laughed.

"Are you ready?" the aide asked.

Jason nodded. Martha and the aide helped him up and to the walker. They held him for a second.

"Do you feel that you are strong enough to stand alone?" Dr. Silvan asked.

Jason's rubbery legs seemed to be holding up.

"Yes."

They released him but remained close.

"Now, can you try to take a step forward toward me?" the doctor continued.

He was already doing it. One step, then another. Walking, with the walker, but walking. What a relief.

"There's your answer. You are already walking," Dr. Silvan said. "Okay, Deandre and Martha, that's enough for today." The other two helped him back into bed.

"Thank God," said Justin.

"And Dr. Silvan," said Jason.

"That went really well and bodes well for your recovery," Dr. Silvan said. "Now, you should probably just rest."

"Just one more thing," Jason pleaded. "Can you tell me anything about Tara Highsmith?"

Dr. Silvan shook her head. "You know I can't disclose anything about anyone else's condition." She started to leave but then added with a frown, "Just try to rest, Jason. It's wonderful to see you walking on your own power."

Jason lay there for a minute, thinking. "It must mean that Tara is still in the hospital too. Try to find out for me Justin, will you?"

"Of course," his bother replied. "I've been trying. There's been nothing in the paper. The cops want to talk to you, too, when you're doing better."

Jason slept through the night. He planned to ask the first person who came in the next morning to be allowed to see Tara, but when someone finally showed up, it was the one he called The Dude. Dan, that male nurse or nursing assistant who was always fondling his own beard.

Dan took Jason's vitals and then asked, "Is there anything I can do for you?"

"Yes. Can I please be taken to see Tara Highsmith?"

"No, she's unconscious and in the ICU."

"I understand that, but can someone just wheel me down there to see her?"

"No, you're not ready for a wheelchair."

"I was walking with a walker yesterday," Jason protested.

"But that doesn't mean you can sit up in a wheelchair under stress."

"God damn it! I think you were the one who wheeled me into this room in this bed!" Jason's hands were shaking. He knew he sounded unhinged, full of some new octave of rage he'd never heard before. "All day long I see people being wheeled in beds past me—and no one can take me to see the woman I love who might be dying three rooms down?"

Dan made a great show of thinking, stroking his patchy dude beard dramatically. So annoying. Was that even sanitary in the hospital setting?

"Let me ask somebody with a higher pay grade," Dan said.

"Thank you, really," Jason replied. "And I'm sorry I lost my temper."

A little later Dr. Silvan came in, frowning. "I understand that you want to be wheeled to see Ms. Highsmith."

"Yes. My God, what's the big deal, Doc?"

"She's gravely ill, and you're still recovering. It's bound to be upsetting. No, it's not something I'd recommend."

"I'm not asking you to recommend, Doctor, I'm asking you to authorize it at my request." Jason's firmness gave way to pleading. "Please, I love her and this may be my last chance to see her."

"I'll need to talk to both the sheriff and Legal."

"Please do. Thanks."

Two hours later, as Jason was just waking from a nap, Dr. Silvan came back in.

"It's all set for tomorrow morning at nine thirty. We're going to keep you in your bed. They may have something for you to sign." She rolled her eyes. "You know, *lawyers!*"

"Thank you," said Jason.

A nurse brought the paperwork that night. Dan came the next morning, and Jason was unhooked from his IVs and pushed down the hallway and through the electronic doorway that guarded the ICU. Going around corners made him woozy.

At the second corner, a fat older deputy was seated, guarding a large plastic bottle of Diet Pepsi. This Shakespeare Fool inspired no confidence.

They pressed down the hall, and it was like in Jason's dreams. A bleakly modern corridor with sick people in rooms with people huddling and hovering over them. Families. Parents. He and Justin had lost theirs years ago. He was floating in a world with no one but Justin to hover around him. Justin and Tara.

Dan angled him in through another doorway, past a tall, dark-haired man with a slightly twitching face, and then there was her thrilling name written in red on a whiteboard. Tara Highsmith.

There was her mother, too, inside. Peg. Dan spoke with her and she came out, trying at first not to look at him. He wanted to greet her. They both nodded briefly. Did she hate him? Seeing Tara's mother,

Jason realized that the man they'd passed in the hallway, the man on the verge of tears, was her father, Bruce, the lawyer.

There was barely enough room for Jason's bed to squeeze into the crowded space, and then there she was, his beloved Tara, seemingly half woman and half machine, but still fully herself as well. A breathing mask covered her mouth. She had her father's nose. It went so perfectly with her sometimes-birdlike movements and manner. How he wished that Tara would twitch her head toward him in recognition.

Her skin was so white it had an aspect of porcelain, and her arms and exposed face had the marble beauty of a statue. She did not move. He'd never seen her so still, even sleeping.

On their few nights together, she'd breathed noisily and twitched restlessly in his arms. But then she would make a deep sigh and say his name— he would say hers back—both breathing in the simple peace of being in each other's arms.

"Can you get me close enough to touch her?" Jason asked abruptly. "I know it's tight."

"I'll try," Dan replied, surprisingly gently. "There."

He angled Jason's bed sharply toward Tara. Jason reached out and touched her lifeless hand.

"I love you, Tara," he said quietly. "I am so sorry this has happened to us. If you can find your way back to me, I will love you forever."

He closed his eyes to let the tears flood in. Then he nodded and was wheeled back to his lonely room, his IV cart his only company.

Chapter Thirty-Six

~~~~~~~~~~~~~~~~~

HOW YOU MAKE ME FEEL

J ason always had his state-issued phone with him during trial weeks, and that was true on the day of the shooting. That phone had been taken by police and was being reviewed for evidence. But Jason had Justin bring him his personal phone on maybe his third or fourth day of having regained consciousness and it was a revelation.

There were three texts from Tara, two of them with pictures that he'd not yet seen. Her glorious smile warmed him like the sun. Oh, if she could only regain that healthy-looking blush upon her cheeks. The other was a picture of a flower that looked, with its little risen pistil, like nothing so much as Tara herself.

"This is how you make me feel, lover!" she wrote.

He felt a warming surge in his own neglected loins.

There was a more ominous-looking message that she'd forwarded, though. The photos. Beautiful Tara joyously on top of him. Twisted round each other in various loving sacraments. Their special love, violated by Earl Franks. The photos must have been what had brought Tara to Lake Joseph, and he knew that he had to share them with the police in their meeting this afternoon.

The meeting was held in a small waiting lounge down the hall from Jason's room. Todd Stevens was in his late fifties, tall and skinny, an experienced former DA. The cop with him was Detective Rollins, whom Jason had met with Skip.

She nodded. "Let's get down to business."

"I'm ready," Jason said.

"This is Detective Rollins's interview of Judge Jason Erickson at University Hospital in Madison, Wisconsin. We are in the sixth-floor waiting lounge and I am recording. Also present is Deputy Attorney General Todd Stevens and Justin Erickson, the judge's brother, who we have determined is not a party or witness to the case and who is here to morally support the judge. Judge Erickson, do you recall attending the Midwest Water Law Conference in June of this year?"

"Yes."

"You've told us previously about an incident that occurred there, is that correct?"

"Yes."

"Okay, Mr. Erickson, could you please just tell us in your own words what happened at the Water Law Conference?" Detective Rollins asked.

"The parties to the case met there, at the Lake Joseph Resort, for a site inspection. We mapped out common areas and looked at the property and lockboxes. When the inspection was over, Franks made several odd remarks that I wasn't sure how to take at the time."

"Please, more specific," said the detective.

"Mr. Franks mentioned that his client had invested a lot of money in the resort, and that he had a lot at stake in the outcome of the hearing . . . I told him we couldn't talk about the merits of the case and he said, 'I *wasn't* talking about the merits, Jason. I was talking about the money. Those are two very different things.' When I asked what he meant he said, 'There's plenty of money to go round, Jay.'"

"Did he usually call you Jay?" Detective Rollins asked.

"No, that was part of what was odd; his tone was very different. Much more familiar."

"What was the next time he did something you thought unusual or inappropriate?" asked Detective Rollins.

"From out of nowhere, he appeared at Myrick Park in La Crosse. I was doing a hearing there; you can check the office website for the date," Jason added. "Franks was quite specific about threatening me—I remember he said, 'These people don't play.' He told me I was in a position to do something that meant a lot to his client and that I should see it as a financial opportunity."

"What was your reaction?"

"Anger and disbelief . . . I told him it was a felony and to tell his people 'No,' and 'Fuck you.'"

Both Stevens and Rollins laughed.

"Good for you," said the detective.

"But he was quite explicit," Jason said. "And that's when he suggested that he had photos of Tara and me from the hotel in La Crosse."

"We'll get more of these details later, when you're feeling stronger," said Detective Rollins. "I want to show you four photographs. We're not saying what it's in connection to, but we just wonder if you have ever seen any of these four men in connection with your dealings with Earl Franks."

Jason looked at the photos. None of them were the guy in the White Sox cap. But one guy was familiar. Yes, he remembered now.

"Him. Number three, with the birthmark. That's the guy who we saw in the elevator in La Crosse at the Charmant. He's probably connected to the younger one who claimed to be putting chocolates in our room as part of turndown service."

"You're sure?" Detective Rollins asked.

"Absolutely."

"That's private investigator Stan Simpson who has been identified as being in the same hotel as the judge and Ms. Highsmith in La Crosse,"

Detective Rollins said for the recording. "Right now, we just want the broad outline of things. What was the next time you had contact with Franks?"

"In Milwaukee, at the Chicago Region USEPA meeting at the Pfister. That's when I made the recording."

"And then?"

"Then I saw him on the day of the shooting, in the men's room at a restaurant in Lake Joseph," Jason said. "I was nervous, because I'd made the appointment to talk to Skip. At lunchtime he cornered me in the bathroom, standing at the urinal. I said, 'Tell them I'm considering it but I need a number.'"

"Cornering you in the john sounds like that son of a bitch," said Stevens. Fortunately, nearly everyone who'd ever had dealings with Franks knew what an ass he was. "Why did you tell him you might go along?"

"Just to get him off my back. I had the appointment with Skip Munson later that day, and I just thought it might buy me some time."

Rollins and Stevens looked at each other, gauging his answers. Rollins, at least, seemed satisfied.

"Then what happened?" she asked.

"Later, I was in the john again . . . In the stall, just getting a little privacy to piss, mind you."

"Of course. Go ahead," Stevens said with a smile.

"A manila envelope addressed to me was shoved under the door. I ran out, but the delivery person was long gone. I decided to walk over to the Lake Joseph Sheriff's Department, to report what had happened."

Jason knew he was talking faster. His heart was pounding.

"We're almost done, Judge," said Stevens. "You're doing fine; this part is hard."

"From out of nowhere, as I approached the sheriff's department, there was a young, thick-lipped white man, over six feet tall, skinny, bearing down on me. He was wearing a White Sox baseball cap. I turned to face him. That's when he pulled a gun out of a paper bag and said, 'You don't really think they're just going to let you fuck them up, do you?' Something like that."

"Would you be able to identify this man if you saw him?"

"Yes, unless—" Unless all the memories he'd been having were just drug-induced hallucinations. Jason decided to keep this to himself. "No, I'm quite sure that I could."

"Just a couple of follow-ups and we're done," said Detective Rollins. "Hair color?"

"Curly black."

"Eyes?"

"Brown."

"Scars?"

"No."

"Facial hair?"

"None."

"I'm sure that's changed by now."

Just then Dr. Silvan stuck her head in and said, "I think we should start to wrap this up." And, a couple of questions later, the interview was over.

"Now I've got a question for you," Jason said.

Detective Rollins said, "Go ahead."

"For God's sake, will somebody please tell me how Tara Highsmith is doing? I went to see her but haven't heard anything since."

"We're going to wait for Dr. Silvan and Dr. Melrose to join us," Detective Rollins said, nodding to her colleagues. "While we're waiting, there's something I need to tell you about the shooting. Based upon ballistics, we're pretty sure there were two guns involved."

"Weird," Jason said. "What does that mean?"

"We're not sure."

Just then, the two doctors entered the room; neither of them looked him in the eye—like a jury that was going to give you a losing verdict.

"I'm Dr. Melrose, Jason."

"Hello, please tell me what you know about Tara."

"Jason, it's very hard to tell you this," Detective Rollins said. "But Tara Highsmith has died."

Each word was harder to bear. He could hear his own pulse in his ears. "Tara is dead?"

"Yes, from what we gather, she was walking right behind you trying to catch up to you. She sent you a text that you never got saying she was surprising you and meeting you back up at Skip's office. She apparently went to the John Muir Wildlife area before coming into Lake Joseph. She sent you two photos and notes."

"I've seen them." He handed them his phone.

"We think someone was following her and shot her with a different gun."

"It's a nightmare." Jason was crying now.

"It's a lot to take in," said Dr. Melrose.

"We were madly in love," Jason sobbed.

"I think that's enough for today," concluded Dr. Silvan, wiping her eyes.

Chapter Thirty-Seven

VISITORS

Jason spent the next couple of days crying and sleeping. Tara was gone. How could it be? Her life was stolen away from her. From him. That comforting voice he could listen to forever—happy just to watch her lips form the words.

Those words. Her potential as a writer. All of her fine thoughts and bad jokes. The blush of desire on her neck and chest. The flutter when he touched her spine. Their love. Gone. Forever.

Why her and not him? They must have thought that they'd killed him too. He'd been in love with Tara since the famous Christmas tree case in Blue Lake. So long ago already.

Four or five days later, Dr. Horton started talking about Jason's upcoming release. On maybe Tuesday or Wednesday, they should be able to send him home. They were hoping to remove the chest tube tomorrow and then they wanted to eyeball him for a day or two, to watch for infection or blood clots. So far things looked good.

"And when can I go back to work?" Jason asked, incredulously. His life would be returning to something like normal soon, but what did normal mean now? "When can I run again?"

"Dr. Silvan should see you in two or three weeks to see if you're ready to work," Dr. Horton replied. "Running, we're looking at maybe a couple of months. No strenuous activity, no heavy lifting, no running at all until your first follow-up. We'll give you something for pain. Any other questions?"

Jason shook his head. "No."

"There will be an exit interview. All of this is a bit premature."

There were two unexpected visitors one day. In the morning, Jason's boss, Steve Hayman, stopped in briefly to get the latest gossip on the investigation and to remind him that he had plenty of sick leave and that he was also properly enrolled in the state's disability insurance, which would pay him eighty-five percent of his salary.

"I'd completely forgotten that I'd signed up for that."

"I thought you'd be happy to hear that," Hayman replied. "And they've paid lots of claims based solely on PTSD, police and others involved in traumatic incidents." He was shifting his weight back and forth uneasily. "I think you should go for it."

Of course, he did. That would make the governor happy.

"I'll think about it," Jason said.

"Thanks. Obviously, you should have told me about some of this beforehand."

"I was going to on the day you gave me that bogus disciplinary letter, but I was too ticked." Jason let Hayman squirm for a minute. His eyelids twitched. "But after that, I was deferring to Skip Munson. He didn't want to get you involved if it wasn't necessary."

"Thanks, I guess," Hayman said. "Do you really think Earl Franks had something to do with this?"

"Yes."

"I never would have believed it. I did many cases with that bastard." Steve was gearing up to leave. "Oh, I brought you some fan mail!" He handed Jason a pile of cards addressed to him in care of his office. "We didn't open anything that looked personal. Especially if there was anything in them that might be a part of your case. I swear a couple of them smell like perfume. Not to be crass"—*that would be a first*—"but you're going to be really popular with the ladies once you're back on your feet."

After Hayman had left, Jason took a look at the cards. He opened one with vaguely familiar handwriting and a postmark from Spain. It was from Madeline. She was in Barcelona with Walter at some kind of world banjo summit. It was sweet of her to write from such august circumstances.

Really, it was.

There was a card that seemed to have been addressed by a crazy person but was from Mr. Borker, the Lake Joseph mailman, who couldn't resist saying something very close to, "I told you so."

And Marge Paulson's handmade card would make a nice bookmark if he ever got around to reading again. It had a retro picture of Blue Lake on it and wished he and Tara a very speedy recovery. Thoughtful. But what useless thoughts.

Finally, there was indeed one that reeked of some flowery perfume. It was from a widow in California. She said she understood the shock of gun violence after her husband's death in Santa Rosa last year. Oddly, that was the one that made him tear up. The poor, sad thing. He was an equally poor, sad thing now.

That same afternoon, Jason was very surprised to see Grace Clarkson's familiar face in his doorway. She must have come from court because she was all dressed up in her blue trial suit.

"Judge, how are you? You look well!"

"Grace, so nice of you to come."

"I've been thinking of nothing else since this happened."

"You're kind."

"It all happened so fast. It's got to be terribly disorienting," Grace said. "I just wanted to offer you my condolences in person."

"Thank you so much."

She hugged him briefly.

"Yes, it was all a whirlwind," Jason said. "Our romance was over almost before it properly began. If you care to know, her husband filed for divorce. I wouldn't have been with her otherwise."

"So, there's no guilt involved. That helps."

"Oh, there's lots of it—just not sexual guilt." He paused. What was it? "I guess just wondering if I'd done enough to prevent it."

"I had loads of guilt, too," Grace said. She looked down and then back into his eyes. "My husband was working late at a bar-and-grill in part to help put us both through law school. His crash was at 2:00 a.m. after closing down the bar."

"I'm sorry. Maybe we can talk sometime?"

"Of course. I'll leave you my personal cell number on my card. I don't want to overstay my welcome."

"You're not, I really appreciate your coming by."

The chief resident, Dr. Valeria Lopez, tall and sharp featured, came in a couple of days later. "You're progressing to where we will consider releasing you by the end of the week," she said. "But, right now, I am more concerned about your PTSD symptoms than the threat to your lungs. You were evaluated by Dr. Hanson and he has recommended an antidepressant for you. Have you ever taken Zoloft?"

"No, but I probably do need it."

Though there was still the constant risk of infection and nastiness of the blood draining out of his lungs, Jason was recovering nicely. But he was deeply depressed and feeling overwhelmed.

"Good. I will see that we start that and give you a sheet for you to sign that describes how it works and the potential side effects, which can include dry mouth, constipation, and sexual impotence in men."

"Now, you're really depressing me, Doc."

She tried to smile. "I've also made arrangements to have a grief counselor stop by later today. Do you have a religious affiliation or practice?"

He thought of all his conversations with Tara, and had to pause to clear his throat before he could answer. "Affiliation, yes, liberal Protestant. But a practice, no. I'm completely agnostic."

"Okay, we'll stick with Dr. Melrose."

Dr. Melrose, the grief counselor, came in just as Jason had fallen asleep after lunch. "Shall I come back?"

"No, that's fine. I still spend a lot of the day sleeping."

"How do you feel you're doing after losing your friend in such a traumatic way?" Dr. Melrose looked him in the eye.

"It's hard. Tara and I were lovers. She was getting divorced," Jason said.

"How long had you known her?"

"We worked together off and on for a couple of years, but we grew really close over the past two and were lovers for just the past couple of weeks after her husband filed for divorce. There was nothing shady about us. But I do have plenty of guilt because Tara was almost certainly shot because of me."

"But you weren't responsible for the shooting, or you would have prevented your own shooting," Dr. Melrose opined. She held his hand.

"Thank you for saying it. But of course, I wonder if I did everything that I could to have prevented it," Jason said. That was usually the first thought in his mind when he woke up. "I might've gone to the police a little sooner than I did. But I wasn't sure that it was even really a threat until fairly recently."

"It's common in cases of traumatic deaths." She let go of his hand. "Auto accidents, suicides, shootings. Everyone always feels that they could have prevented it, but that is often just their desire to try to restore a sense of order to what was fundamentally outside of their control. Do you follow me?"

"Intellectually, yes, of course," Jason said. "But only intellectually."

"Okay. Then a good place to start is just to reinforce what you know to be true," said Dr. Melrose. "I want you to write down what you know to be true intellectually, and when you have that feeling of guilt, take it out and repeat it to yourself over and over again like a mantra. Are you physically able to write?"

"Yes, and I will do it this afternoon."

"Okay. Start there. I will be back on Tuesday, and you tell me what you have written and how the rest of you responded to this good advice from your brain."

"Thank you!"

"Of course." She reached down to shake his hand and then held it in hers. "You have been through something horrible, Judge, but you will get through it."

The next day Tara's husband, Michael, stopped by. Jason wondered how much he knew about their relationship.

"How are you doing?" Michael asked, betraying no animosity.

"They say I might be able to leave next week. I'm really sorry about Tara."

"It's so awful. Look, I've got something to show you. A piece of Tara's called 'The Blue Smell of the Pines.'" Michael had found a copy of Tara's last essay. "I made a copy for her family. But the original was addressed to you. We were also wondering if you would read one of her poems at her funeral. If so, I put a copy of that in there too."

Was that why he'd come? Maybe he wasn't such a bad guy. "Yes, thank you, I'd be honored."

"Her parents are on board."

"Okay, thanks. How is it with you and her parents?" Jason asked.

"Awkward, as you might imagine, given we were in the process of a divorce. You knew about that, didn't you?"

"Yes, Tara told me."

"I figured. One of the cops told me off the record that he thought you and Tara were an item too?"

"Only after your counseling didn't work out."

"I'm sure, I know, knew, Tara." Michael paused. "If you're up to it, I also have a legal question for you."

"Go ahead."

"What happens with our divorce now?" Michael asked. "I haven't been able to get through to my lawyer."

"Well, you should consult with your lawyer. You filed it, right?"

"Yes."

"Talk to your lawyer, but you could probably simply drop the case." Jason's voice trailed off. Why should he help this jerk?

"And then the house would be mine as marital property, right?" Michael asked.

"Her parents may have some right to intervene. I'm not sure. You better talk to your lawyer."

Michael's last line of questions left a bad taste in Jason's mouth. After Tara's husband had left, Jason thought about it all day. It unsettled him enough that he called Detective Rollins to talk about it.

She came up the next morning, with her tape recorder and a uniformed officer.

"We want to talk things through with you to get a sense of covering all possibilities. Besides Franks, did you have any other professional enemies?"

"Yes, I'm sure I did," Jason replied. There were so many.

"We need names, and the reasons they didn't like you."

"My job involves stepping on people's toes and saying no to people who are used to only hearing yes. Just recently, White Farms Dairy was upset about my comments about there being a massive regulatory failure relating to CAFO manure runoff. They were verbally going after me by name."

"Others?" Detective Rollins searched his face.

"I called out State Senator Lucke for what I thought were his Joe McCarthy-like comments at another hearing. Both of those were in just the last few months."

"I know him," said Detective Rollins. She shook her head. "Do you think either of them was so upset that they would try to kill you?"

"No, I don't think so. They're more likely to attack me in the press or just try to limit my authority in the legislature. But really, how do I know?"

"What about Franks and Calandro?"

"The timing is a little bizarre, given that they'd given me a deadline, as I've said. But I was on my way to the police station, so maybe they were following me," Jason said.

"What was the deadline?"

"The next Friday. The shooting was on . . . " Jason couldn't remember. "The week before."

"The shooting was on Thursday. What about Tara's husband? Did you get a sense that he had any animosity toward you?"

"Well, I never met him or spoke to him. Their divorce was his decision, and he was already seeing another woman from his job. So, frankly, I doubt it. But he was up here yesterday asking me legal questions about their property and so forth, which was weird."

"Did Tara ever mention problems in their divorce settlement?"

"Yes, she did. Some brokerage accounts that she'd had since before their marriage. She was upset that Michael was pursuing them because she'd contributed marital assets to them over their years together."

"Would you be surprised to hear that Tara had nearly four million dollars in her brokerage accounts?" Detective Rollins looked at him closely for his response.

"Very much so, yes." Though she did tell him she had money. "She drove around in an old Prius and bragged about buying clothes at secondhand stores, which she said was recycling."

"Now, you mentioned that Tara's husband visited you here at the hospital yesterday," said Detective Rollins.

"Yes."

"What did he say to you?"

"Well, we talked mostly about Tara, and he gave me some things that she'd written," Jason said. "But then the conversation seemed to pointedly swerve to what the implications of her death were for their divorce. For their joint assets."

"Specifics, Judge. What did he say in that regard?"

"He asked me if the house and other assets would remain in his name now that she had passed." Jason's eyes stung again. "It was pretty callous."

"Anything else?"

"No, it was just that question, which he posed as getting free legal advice."

"Okay. Well, thanks for talking tonight," said Detective Rollins. "We know how hard this must be for you."

Chapter Thirty-Eight

~~~~~~~~~~

THROUGH A CAPPUCCINO, DARKLY

Earl Franks was pitching to little Laurie at their place on Blue Lake. How cute Laurie was, swinging a giant Wiffle ball bat and running with delight straight past him and on to second base—to hell with first! The alarm clock—no, it was the damn doorbell—interrupted his reverie from the glory days with Maggie and Laurie.

Cursing the obnoxious doorbell, he reluctantly got out of bed. He'd wisely deeded the Blue Lake place to Laurie as part of his divorce. It was Franks-family property and none of these assholes could take that away from them.

It looked like a beautiful sunny day as he peeked out the living room window. But then he saw Tommy C. standing there, looking lumpy in a running suit with white stripes down the side. Fuck.

"I'm glad to find you in—"

"In, but not up," Earl interposed. "There's a difference, Tommy."

Tommy took out a cell phone. "Earl wants a skim cappuccino from Starbucks."

"A double," Earl groaned. "Give me a minute to get dressed."

Earl went into his bedroom to put on pants, and by the time he was back in the living room, some flunky had already brought the coffee, and a blueberry muffin to boot. It was a none-too-subtle statement. Tommy the Great can make coffee appear—or, say, people disappear—with a mere clap of his hands.

Big deal. There were three Starbucks on Dempster Street in Skokie.

Earl chugged the foamy brew for a brief moment as he thought of what to say.

"I don't necessarily think it's such a good idea that we talk, Tommy."

"Chill, Earl," Tommy replied casually. "We can talk, once. We need to wrap up a few loose ends on the Lake Joseph case."

"Somebody's probably ordered me off the case by now," Earl lied, taking another slurp. That wouldn't faze Tommy. The law was for other people. Loyalty was Tommy's law. "Anyway, you know I'm a firm believer in making the state prove any criminal case."

"Very smart," said Tommy. "Fuck 'em."

"Nobody gets a word out of Earl Franks."

Tommy put his paw on Earl's shoulder. The sunlight was streaming in through the living room window. The world was often disingenuously bright.

"By the way, I'm outta here. I'm going back to Italy, Counselor." Tommy smiled. "The sun shines like this every day out on my island there."

"Good move," Earl said sincerely.

"And I wanna quit while I still have my perfect record."

"What's that, Tommy?" asked Earl. It'd just dawned on him that maybe this was in part a social call on Tommy's part.

"Still haven't killed anyone yet." Tommy smiled, showing his big, mismatched teeth

"Well, that's great, Boss," said Earl. That was just the word to bring an approving look to Tommy's ugly mug.

"I wasn't lying when I said we had nothing to do with the shooting," Tommy said. "I even double-checked."

Was he wearing some kind of recording device?

"Yeah, I mean no—of course not. I know you better than that."

"I wasn't sure if there would be hard feelings with you, but I've got something for you." Tommy handed Earl a little shaving bag full of fifty- and hundred-dollar bills.

"No, Tommy, I'm okay, really." He was stalling, trying to figure out if this was some kind of elaborate setup.

"You don't want it?"

Tommy was being grand and saying he was sorry. He probably saw Earl as an ingrate. Earl took the bag to smooth it over.

"Of course, I can use it. I hired Myron Rosenberg," Earl said. "And the lawyer's fees are killing me."

"Welcome to my world, Counselor." Tommy smiled. "You've been sending me those bills for years."

"Thanks, Tommy. Really. I just didn't want you to think I'm greedy."

"Naw, I got plenty." Tommy's face brightened. "Stashed away. Here and over there."

"Very classy. Thanks, old friend," said Earl, moved despite himself. A lump was in his throat constantly since the shooting.

"Some for you, and more for me and my lady friend in Italia." He put his hand out and Earl shook it. "Look, you let me know any time anyone's going to lay a hand on you, all right? Inside or outside prison. You get me?"

"Yeah, sure. You bet." How the hell would he get in touch with Tommy from prison? Maybe through Stan?

"Look, you keep your mouth shut and we're even," Tommy said. "You're free. That's a promise."

"Thanks, Tommy." Earl sat down on the sofa.

Gee, how generous—they might both be in their seventies or eighties before Earl would get out of prison.

"Ciao, Counselor."

So that was it. He was on his own now. The designated fall guy. Some prison time for sure in the pound of flesh they'd want for all this.

He sat there feeling doomed, sipping his cappuccino and watching the cardinals stuff themselves at Mrs. Schwartz's feeder.

Chapter Thirty-Nine

~~~~~~~~~~

BLUE LAKE BLUES

Jason was sitting up in his chair, drinking the crappy hospital coffee, when Justin called. His little brother managed to call almost every morning. A couple of days ago, Jason had kept him on the phone for almost an hour. He was determined to keep it shorter today. He told Justin that he might be discharged tomorrow and wished him a good day.

Tara's father poked his head in the door at that exact moment. Had he been listening?

"I'm Bruce Morton, Judge, Tara's father." He extended his hand. "Wanted to introduce myself."

"Jason Erickson," he said softly. "So sorry for your loss."

"And yours too, Jason."

They shared a silent moment.

"Thanks for coming over. Tara told me a lot about you and Peg."

"Not Peg!" Bruce's head jerked involuntarily. "You better go with Margaret. A word to the wise." Bruce forced a smile. He had some of Tara's quick, birdlike, nervous energy. "Margaret doesn't know I'm here, and I'm not sure she'd approve." He paused for effect. "But even she knows that none of this is your fault!"

"Very kind of you to say, Bruce." Jason looked into his sad, Tara-brown eyes.

"It's the truth."

"Maybe I didn't see it coming soon enough? Because I was too busy falling in love with Tara?" Jason wondered. "That's my one regret. We were both on our way to the police when we were shot."

"I know." Bruce reached for something in his sport coat pocket. "Tara was also busy falling in love with you." It was a greeting card, addressed to *Jason, My Love*. "I found this in a book of nature poetry at her place, and I thought you should have it. The police should probably see it at some point, too."

Jason held the precious card, bright with Tara's distinctive cursive handwriting.

"Shall I read it now?" he asked.

"No, savor it in private. It's clear that the two of you had a deep connection. I wanted you to know that I get that and I don't blame you. You could have just as easily died too, from what I've heard."

"Thanks, Bruce. You're just as amazing as she said you were."

"No, I'm not. I'm not as great as Tara said I was, and her mother's not as bad. Remember that. Margaret always loved Michael." Tara's father shook his head. "I'm sorry, but I read the card addressed to you. The envelope was not sealed."

"That's fine." Or was it? Tara was pretty candid about their connection. "Can you leave me your contact information?"

"Of course. I'm going to insist that you have some role in Tara's memorial." His voice broke a bit with that last word. Bruce found a business card, wrote his personal phone number on it, and then quickly left the room.

When Bruce had left, Jason pulled out the card. It was silly. Tara's juvenile sense of humor. There was a drawing of a Dr. Frankenstein figure who had just made two monsters, one male and one female.

Inside it said, "We Were Made for Each Other."

There was her beautiful cursive scrawl, still full of her energy.

Jason, My Love:

I like the sound of that—if you get a text from me that says JML, you'll know what it means. So much, so fast. Or maybe not? We spent almost two chaste years getting to know each other before our love had a chance to bloom. Now, there it is, a world-record white pine still not hit by lightning.

What a sight!

Let's put Franks and company in prison and then spend the rest of our lives together—what do you say?

I was thinking that it would be fitting to buy a place together in Blue Lake someday. It's pristine there, like our new love. (And I hear that the schools there are good!)

So much love, always,

Tara

Everyone was dressed so formally at Tara's memorial service. Very Catholic. This was all her mother's doing, and who could blame Margaret for anything now?

But it all seemed a little stiff and hard to reconcile with Tara's casual, earth-tone style and crunchy manner. Jason himself had worn a black suit, white shirt, and black tie, and that was pretty much the uniform for all the men in her life.

Tara's kind and broken father, Bruce. Her brother, Jack. Her not-quite-ex-husband Michael. The women were a sea of black dresses too.

There was a bluish-black casket. Tara would have no doubt opted for cremation and a biodegradable paper bag on high ground away from water, but she was only thirty-seven and hadn't made her wishes known. Thank God, the casket was closed. But there it was, up in front of the room, with the elaborate flower arrangements and a wonderful photo of Tara in the woods in her field gear clothes. That sleepy smile on her face.

How could he live without her?

There were two separate lines of greeting—a long one with her parents, sister, and brother, and a short one that led to Michael. To get it over with, Jason went through the short line quickly, and Michael embraced him.

"Sorry for your loss," they told each other.

"She was an amazing woman," said Jason.

"Thank you for reading her frog poem," Michael said. "She would've loved that."

Jason nodded and made his way to the longer line and to Tara's sister, Catherine.

"I'm Jason Erickson and I am so sorry for your loss, Catherine." He wasn't sure of how she would greet him, but she gave him a warm embrace.

"I'm sorry for yours," said Catherine. "Tara has told me so much about you over the past year or so." She pulled him close and whispered. "I know how much Tara loved you, Jason. This must be impossible for you, too."

"Yes," he said. Holding her, fighting back tears. "Thank you so much for saying that. I loved her. And I know how close you two were."

"How are you doing with your own recovery?" Catherine asked.

"Still healing, but back home." His standard answer. He still had the plastic tube and a drain full of bloody crud that he had to clean out every night.

"Good luck with everything," said Catherine.

Her brother, seeing Jason's tears, averted his eyes and just extended his hand in greeting.

Then formidable Margaret. In so much pain.

"You're the judge she was chasing after when she was murdered," she said coldly. "I recognize you from the papers."

"I'm sorry for your loss. She was—"

"My daughter!" She cut him off. "Please don't try to tell me who she was."

Jason must have looked shaken, because Bruce Morton embraced him quietly.

"I know, I know," Bruce said.

Catherine read excerpts from Tara's last essay. It'd just been accepted by *The Sun*. That would have pleased Tara because they'd rejected her numerous times.

To Jason's surprise, the excerpt included their debate about Emerson and Melville's response to the "all feeling." It was so like Tara to include and parry an opposing point of view.

Was the *all* connection a temporary feeling, or something to build a philosophy around? She concluded it was both, that temporary insights were like the individual data points underlying all of science. Jason would have loved to debate this with her.

Then Catherine followed Tara's essay on to Aldo Leopold, and what Tara called his "biological imperative." She compared Leopold favorably to Kant. Kant said to treat every person as an end unto themselves and never merely as a means to an end.

Leopold's ethics went further: "A thing is right when it tends to preserve the integrity, stability, and beauty of the biotic community. It is wrong when it tends otherwise." Leopold said, "an ethic, ecologically, is a limitation on freedom in the struggle for existence."

Catherine paused.

"Tara lived up to Leopold's ethic in her own life. She gave up eating what she called 'her fellow mammals' years ago, as a young woman, after learning how much meat contributed to climate change. That was my sister," Catherine concluded. "I want to close with the question Tara asked in her essay: 'Which part of us will win out—our ability to love the nature of which we are a part, or our seemingly endless need to prop ourselves up by dominating it? With the crisis of climate change, the answer will be apparent soon enough.'"

Catherine sat down.

The old priest weaved Tara's essay into his homily. Tara loved nature, God's creation, and that love had led her back to her faith in God.

Mysterious ways and all of that. The priest had known Tara since she was a little girl and was proud to call her parents his friends. She was fierce and intelligent and had integrity beyond measure.

In her teens, Tara had told him openly when she stopped believing in God. Margaret seemed to wince upon hearing this. But, the priest intoned, her love of nature had been just the right thing to bring Tara back.

"God doesn't expect all of us to become priests or nuns," the priest said. "God wants us to love Him just enough. We know that our beloved Tara did and is now in God's loving embrace. But can the rest of us, seared by this violent and untimely death, still feel that embrace?

"How do we make sense of this violence?

"We don't. We can't. This evil, too, is beyond our understanding. We know that it happens, that it has always happened, but we will never understand it until we solve the riddle of evil itself."

Jason had been with him for a while, but this last seemed a bit circular and the ending abrupt. So abrupt that it took Jason a moment before realizing it was now the time for him to read Tara's frog poem.

No Mutants Yet in Baxter's Hollow

No mutant frogs yet in Baxter's Hollow . . .
Yes, there are still the long hind legs,
perfectly adapted for leaping,
the unblinking amphibious eyes,

The moist, green, yellow-spotted skin,
and still the same timeless desire
to sit meditating in the midday sun . . .

Ah, to eat the things that are there for you,
to breathe the unembellished breaths
of simple biology, to be so full

Of uncomplicated purpose—
before belching out a more or less
joyful noise, high to the bright sky.
The frogs here still have all of their legs!

Instead of returning to his seat after speaking, Jason went directly to a stall in the men's room and let himself cry. His mother used to say that about half the time that men cried, it was because they felt guilty or sorry for themselves. He definitely felt guilty. And, with a tube still draining blood from his lungs under his suit coat, sorry for himself as well.

He thought of losing his own parents so young. Bruce had reminded him of his own father. And Jason's mother had been so fun-loving and kind.

If he'd listened to Tara early on and gone to the police right away, would any of this have gone this far? Would Tara still be there in the morning, waking up next to him and writing her essays and just living the amazing life that all of the other speakers had movingly recounted?

Either way, it was too much to bear.

Chapter Forty

A BEAUTIFUL TAN
LEATHER CASKET

As the weeks dragged on, Earl just sat around his condo, more and more depressed. He couldn't figure any way out of this one. His new lawyer, Myron Rosenberg, couldn't either.

"You've been around, Earl," Myron said at their first meeting. "This looks like something that will get you time, especially with Tommy C. cutting out."

"I appreciate the candor, Myron."

What kind of life would he have the rest of the way through? He was sixty-seven years old! The best case would be for him to end up a washed-up lawyer with a felony conviction, but the worst—and most likely—was to spend the rest of his remaining life in prison.

Tommy had come to give him cash for a lawyer and to make sure he kept his mouth shut. That's what that visit was all about. Tommy's flight made it pretty certain that Earl was going to be doing some prison time.

He'd never admit it, but Earl was scared of prison. Scared of both the disgrace and the brutal, empty days. He could try to run, but he was being shadowed. Running would only postpone the inevitable. And add more time.

How could he ever look Laurie in the eye again if he was involved in a conspiracy to commit murder? In short, he couldn't. Finally, Earl more or less resolved that he was going to kill himself. The only question left was how. He spent a couple of afternoons considering his options.

He was pretty much down to sticking a gun in his mouth—something a couple of trial lawyers he knew had done—hanging himself, or taking a chance that someone would find him before the job was done if he left his car running in the garage. He didn't want Laurie to see him with his head blown off or his tongue sticking out. So, the garage won by default.

He had a few things left to do. He wanted to FedEx most of Tommy's cash to Laurie, and he wanted to tell his ex-wife, Maggie, how sorry he was.

The conversation with Maggie was short, bittersweet.

"Maggie Magpie, I guess I've finally hit the bottom of that abyss."

"Oh, Earl, I'm sorry. I feel so bad for you." She paused. "I know you'd never kill anyone."

"No, I wouldn't. And I'm sorry, too—for everything."

"I know—"

"I—"

"Don't, Earl. I can't really talk, but I need to tell you two things. One is that I'm getting remarried, to a nice accountant named Joel Goldberg."

"I'm happy for you." It was true. Would she try to make Goldberg a Catholic too?

"I didn't want you to hear about it from someone else that I'd changed my name."

"Thanks. Can't blame you right now. So, what's the other thing?"

"Don't give up hope," Maggie said, her voice breaking a bit. "I'm praying for you and that judge too."

"Thanks, Maggie."

Then Earl wrote Laurie a short note that made him cry. He dodged the traffic on Dempster and stuck the cash in a large envelope in the FedEx box a couple of blocks down. Earl went home and into the garage to get it over with—before he changed his mind.

He sat in Black Beauty, his smooth Lexus, and turned on the radio. Dexter Gordon's "One Flight Up" was playing on the Real Jazz station. Perfect. Or was he going "One Flight Down?"

Earl didn't believe in any of that crap and never really had. Nice of Maggie to give it a shot for him, though. Pascal's Wager and all of that.

The car was so quiet and the music so full of juice. And what a beautiful casket the tan leather seats made. Put that on his tombstone: He Went Out with Class. In a car that he'd won in a bet. It wasn't all losing, not by a long shot.

Earl thought he heard someone rustling around just outside the garage. Yes, someone was at the fucking door, banging. Dammit. What were the odds? He lumbered out. It was Mrs. Schwartz, the condominium board president, standing imposingly before him.

"Hello, Mrs. Schwartz."

"Earl," she replied coolly. What a sea change from meetings past, when she'd fluttered over him and called him Mr. Justice. "Earl, the Association Rules include a Moral Conduct Provision—"

"I'll be sure to let you know if I see anything immoral going on, Mrs. Schwartz."

"Earl Franks, you know I'm talking about this criminal case business," she said. He was reminded, by her face and stern manner, of some over-the-top Lily Tomlin character. What was it about condominiums that attracted the cranky and officious?

"Okay, I hear you. And thanks for warning me. But the last time I looked, a person is innocent until proven guilty, Mrs. Schwartz."

She went off in a huff. Earl went back to his car and the task at hand. She was probably already on the phone, justifying her every word. *Earl Franks tried to make a joke of it. Not so funny if it hurts our property values. Blah, blah, blah.*

Meanwhile, Earl sat there pondering his fate, waiting and waiting.

What had his life added up to? What had it been *for*? Five minutes went by and then ten. He'd been a great linebacker, a decent father, and a rugged and skilled trial lawyer. Football and then OTB had been his gateway drugs. His juice. He liked winning too much to admit what a loser he was!

Twenty minutes later, he was still reminiscing and feeling fine. But, after twenty-five, it finally occurred to him and he started laughing. The Lexus was a hybrid and the battery kept kicking in. There was never going to be enough exhaust to kill him!

That had to be something like fate. Still chuckling, he turned the engine off, got out of the car, and went into his sunny kitchen. He'd always liked the kitchen of his little condo.

Earl made himself a batch of oatmeal, with raisins, walnuts, and plenty of brown sugar. The absolutely most delicious fucking bowl of oatmeal that he'd ever had. Then his cell phone rang. Laurie.

"Hi, Daddy. Did you call me?" Laurie asked.

"Just wanted to say I'm sorry, Lauralee."

"I know, Daddy." After all these years, and they both still used the same names with each other as when she was three.

"It must be embarrassing for you."

"Yes," she admitted. Silence. She was either letting it sink in or measuring her words. "I may start using Steve's last name."

"Laurie Little."

She laughed. "Oh, that's awful."

"Sounds like Stuart Little's sister mouse," he said with a chuckle. "Look, I accidentally sent you something in a FedEx. Can you just return it to me unopened?"

"Okay, sure. Hey, you probably know, but Michael Highsmith, Tara's husband, is going to be on TV tomorrow night. On that sleazy crime show *Nightzone*. Maybe I can come over and watch it with you?"

"I didn't know!" Earl said. "That'd be great!"

"One more thing. It's the reason I called last week." She paused a second, controlling her emotions. "Whatever other ways you've screwed up, wasted your talents, messed things up—"

"Okay, I get the idea."

"Whatever else you've done or not done—you weren't a bad father."

"Thanks, though I don't deserve it." Earl hoped she couldn't hear his sniffling. "I love you."

"And I'll always love you, no matter what."

"I had nothing to do with any violence!" It was true, and it felt good to say it. "Will you visit me in prison?"

"Sure! You'd be a hit there; you can help everybody with their cases. But you have to listen to this Michael before you even think about prison. If he messes up at all, Myron Rosenberg will pounce on it."

"Okay, come over here and I'll make popcorn." He'd lost Maggie, but he still had Laurie! "Thanks for calling, Lauralee."

"Don't you go killing yourself or anything lame like that." She knew him so well. "You hear me? Dad?"

"I wouldn't think of it." It was now true.

"If you do, I'll take back what I said about you being a halfway decent father. There's an old story that anyone can be redeemed if they just love one person right in their lifetime."

"I know, I'm the one that told you that!"

"Yes, you did! I'll bring the FedEx when we watch *Nightzone* tomorrow."

"That sounds grand."

Meanwhile, Earl had received both a text and a voicemail for him to urgently call Stan, the private investigator. He did.

"Earl, I found out some things that could be really helpful," Stan teased. "It's kind of crazy—isn't anybody faithful to their wife anymore?"

"I wasn't—were you?"

"Nah, but listen, here's the thing—neither was Tara's husband."

"Not earth-shattering, but something to work with."

"There's more. Tara's estate got bumped into the big-league probate court because little Ms. Prius had almost four million bucks in brokerage accounts—"

"Wait, working for the Green Bay paper?" Earl asked.

"Yes, she got a big stake from her grandmother dying right when the market crashed. Then, whenever she learned of any good tip from her job, she would put down some money for the securities. And she was fighting tooth and nail to keep those accounts from Michael in their divorce! Damn, that's a reasonable doubt right there, old friend."

"It's pretty fishy, at least."

"She put it in a trust in her own name because she'd started it before they were married. And guess who gets one hundred percent of it free and clear now?"

"The husband, of course," Earl said. "Myron can carry that way beyond reasonable doubt."

"Yeah, and I leaked the information all over the fucking country," Stan said. "Starting with *Nightzone* tomorrow night."

"Thank you, Stan. I'll be watching."

"You're welcome, but you should also thank Tommy C. He gave me a fat advance to try to get you sorted out properly."

"He came to see me, too. He's stepped up. I was loyal to him, and he came through for me."

"I'm still digging for more; you know how I am when they give me carte blanche."

"Keep digging, Stan. Keep digging."

Suicide? That was for losers. What the hell had Earl been thinking?

Chapter Forty-One

~~~~~~~~~~~~~~~~~

THE NIGHTZONE NEWS

From the eye of the storm, Jason watched the case go viral and explode into the national media. First, the "jealous husband versus the mafioso and former state supreme court justice" was in the local papers. Especially Tara's, which meant that it got picked up by the whole national chain. When the police confirmed that there was a sex tape, the story made national crime and news TV.

Then came the social media memes. The country seemed to have nothing better to do. Many former political allies of Earl Franks were now making the rounds of the television gossipmongers, righteously proclaiming his innocence, and Michael's guilt.

Jason knew it would have all hit the very private Tara very hard.

One morning, when Justin and Sunny were visiting, Jason woke up and saw the headlines in the Milwaukee and Madison newspapers that Justin had brought in for him. "Murder Mystery" blared one and "Jealous Husband or Supreme Corruption?" asked the other.

Someone had leaked some documents to the papers that showed that Tara had millions of dollars in her brokerage accounts.

"That kind of puts it back on Michael, no?" asked Sunny.

Jason nodded.

"You better call that detective," said Justin.

Jason did. And Detective Rollins, though she said very little, made it clear that they were looking closely into Michael as well as Earl Franks and Tommy C. She also was emphatic that the leak had not come from the sheriff's office but was more likely connected to lawyers for Earl Franks.

"Earl seems to be sticking around, but Tommy is nowhere to be found," she told him. "Do you remember anything Tara said about Michael or her brokerage accounts?"

"No, not really. She told me that she'd always bought a few shares of any good tips she'd gotten from her years in journalism but, wow. Four million is a lot." Then Jason remembered something. "When I think about it, I remember her telling her attorney about standing firm on those accounts."

"Did you know that Tara was that rich?" Detective Rollins asked.

"No, of course not. She drove an old Prius full of dog hair," he said, his voice catching. Jason could see Tara seated next to him there, her head bobbing happily. "But she did say her grandmother left her some money that she'd invested wisely. She bought a lot of it in 2009 when the market had collapsed."

Later that night, Jason, Justin, and Sunny watched Michael Highsmith on *Nightzone*. For some reason, it did not strike Jason as odd to see Tara's handsome ex-husband sitting next to Walter Shaw, the familiar but slightly creepy true-crime show host.

The camera suddenly panned to reveal Susan, Michael's attractive, blonde girlfriend. Shaw called her Michael's beautiful fiancée. Shaw did his best to dress up the tabloid aspect of his subject with his splendid voice and supercilious manner.

"Our subject tonight is former Wisconsin Supreme Court Justice Earl Franks and the shooting of Judge Jason Erickson and the murder of his married lover, Tara Highsmith. In that case, some have sought to deflect attention and hence suspicion from the former supreme court justice by implicating Michael Highsmith, the ex-husband of Erickson's intimate companion, Tara Highsmith. Tonight, on the *Nightzone,* you will for the first time hear Mike Highsmith's response to those charges."

They played the melodramatic *Nightzone* theme, and Jason and his brother sat through the commercials.

"Mr. Highsmith, I'll ask the question I'm sure many of our viewers have on their minds tonight. Did you have anything to do with the shooting of your late wife or the judge?"

"No," Michael said, his eyes welling up. "Nothing whatsoever."

"Did you bear Judge Erickson any grudge—or let me back up first," Shaw said dramatically. He raised a bushy blond eyebrow. "It's been suggested that Jason Erickson may have already been intimate with your then-wife, Tara. Was that known to you?"

"That was not known to me then. Nor do I know that now, though I certainly did know that they were work friends."

"And what did you make of that friendship?" Shaw asked.

"I encouraged it, if anything. At that time, Tara and I were pretty distant. She and the judge were in a book club together." Michael paused. "And I do a lot of traveling for my job."

"In the software business?"

"Correct. And, frankly, by that time I was already seeing Susan. This whole jealous husband thing doesn't make sense."

Something in Michael's voice made Jason suspect him more. Liars often got impassioned about side issues about which they were *actually* telling the truth. The camera zoomed in on a glamour shot of attractive Susan, and displayed in a side panel a picture of Tara—looking a little tired, casting for trout in her hip-waders—as if to say, which would you choose?

"When did you start seeing Susan?" Shaw asked.

"Over a period of more than a year," Michael replied. "Tara and I were, as I've said, quite distant, and Susan and I worked a lot of hours together. I focused way too much on my career. We went to marriage counseling. But Tara and I no longer shared the same interests. She is, she was . . . interested in books and nature, and I'm excited about technology. We didn't see much of each other the last two years of our marriage."

"What do you say to those who have implied that you had something to do with the shooting of your late wife and Judge Jason Erickson?"

"It's an absolute lie. And an absolute disgrace for political operatives and spin-masters to slander and libel a person whom they don't even know. People need to take more care with what they say in this country," Michael said. "It's not all a game; real people are involved, are damaged, in these national scandals of the moment. Our lives are not a soap opera."

"But Michael, I have to ask you about these large brokerage accounts in Tara's name."

"Go ahead." Michael's eyes shifted. "Anyone who thinks I would kill Tara for money has no clue who I am."

"Have those accounts now passed to you?"

"Of course. We were still married, and that's the way Tara herself had set them up. I haven't touched them, if that's what you're suggesting."

"But you were going through a divorce?"

Michael nodded, his eyes looking everywhere but the camera.

"Incidentally, Michael, where were you for the past month?" Shaw probed.

"Susan was with me part of that time, on a hiking trip in Patagonia."

Susan seized the opportunity to speak. "Yes, for two weeks, or seventeen days with the long-distance flights. I thought it would be good for Michael to get away."

"Susan, do you agree with Michael's comments?" Shaw asked.

"Absolutely. Michael and I worked together for three years, and our feelings for each other slowly grew. We were well on the way to falling in love before the shooting of Tara and Judge Erickson." Her voice was sincere and intelligent, but she ended her sentences like they were questions.

"Michael, I have to ask you about one last thing," Shaw said. "The life insurance. Have you received any life insurance proceeds?"

"No. Well, the insurance company has paid it into my attorney's trust account, and Tara's divorce lawyer has been opposed to them releasing it to me."

"Okay, that's all for tonight's show. We'll be back next week to look into a strange case of sexual harassment some are labeling with the new hashtag #Me3."

"Well, he did pretty well," Jason said, a little tentatively.

"Really? He seemed guilty as hell to me," said Justin. "No doubt in my mind."

Chapter Forty-Two

~~~~~~~~~~

TIME FOR IT TO STOP

Tom brought Grace the envelope from the State Division of Environmental Appeals with a bunch of the day's mail. He waved it in front of her.

"Look what I have in my hot little hands." Tom set it down on her desk. "What do you think it's going to be?"

"No idea, but probably the project approved with some conditions," she replied. "That's how most of them have gone. Hopefully, to include groundwater monitoring." Grace's hands were trembling as she opened it. "Oh my God, he's denied the whole permit! We won, Tom! We won!"

"Congratulations!" Tom held out his arms and they hugged. They'd spent countless hours together, organizing exhibits and shaping the arguments that had carried the day.

"Thanks so much, Tom. It truly is a shared victory. I can't wait to tell Irene Douglas!"

Grace read the decision through thoroughly. Seeing the words on the page confirming one's view of things was deeply affirming. Amazing, even. Then she called her client. One of her greatest joys was telling clients that they'd won their case.

"Hello, Irene? It's Grace Clarkson."

"Yes, hi. Have you heard something?" Irene asked eagerly. "I checked the website this morning and there was nothing."

"Yes, I got the certified letter with the decision in the mail just now. Good news, Irene. We won!"

"Monitoring and costs?"

"For now, the permit request was flat-out denied. There can be no expansion without them establishing that there have been no Clean Water Act or groundwater violations."

"Oh, that's wonderful, Grace." Irene sniffled. Her voice broke a bit. "I felt like my late husband and your late uncle were guiding us all the way through this. Does that strike you as odd?"

"No, it's sweet. And who knows about any of that?" Grace was agnostic about such things anyway.

By lunchtime, her phones started to ring. Reporters and potential new clients. A lawyer from the Carolinas who was planning to sue pig farm CAFOs after their manure storage pits were washed into rivers and groundwater as a result of a recent hurricane. Even a couple of old clients who were proud of her accomplishment.

It was heady and exhilarating, but Grace needed some time to herself to make sense of it. She looked at her calendar and the whole afternoon was free. It was as good a time as any.

"Tom, it's a beautiful day. I've nothing on my calendar. I think I'm going to take the afternoon off." Damn, that sounded good.

"That's a great idea." Tom smiled. "Louisa and I will hold down the fort."

Grace went home, threw on a pair of jeans, grabbed her backpack, and headed out to the big bluffs and on to Perrot State Park outside of Trempealeau. Her favorite hike was there, and in the backpack was her sketchbook. She would make some sketches up on Brady's Bluff. Maybe some kind of inspiration would strike?

She hiked up the crooked diagonal path that went straight up the bluff. It started in a narrow green ravine and had switchbacks that led to a wooden staircase where she rested. She took out her book and her sketch pad. From here, she could sketch verdant little Trempealeau Mountain. She took out her pencil and had at it. The view from up here was spectacular, with the green marsh and hills across the river in Minnesota.

From here, the first French voyageurs would scan the water for trading prospects, thinking they'd discovered something. At the end of the Ice Age, as the mile-thick glaciers were just melting to form the Great Lakes, the Driftless Area along the Upper Mississippi was flowing open and already inhabited by a hardy band. The Paleo People shared the lush river valley with mammoths and mastodons.

Hundreds of years before Jesus, the Woodland People were farming squash and sunflowers to go with the smoked fish that got them through the brutal winters. Why did they stay so far north when even the river itself beckoned them further south?

And why did this history have such meaning for her? Was she just getting old? Or was she starting to embrace her own roots?

Did that mean she'd have to turn down the life-changing offer on her property? Was she stuck here? Was it such a terrible thing if she was?

Chapter Forty-Three

~~~~~~~~~~~~~

SHALOM

Jason pulled his car into the parking lot outside his office and sat there for a minute, meditating. His grief counselor had strongly encouraged him to go back to work when his blood drain had been removed and he was at last truly on the mend physically.

"The first day will be emotionally exhausting. Don't expect to get much done," Shalom, his counselor, had warned him.

But was Jason ready mentally? He walked into the unimpressive building, a converted warehouse with funky, low wooden ceilings and exposed beams.

"Hey, welcome back!" Judge Scott Parker greeted him with a high-five as he went to the elevator. "So nice to see you looking good."

Similar expressions of support poured out from his friends and colleagues when he made it upstairs. No fewer than ten of them came out to greet him. It was great to see them. Many of them had sent cards, flowers, and magazines. Jason finally tore himself away and had just settled into his stylish new desk and chair when his boss came in.

"Wasn't expecting to see you back so soon." Steve frowned. Hayman was the only person who hadn't either hugged him or shook his hand.

"It's been over six weeks, Steve."

"How are you, anyway?"

"Feeling much better, and I haven't had to take a nap for over a week. So, that's a good sign."

"What about the PTSD-type stuff?" Hayman asked.

"I've been seeing a counselor for that and my grief, a very nice woman on the Near East Side. She's been encouraging me to come back."

Hayman was shifting back and forth on his feet again.

"Look, I was planning to talk to you about something. I think I could get you a full disability pension, that's about ninety percent of your current salary. Permanently and with no red tape."

Kind of tempting. But most likely, just BS or illegal.

"I'm sure the governor's people would prefer that someone else do the White Farms Dairy decision, but it's my case and I'm looking forward to writing the decision."

"Well, maybe go home and think about it a couple more days." Hayman forced a smile. "It's the kind of sweet deal that they only give to cops shot in the line of duty. If you write that decision, it'll be hard to argue that you're too messed up to function."

"Almost sounds like another threat or bribe, to me."

"No, no, no! Everyone feels really bad about what you've gone through." Hayman paused. Jason could see a couple of his nosy colleagues fluttering about in the hallway, trying to overhear what was being said. "And I was seriously thinking of reassigning the thing to Jake to review the record and briefs."

"No, I'll do it." Of course, he was. Jake was a well-known Republican loyalist who would never rock the boat. "I'm not much the malinger-type."

"Just think about it. Nothing will be decided until you send something major out of here. I can cover for you until then."

"Okay. Thanks, then. Obviously, I can't do Lake Joseph Resort anymore. So, feel free to farm that out."

"I will." The rocking back and forth on his heels had ended and Hayman had turned a shoulder toward the door to leave. "Maybe, since you're here, do a memo to the file telling me where everything stands?"

"Yes, of course. We still had a couple of days of testimony remaining." Jason pointedly turned his back to Hayman to look at his files. When he turned around, Hayman was gone. It didn't matter. Jason was excited to find that he'd done a really detailed draft of the White Farms decision before the shooting, and he had the final decision out the door two weeks later.

～～～～～

Was it 315 or 319 Williamson Street? This was the fourth time Jason had been to see Shalom Garcia, his hipster grief counselor, but he could never remember. Oh yeah. There it was, the building with the bright red door. She'd said it was a symbol of openness to change or some kind of mumbo-jumbo like that. He found a parking spot and made his way to it.

"Welcome. You're right on time. How was work this week?" she asked, closing the inner, electric-blue door, behind her.

"I sent out the White Farms Dairy decision. Maybe you saw it in the paper?"

"I did." Shalom wrinkled her nose and smiled. The silver nose ring that had put him off at first sparkled in the sun. "Sounds like you just said no."

"I'm not sure if I would've had the guts before all of this, but it seemed obvious afterward. They're poisoning children, just the same as in Flint," Jason said. "Those people are going to prison, so I guess my decision is pretty moderate after all."

"You tried to do what's right." Shalom looked into his eyes a little intensely. "How are you doing with your grief?"

"I seem to be getting over some of the numbness, but part of that is that I'm feeling better and starting to get over my own injuries. Going back to work to finish my old decisions was a great idea, thanks." Jason paused, knowing she would wait patiently for him to resume. "I liked what the pamphlet said about numbness being nature's insulation against the shock and pain."

"Yes, it sort of cushions you until you are gradually forced to accept the new reality." She paused, taking a sip from a Café du Monde mug. "What do you find yourself missing the most about Tara?"

"I miss our conversations the most. Even her texts. We used to text each other twenty or thirty times a day after her divorce started. It's such a loss; we told each other every little thing." Jason sank into Shalom's orange sofa and sighed. "And the guilt is still the hardest part. If it hadn't been for me, she would still be here."

"You don't know that for sure." Shalom frowned. "I mean, it could have been a random act of violence or . . . "

Jason gave her a look. "I doubt that very much."

"But even if it was from one of your cases, your guilt is disproportionate, especially given that you also nearly died from this violence," Shalom said. "I think you have various sources of guilt that you need to unpack."

"Unpack away, Shalom." It was probably a fake name but it made Jason feel better just to say it. He genuinely valued her insights.

"Well, there's obviously classic survivor's guilt. Why did you survive when Tara didn't? Especially because it may have been your job that had put you both in danger."

"That's often the first thought that strikes me when I wake up in the morning."

She gave him a slightly mysterious look. "But do you think you also have any residual guilt over having had an affair with her?"

"Yes, I felt awkward speaking at her memorial service. It was very gracious of her family and ex to include me, but I felt like a bit of an interloper—even though my feelings for her were so deep."

"That's hard, feeling so much and also feeling marginalized."

"It's weird. I've always tried to live my life in such a way that guilt and regrets were not major factors—so these are new feelings." Jason was used to feeling like a man with principles, but now, he felt like just another asshole.

"You didn't do anything to cause Tara to lose her life. You're a victim, too," Shalom said.

"Yes, that's helpful, and getting justice for both of us is so important to me. I've spent hours with detectives and prosecutors, and racked my brain for every suggestive or threatening conversation."

"I think your whole life has been about getting justice, Jason, and now you have to struggle with this profound injustice that impacts you so personally. But give yourself justice too, and let go of this guilt. Try that the next time you meditate."

"I will. The meditation really helps. But getting justice for Tara would help even more!"

Chapter Forty-Four

THERE'S A COP OUTSIDE

Grace was sitting in her office, drinking coffee from the Pearl and looking at her calendar, when Tom came in with a troubled look on his face.

"What's up, Tom?"

"There's a cop outside who wants to talk with you."

"A cop?" That was weird. "Send him in."

He was a tall redhead about her age. He politely shook her hand. "I'm Detective Martin Griswold and I'm investigating the Judge Erickson matter."

"Okay. Come in, but please close the door." Grace sat down behind her desk and motioned to him. "Please have a seat."

"Detective Rollins and the DA gave me a couple of topics that I'd like to explore."

"Go ahead."

"The first is that you were socializing with Judge Erickson in a bar here in downtown La Crosse? Is that right?"

"Yes and no. It wasn't planned. We just ran into each other at the Bodega Bar downtown."

"Had you ever socialized with Jason Erickson before?" Detective Griswold made it sound like some kind of scary health risk.

"Maybe once or twice in law school. But we were never close, if that's what you're suggesting."

"I'm not suggesting anything," he said with a bland smile. His face had boyish patches of orange and greenish freckles. "When you were at the Bodega, the judge told you something about an ethical issue, is that right?"

"Yes."

"Can you remember exactly what he said?"

"We talked about the ethics of our having a beer with our case pending, and both of us concluded that it was okay if we didn't discuss the case," Grace replied.

"For the record, do you still take that position?"

"Yes."

"And then?"

"Judge Erickson said something like 'I've got bigger ethical issues than this right now, trust me.' I offered to help him think it through—and that's when he said what I told Detective Rollins, 'It's really more like a threat than an ethical issue.'"

"That's pretty unusual, isn't it?" He was staring intently at her. Taking her measure.

"Yes, it is."

"How did you respond?"

"I told him that I'd been on some ethical committees and that he could run it by me," Grace said. "But the judge said, 'It's really more of a threat than an ethical issue.' That's pretty much an exact quote, as far as I remember. Obviously, it stuck with me. He changed the subject to small talk after that."

"Before we move on, anything else you can remember about meeting the judge at the Bodega?" The detective looked directly into her eyes. His were green and searching.

"Nope. Do you have any idea when this might go to hearing?" Grace asked. She hadn't really looked very far into her calendar lately.

"Yes, I have an exact time and place for you." The detective slapped down a piece of paper with a thump. "It's all in this subpoena. Just so you know, the DA has separated out the public corruption and the murder and attempted murder cases. Officially you're witness for both. But Scott Horner said to tell you that you'll likely only have to testify at the first, even though you're technically under subpoena for both."

The preliminary hearing on the public corruption case was set for the following week. And that was the same week that the realtor was demanding an answer about the offer on her building.

~~~~~~~

When the day came, Grace was surprisingly nervous. She was a witness in a murder case. A relatively minor witness, but her corroboration of Judge Erickson could be important. Her credibility was crucial, but she'd withheld the fact that she'd kissed Jason that night outside the Bodega. Was it going to haunt her?

She was up second, after Skip Munson, a prosecutor friend of Jason's. Munson was as cool and calm as Grace wished she was. His testimony was brief and seemingly painless. Jason had called Munson on the Sunday night after the last day of the White Farms Dairy trial. He'd told Skip, who was putting his mother in a nursing home that same day, that it was Earl Franks who had threatened and attempted to bribe him. The cross-examination didn't lay a glove on him.

Her turn. Grace's direct went fine. No hiccups at all. She'd done a practice run with Horner's paralegal, and it was almost sentence by sentence. But then came the cross.

"Ms. Clarkson," Myron Rosenberg said. He bolted toward her. Grace had the instinct to flinch, to put her hands up to protect herself. Then she heard Horner's voice.

"Your Honor!" the prosecutor said, exasperated. "Can you tell Counsel to back off a bit?"

Myron was always macho, territorial, but for a second, Grace had wondered if he was going to pee on her leg.

"Mr. Rosenberg, knock it off, please!" Judge Cole was the epitome of the small-town judge, with his gray-white hair, horn-rimmed glasses, and genial manner. No nonsense.

"Ms. Clarkson, did Jason Erickson ever mention a name in connection with this conversation?" Myron asked.

"No."

"So, for example, he didn't mention Earl Franks."

"No, he didn't," Grace said.

"Don't people also use the word *threat* as in 'I feel threatened' by something? Say, a spouse 'threatened' by another woman or man?" Myron asked.

"Sure, they do, but that wasn't the vibe I was getting."

Myron paused and looked at her with skeptical drama. "So, now this is all about a vibe?"

"Yes, it was obvious that he felt he was in trouble."

"But no idea of *what* trouble or with whom?"

"No, he expressed very clearly that it was a quasi-ethical issue that he felt was more akin to a threat," Grace said.

"Incidentally, you are on a bar ethics committee, isn't that right?" Myron took his glasses off.

"Yes."

"I was wondering how you analyze the ethics of drinking beers with the judge with whom you have a pending case?"

"We didn't talk about the case, so there was no actual ethical issue," Grace began. "But the concern would be about whether it gave the appearance of impropriety."

"It looks bad, doesn't it, the two of you sitting there drinking beer together?"

"It could," said Grace. "A gray area is how I would characterize it."

"Did you walk out of the bar together?"

"Yes."

"Did you hug or kiss goodnight?"

"No." She'd been bracing for it and looked blankly ahead. What did Myron know?

"So, if Judge Erickson testified that he kissed you on the cheek, that would be inaccurate?"

"I don't recall that." She felt her face warming. Her uncle Ray had always told her she was the most honest person he knew because, whenever she lied, her face changed color. That damn kiss again.

"No, I'm sure you don't." Myron looked directly at Judge Cole. "Now, I want to turn to this conversation about supposedly seeing Earl Franks in La Crosse."

"I did see him."

Myron shook his head. "Where exactly were you, and what exactly do you claim to have seen?"

"I was on a run along the path in La Crosse," Grace began. "It goes from Riverside Park downtown across the causeway and back through the woods toward the university and Myrick Park. It's convenient for me because my office is very near Riverside."

"And?" Myron asked.

"And, when I'd made it down near the Myrick Park parking lot, I observed Earl Franks pacing around near a black Lexus with a University of Michigan decal on it."

"What time was this?"

"A little after eight a.m. I always try to get back and shower by nine a.m."

"What made you think the man was Earl Franks?" Myron asked.

"I'd just seen him speak at the Water Law Conference in June, and he's a tall and distinctive-looking man. He was wearing a yellow golf shirt and tan shorts. He has really hairy legs."

"So, it was his hairy legs?" Myron asked sarcastically.

"Well, I understand that it has been corroborated that Mr. Franks drives a black Lexus with a University of Michigan decal," Grace said. She was trying to respond in a very understated manner, and it seemed to work.

Myron stood up, his face flushed. "I object; she is reaching a legal conclusion talking about what is or is not corroborated."

"Your Honor," Scott Horner implored. "Counsel asked her a general question, and the witness simply answered it truthfully."

"Overruled," said Judge Cole. "Go ahead."

"You saw this man get in a black car?"

"Yes. A black Lexus SUV hybrid with a Michigan decal."

"Were you still running?"

"No, I thought he was acting unusually, and I made a point of stopping for a drink of water at the bubbler near the park," Grace said.

"Bubbler?"

"The water fountain. I got a drink of water, mostly because I wanted to see what he was up to."

"Was he doing something you thought suspicious?"

"Just pacing around nervously," said Grace. "But it was weird enough that I told Judge Erickson about it that morning when I ran into him in the hotel lobby."

"Nothing further."

"Redirect, Mr. Horner?" Judge Cole asked, clearly hoping that the answer would be no.

"Just one. Why did you tell Judge Erickson about seeing Earl Franks?" Horner asked.

"Because Franks was acting strangely," Grace replied. "And I couldn't figure out why Earl Franks would be in La Crosse, until I began to wonder if it had to do with that threat to Judge Erickson. Then I began to worry."

"Motion to strike," Myron said.

"Denied, but it's clearly speculative," said Judge Cole.

"But you never spoke to this mystery man, isn't that true?" Myron asked.

"No, I never spoke with him."

"And what was the closest distance you got to this fellow?"

"Oh, maybe one hundred fifty feet," Grace said. She was terrible with distance estimates.

"Maybe, or that's your best estimate?"

"That's my best estimate."

"So, that's fifty yards. Half a football field away?"

"Sounds right."

Myron smiled. "And you're a lawyer, right?"

"Yes."

"So you're familiar with the statistics on the number of people falsely convicted due to mistaken identification?"

"Exact numbers, no. But that it happens, sure. Yes."

"That's all I have."

"You're excused, Ms. Clarkson," said Judge Cole. "Any objection to releasing her from her subpoena for tomorrow?" There wasn't. "Let's break for lunch."

All witnesses were sequestered, so she wasn't allowed to stay.

Grace just got in her car and drove back toward La Crosse. She was anxious and couldn't quite place what she was feeling. A mix of dread and disbelief.

It was still hard to imagine that Tara had been murdered. That she had just testified in a murder prelim. When she got to Madison, she decided to get off the interstate and onto Highway 14, the scenic route.

She decided that she would grab dinner at the Driftless Café. She had to call the realtor before then. She'd made her decision during her testimony. She was going to walk away from one million dollars. What was it about the trial that had helped her decide?

She had the number in her phone contacts and called as she drove through the bluffs outside of Richland Center.

"I'm going to have to say no to their amazing offer."

"What?" The realtor sounded almost angry. "Can I ask why?"

"That building means a lot to me. It's family. It's roots." Grace paused as she approached an Amish horse and buggy up ahead. "It's my life, as much as I might sometimes long for a different one."

Chapter Forty-Five

~~~~~~~~~

EX PARTE CONTACTS

District Attorney Scott Horner was a short man who'd been a college wrestler at Iowa and was still stocky and strong in his mid-fifties. He asked Jason one question after another with the same understated directness. It was a masterful performance from a small-town lawyer who knew his judge and knew the facts of his case.

Jason had been threatened in several conversations with Earl Franks over the course of last summer. No one else had ever threatened him in all his years as a judge. Jason was shot, going to the sheriff's department, trying to do what was right.

Laid out like that, the nightmare of the past year was all so clear and simple. Yet Jason couldn't quite square its clarity with his own messy experience. That was all gray.

Now, sitting at the table beside Earl, Myron Rosenberg looked a little off. Momentarily. Then he stood up and charged ahead.

"The remark about money and the Lake Joseph Resort was ambiguous. Wasn't it?" Myron asked.

"To some degree," Jason replied.

"You thought at the time that you may have misconstrued it?"

"Yes."

"And then there was this supposed conversation at a parking lot at the county park in La Crosse?" Myron asked.

"Yes."

"For the record, where is La Crosse?"

"Western Wisconsin, several hours from Lake Joseph," Jason replied.

"And even farther from Earl Frank's office in Chicago?"

"Yes, another hour and a half."

"And Earl Franks just shows up there, out of nowhere, and tells you he wants to bribe you on the Lake Joseph case?" Rosenberg's tone suggested it was preposterous.

"Yes."

"But, after this conversation, you still don't go to the police to report this threat; is that what you expect the court to believe?"

"Yes," Jason responded. But Myron had a point. Why hadn't Jason gone to the police?

"Are administrative law judges bound by the judicial ethics code?"

"Not specifically, but we are bound by the attorney's code," Jason answered. "And we have our own draft, non-binding code, which I voluntarily follow."

"Do they both require that you disclose what are known as *ex parte* contacts?" Myron asked.

"Yes."

"What's your definition of an *ex parte* contact, Mr. Erickson?"

"Any conversation about the merits of a pending matter that includes only one side of a contested matter."

Myron looked directly at Judge Cole. "Would that include an attempt to improperly influence a decision-maker?"

"Yes, of course," Jason said.

"So, you were ethically bound to report this supposed conversation at Myrick Park parking lot," said Myron, raising his voice, "But your testimony is that you didn't report it. Is that right?"

"That's right," Jason said calmly. "I was pretty scared. And there was this whole sex-tape thing. It was a lot to take in. I wanted to discuss it with Tara."

"Did you tell the other parties in the Lake Point resort case, the so-called slipominium case, about this *ex parte* conversation?"

"No."

"Would this be required ethically under either code?" Myron asked.

"Yes, under both."

"Were you planning to ever do so?"

"Yes," Jason said again.

"But as of the date of the shooting, you hadn't?"

"That's correct."

"You wanted to talk to Tara but didn't care about the parties to the case you were presiding over," Myron said.

"Is there a question?" Horner asked.

Myron Rosenberg paused, shaking his head. "Mr. Erickson, do you expect the court to believe that a former chief justice of the state supreme court would ruin his legal career over one small case about pier slips?"

"The case involved something like twenty-five million dollars," Jason replied. "Earl Franks said he didn't want to do it, but suggested that he was being forced into it."

"Your Honor, I ask that that last answer be stricken," Myron fumed. "Fair is fair. If there is some specific evidence, put it on the table, otherwise—"

"Sustained," Judge Cole ruled. "The last sentence is stricken."

"Let's talk about Milwaukee," Myron continued. "You've shown that you were both at the USEPA Delegation legal seminar at the Pfister Hotel, but then you say you went to get a drink together?"

"Yes," Jason answered. "But the more important conversation was the one in the lobby, the one I taped—"

"Objection!"

"Sustained," Judge Cole ruled. "Judge Erickson, as you know, that tape has been excluded from evidence."

"But Your Honor," Scott Horner said. "He's not addressing the truth of any matter asserted in the tape; he's just referencing that there were two distinct conversations."

"I understand, but my ruling and your objection stand, and the record we're making requires no further references to it," said Judge Cole.

"I'm asking about the second conversation," Myron probed. "It simply strains credulity that you would have a drink with someone you say you were afraid of, who you also say has just tried to bribe you. Can you explain that?"

"It was an error of judgment on my part," Jason said. "But I was trying to give Earl the impression that I might go along," Jason said. "I felt safer that way." Was part of it that he just needed a drink after taping Earl? It was a stupid move on Jason's part.

"Let's go back to Tara." Myron Rosenberg leaned on the courtroom banister melodramatically and raised an eyebrow. "How would you characterize your relationship with Tara Highsmith over the past year?" Such a hammy putz. So, of course, Earl Franks had hired him.

"I would describe Tara as a professional colleague first and then a close friend," Jason began. He paused, finding the words. "And then lovers after her husband filed for divorce. Briefly, so briefly. Before Tara was murdered."

Murdered. How could she be in his arms one day and then gone the next? Everything about Tara was so special, so dear to him.

Those amazing book club emails. All of her beautiful words. She had so much to say, and felt things so deeply. That electric feeling, holding her hand during their walks around the lake. Kissing her, being in her arms! The way her earnest voice would burst into her earthy laugh. Their dream of a house on Blue Lake. Her last letter. *I've heard the schools there are good.* He hadn't let himself think of the kid that they both knew they were going to have together.

Then, there it was, the sudden storm of his grief for Tara, for that life they would never have together. Everything that had been welling up in him came pouring out.

"Judge, Judge, would you like to take a minute?" It was Judge Cole. "Ten-minute recess."

Judge Cole went back into his chambers. The others got up and started milling around.

Jason just sat there. There was nowhere to hide. He closed his eyes and let himself cry.

Chapter Forty-Six

~~~~~~~~~~~~~

THE VIEW FROM THE DOCK

Earl looked around the courtroom, still hoping that Laurie had come, though he'd told her not to. Nope. No sign of Laurie Little.

Jason Erickson was putting on a good show, blubbering from the stand. Maybe it wasn't all show, but the timing was suspicious.

Earl went up the steps to the men's room on the third floor and made it back just as Judge Cole's clerk, Judy, brought Jason a box of tissues. A couple minutes later, Cole peeked out from his chambers, and Jason nodded that he was ready.

Myron Rosenberg was ready too. Damn, Myron was *good*. The guy was like fucking Johnny Appleseed, planting seeds of doubt everywhere. Myron had all the time-honored moves too—even that rare, deadpan, I-don't-believe-a-word-of-this-crap look that Earl himself used. It wasn't clear what Old Judge Cole would make of it, but a lot of juries would just eat it all up if Earl's case ever got to trial.

"Now, you admit you were seeing a married woman at the time of this shooting?" Myron asked Jason.

"Yes," Jason replied. His eyes were still puffy and he looked sincerely depressed.

"Did Mr. Highsmith—Tara's husband—did Mr. Highsmith know about your relationship with his wife?"

"He knew of our friendship. Yes."

"Did he know you'd become lovers?"

"No, as far as I know, he did not."

"Would that knowledge be embarrassing to you professionally?" Myron asked.

"Yes. It's been difficult."

"Was it also embarrassing to Ms. Highsmith?"

"Yes," Jason said.

"And someone—we don't know who or why—took photos and a video?"

"Yes, but it's a pretty strong inference on why."

"But that's the most embarrassing of all, right?" Myron asked.

"Yes."

Myron suddenly raised his voice. "Isn't it true that you concocted this whole previously unreported story about Justice Earl Franks, just to divert attention from what really happened?"

"No," Jason said. "Absolutely not."

Horner was on his feet. "Your Honor, pursuant to your ruling on the highly incriminating tape recording, I think it's only fair that you reconsider it if Mr. Rosenberg pursues this line of questioning."

"I'll rephrase it," Myron said quickly. "You don't know whether or not Tara's husband found out about your affair—from the photos or otherwise—and hired someone to shoot you?"

"Objection." Horner stood up.

"I'll allow it," Judge Cole ruled.

"No," Jason said.

"It would be natural for a husband to be angry at the man who was so 'intimate' with his wife," Myron said, in a very licentious way. "To be angry with the man who was making love to his wife, wouldn't it?"

"Perhaps, but it didn't happen that way. Tara and I did nothing until her husband said their marriage was over."

"You don't know for sure that Earl Franks was responsible for your shooting, do you?" Myron asked.

"No, but I think it would be a reasonable inference. As you know, case law supports that inference where there were demonstrable threats."

"You weren't even sure, at first, that he attempted to influence you?"

"Not at first, but there was no doubt whatsoever after the conversation in La Crosse," Jason replied. "And Franks had made considerable effort to corrupt the process, including threatening Tara and myself about the sex tape."

"Let me back up a minute," Myron said. "Were there any witnesses to this supposed conversation on the running path and in the parking lot of the county park?"

"Not that I'm aware of—"

"And the same thing for that somewhat ambiguous remark at Lake Joseph?"

"Yes."

"And, even by your own testimony, Mr. Franks never explicitly said, 'I will have you shot if you don't accept a bribe'?"

"That's right," Jason said. "But I wouldn't have expected him to."

"Incidentally, what possible good to him would you be dead?"

Damn it. Myron had overreached. What was he thinking?

Erickson, regaining his courtroom bearings, looked directly at the judge. "I was on my way to the Lake Joseph Sheriff's Department with an envelope full of what felt like cash, and Mr. Franks had recently threatened me. It would be better for him if I was dead, because this fact would not have come out." There were scattered nods around the courtroom, and Jason went on. "He probably wouldn't be sitting here charged with a felony if they'd succeeded in killing me."

"Move to strike, Your Honor," Myron said.

"But, Counsel, you asked him a why question," said Judge Cole, amused. These small-town judges sometimes enjoyed seeing the city slickers falter. Earl's hopes sank.

Myron went back on the attack. "Back to that envelope—none of that cash was ever recovered, was it?"

"I don't know."

"I'm sure you would know if it had?"

"Objection!" Horner said.

"I'll rephrase it. Would you expect to be notified if any cash had been recovered?"

"Probably. Mr. Horner has been extremely courteous and professional in all aspects of his investigation."

"I have nothing further, Your Honor."

"No redirect." Horner smiled.

"Okay, let's take a break." Judge Cole looked weary. "No contact between possible witnesses. Court reconvenes in sixty minutes after our lunch break. Please be on time."

Earl went to lunch with Myron, and they talked about the possibility of putting on any witnesses of their own—rare at a preliminary hearing—but something Rosenberg was prepared to do.

"What do you think? Do we have a shot?"

"You're an experienced guy. I'm not going to sugarcoat it." Myron shook his head frankly. "Could go either way. Their case is a little thin, but this is just a preliminary hearing. They still can't completely tie you to the second so-called threat. Clarkson and Munson hurt you, no doubt. Both were good witnesses, even if Clarkson was a little vague. I'd put in your daily calendar to rebut them, but they'd want to grill you. We can't let them do that."

"Let's just take our chances on these charges and then clobber them tomorrow on the . . . " Earl couldn't even say the words . . . "the serious charges."

In the hallway after lunch, Scott Horner was huddled with a blonde woman who looked familiar. Earl had seen that forlorn face before, but where? Horner was furiously taking notes. An old law clerk? Then he remembered.

It was that blonde woman from that trashy bar in the hills. Damn. How would she even know about this? Earl ran to find Rosenberg.

"Myron, we've got a problem!" Maybe he shouldn't tell him. "They may have another witness. I was in a bar around that day that Erickson claims I threatened him. But not in La Crosse."

"Where?"

"Some town an hour east of there. But the woman thought I was hitting on her, and she's over there, talking to Horner."

"What's the gist?" Myron frowned.

"The timing might be a little awkward. It may have been that same night."

They went back into the courtroom.

"Any witnesses on behalf of the defendant?" Judge Cole asked.

"No, Your Honor," Myron answered.

"Excuse me, Your Honor," Horner began. "Over the break I became aware of another witness, one who can tie Franks to the La Crosse area on the day Erickson alleges they spoke in the parking lot."

"I object, Your Honor. We put on no witnesses," Myron said. "Surely there is no basis for a rebuttal witness."

"I just became aware of this witness," Horner countered. "This is a prelim; I think it's appropriate that you have all the evidence before you make your decision, Your Honor."

The woman came forward and was sitting at the counsel table next to Horner and Jason. She was very pale. It was hard to tell whether her fine, thinning hair was dyed platinum or naturally whitish-blonde.

"The objection is overruled," said Judge Cole. "The state never formally rested, and, if they did, the court formally relieves them of it. The witness can come forward."

She was wearing a flattering, out-of-date, blue-and-white polka-dot dress.

"Could you please state your name for the record?" Horner asked.

"Jennifer Johnson."

Her eyes were slightly crossed and pinkish blue. Earl remembered that he liked her voice.

"Where do you reside?"

"Outside Viroqua, in Vernon County," Jennifer answered.

"And where is that in relation to La Crosse?" Horner posed.

"Maybe thirty-five to forty miles east and south," she replied.

"What is your date of birth, please?"

Jennifer paused and then smiled. "In front of all these people?"

Horner nodded. Judge Cole and the spectators laughed. Earl felt a little ill.

"July 18, 1953."

"Did you celebrate your birthday this year?"

"Yes."

"How?"

"Well, I met some friends at the Drop On Inn in Wellsburg," Jennifer answered. Earl hadn't seen her with any friends. If they'd been there, Earl would have never hit on her.

"And where is that?" Horner continued.

"About twenty miles south of Cashton."

Cashton, that was a blast from Earl's own past. A high school friend used to play a cover of Nashville Cats as Cashton Cats, to the delight of all the locals.

"And in relation to La Crosse?"

"Like I said, maybe forty or so miles east."

"What time did you go there?"

"I was supposed to meet a couple of my friends there at six o'clock."

"Do you recall seeing the defendant, Mr. Franks, on that evening?"

"Objection," said Myron. "No foundation."

Earl noticed a young man get up and simply leave the stuffy court-room, free to head out into the sun. Would Earl ever be that free again? He suddenly longed for that more than anything.

"Sustained," said Judge Cole.

"On July eighteenth, the night of your birthday," Horner began, "did you encounter anyone in this courtroom at the Drop On Inn in Wellsburg?"

"Yes." Jennifer pointed directly at Earl. "That man sitting at the table in the blue suit."

Horner slowly turned to look at Earl, and then back at Judge Cole. Earl felt cornered.

"Let the record reflect that the witness has identified Mr. Franks," Horner said.

"What were the circumstances of you seeing the defendant?"

"Well, he came into the bar and kept trying to get really chatty and friendly, you know, the way men do in bars," Jennifer said. "And then he tried to buy me a drink. But I told him I buy my own drinks."

Yeah, and she drank one Earl bought for her anyway.

"Do you recall what time that was?"

"A little after six p.m., maybe six fifteen p.m. My friends were a little late and they hadn't arrived by that point."

Horner looked at the judge. "And you're sure it was the defendant?"

"Yes, when I saw his picture in the paper, I said, 'Aha, that's that creep who hit on me on my birthday!'"

"Objection, Your Honor." Myron stood.

"The witness is urged to refrain from name-calling," Judge Cole ruled. Smiling.

"Did the defendant say anything to you that night?" Horner continued.

"Yes. I told the bartender that he was, you know, pestering me, and then I called him—it's a couple of names. Can I say them?"

"Yes," Judge Cole said.

"I called him a loser and a Harvey Weinstein-wannabe," she said with a smile. How many times had she told this story by now? "And he says, 'I'm not a wannabe. I used to be on the state supreme court.'"

"And you're sure it was July eighteenth?" Horner said.

"Absolutely, wouldn't forget my own birthday. And it was a big one, since I turned sixty-two and became eligible for Social Security." Jennifer smiled her annoying smile. "Not that I can afford to retire."

"And you're certain it was the defendant?" Horner asked.

"Yes."

"How did it come about that you became a witness in this case?"

"Like I said, I saw his mug in the local paper and that he said he was nowhere near La Crosse. So, I called your office to let them know that I'd seen him half an hour from La Crosse on my birthday."

"No further questions."

"Counsel?" Judge Cole inquired.

"Your Honor, I move to strike all of this testimony as being non-probative and prejudicial," Myron said. "Even if it were true, it doesn't provide you with any information that you need to decide whether to bind Justice Franks over."

"Your Honor," Horner put in. "That goes to the weight you give the testimony, but it's clearly relevant. The fact that Earl Franks was in the area on the exact night."

"Objection overruled," Judge Cole ruled. "It corroborates earlier witness testimony. Do you have any cross?"

"No," Rosenberg replied.

That was a very bad sign indeed. There was a short break. Myron went out to his car and made some phone calls. Earl was feeling doomed again. If he was an embarrassment to a hard-boiled criminal defense lawyer like Myron, what would he be to Laurie and Maggie? If he felt like shit now, facing the bribery charge, how would he feel tomorrow facing murder and attempted murder?

It was time for Judge Cole to rule. He appeared animated, enjoying the attention.

"There are two separate felony charges, and I'll take them one at a time. First, I find that there is probable cause to believe the felony crime of Bribery of a Public Officer has occurred. I base this finding on the testimony of Mr. Erickson and Mr. Munson. Mr. Munson's testimony was very important corroboration of Judge Erickson's testimony.

"Now, with respect to the second charge, I must say that the record is far less clear. However, I do find probable cause to believe the defendant has committed the Class D felony of Threats to Injure, relating again to attempts to influence a public officer. I find, on the testimony of Administrative Judge Erickson, and specifically on the basis of the conversation on the running path. This is corroborated by the testimony of both Ms. Clarkson and Ms. Johnson, tying Earl Franks to the scene.

"I found Ms. Johnson's testimony particularly compelling," Judge Cole continued. "She credibly remembers an agitated Earl Franks in a bar not far from where Judge Erickson said the threat occurred.

"Accordingly, the defendant is bound over on this count and the hearing is adjourned. The Motion to Dismiss and related Preliminary on the Murder and Attempted Murder Conspiracy will be heard tomorrow morning pursuant to the terms and time agreed to by the parties. The defendant will remain free on his bond. Thank you both for cooperating and working well together."

Myron had already packed up and left with barely a grunt. Earl sat there, stunned. He was facing two felonies. There was a dead body. Erickson, a very sympathetic witness, wanted his ass in prison for the rest of his life. And tomorrow, Earl was up for conspiracy to commit murder. Maybe he should've just hit the road when Tommy C. had? That bastard was drinking limoncello in Capri with his lady friend while Earl was looking at a stretch in prison.

"Hang in there, Earl. Tomorrow will be better. I promise. I just got a text from Stan," Myron whispered to Earl. "He's found something that could blow their case right out of the water."

Stan was doggedly thorough, especially when he had an unlimited budget.

Earl knew not to hang his hopes on some Perry Mason moment

where some game-changing evidence comes in during the actual trial. But what if Stan had actually found something?

Earl pushed it away. He'd been around the law long enough to know better.

Chapter Forty-Seven

~~~~~~~~~~~~~~~~

MURDER AND
ATTEMPTED MURDER

Aided by an extremely dull PBS feature on the American woodchuck that was in heavy rotation, Jason had finally slept through the night after his emotional day on the stand. Part of his breakdown yesterday had been a lack of sleep. But he was feeling much better as he made his way back to the courtroom and his seat next to DA Horner.

Scott Horner and Detective Rollins had given Jason a heads-up by text that the murder and attempted murder hearing was going to have some twists and turns. They couldn't say any more than that.

Jason looked around the room. He had plenty of moral support today. His brother, Justin, and his friend Ben were sitting together in the back, and Justin gave him a thumbs-up. Grace Clarkson smiled to him from a couple of rows up. She must not be a witness because all of the witnesses had been sequestered.

"All rise," called the clerk as Judge Cole entered the courtroom.

"Call the case of State v. Franks Motion to Dismiss Murder and

Attempted Murder charges," Judge Cole said solemnly. "The parties have reached certain agreements about how this motion will proceed."

Myron Rosenberg was up first to describe the agreement of the parties. Myron was impeccably dressed, tall, with just a touch of gray at the sides of his longish hair.

Myron said that he knew that Judge Cole would listen carefully to the evidence presented that would show that there was simply no basis for charging Earl Franks or Tommy Calandro *in abstentia* with murder or attempted murder. It was the rare motion hearing with witnesses, by agreement of the parties. The State had overcharged his client because of the threats that had allegedly been made against Judge Erickson. This was understandable, but there must be no rush to judgment. Obviously, his client maintained his right to appeal the determination yesterday on the public corruption charges, but that was a separate issue.

"Your Honor, even if one assumes *arguendo* that that is all true," Myron continued in his soothing, deep voice, "it's a long way from making vague threats to carrying them out with murder. We are going to establish not only that the State's evidence is insufficient on this charge, but we believe there is enough evidence to establish both another motive and strong likelihood that the murder was purposefully undertaken by another actor who knew of the threats. That person saw it as the perfect opportunity to accomplish this heinous crime for his own financial gain."

"Thank you, Counsel," said Judge Cole. "Mr. Horner?"

District Attorney Horner stood up. "It's highly unusual that we have agreed to let Mr. Rosenberg call witnesses, but we did so that there would be no suggestion that we have predetermined who has committed these crimes that took the life of Ms. Highsmith and came close to taking Judge Erickson's life as well."

"All right. Let's get to it," said Judge Cole. "Mr. Rosenberg?"

"We call licensed Private Investigator Stan Simpson to the stand," Myron said. The witness was sworn and identified himself. "How are you employed, sir?" Myron asked in his velvety, I'm-going-to-win-this-thing voice.

"Private investigator, for the past twenty-five years. Currently professionally licensed in eighteen states."

Stan had prepared a written report of what he found relative to the divorce of Tara and Michael Highsmith and the exhibit was marked. Tara had brokerage accounts in excess of 3.6 million dollars and Michael was the beneficiary.

Stan continued, "Some portion of this was likely due Michael because investments were made with marital assets, but only fifteen percent at the most. But with Tara's death, it all now presumably belonged to Michael because their divorce proceeding was now moot."

"Did you do an investigation of the scene of the shootings on Main Street in Lake Joseph?" Myron asked.

"Yes," Stan replied.

"Were you able to find any video surveillance footage that assisted you in your efforts?"

"Yes. As it happened, a colleague of mine, Ed Christianson, represented a client who co-owned a hair salon in that area with his wife. He was under the impression that his wife was meeting her lover at the salon on the evenings that he went to visit his mother in an area nursing home. My client lawfully placed a surveillance video that included footage of a man who is likely the shooter."

"Your Honor, can we play some of it?" Myron asked.

"No objection," said Horner.

"Mr. Simpson, will you describe for the record what we're going to see?" Myron said.

"Sure," Stan replied. "The first shooter emerges from a black SUV with a clearly visible Illinois plate. He is wearing what appears to be a Chicago White Sox cap."

Jason saw himself hurrying down the street. Soon the skinny guy with the White Sox cap got out of his SUV in hot pursuit. The footage was grainy, but watching himself become prey made Jason's stomach churn. It was like all his dreams in the hospital but somehow both more banal and terrifying.

Did this guy listen to a Sox game before hopping out of his van and tracking Jason down? Did he go back to it after he tried to murder Jason? How do such people live with themselves? And how did the rest of us live knowing that people like that were among us?

"Did you follow up on the plate number?" Myron continued.

"Yes, and the man, Dale Lancaster, is a former high school acquaintance of Michael Highsmith. I have just done this research this morning, but I have included photos of the car and Mr. Lancaster in my report, as well as information documenting his connection to Michael Highsmith. I suspect that if Detective Rollins checked their bank accounts that there will be some further proof."

"You said first shooter, Mr. Simpson, what did you mean by that?" Myron continued.

"Our investigation has led us to conclude that Mr. Lancaster's brother, John Lancaster, was also involved and that he was hired to shoot Ms. Highsmith. The two employed two different guns and shooters in an apparent effort to make the killings look contracted."

It wasn't Franks or Tommy C.! Michael had paid to have them both shot. Jason was stunned. He had no clue what was going to happen next. Myron asked a few more questions and then sat down.

Scott Horner jumped to his feet. "We agree that there have been several developments in this case, Your Honor, that merit further consideration. Instead of cross-examining Mr. Simpson, the State would like to defer on that and call Detective Rollins to the stand for *voir dire* and to explain these new developments while under oath."

"No objection," Myron replied. Unable to contain a smirk.

"Before Mr. Simpson is released from his subpoena, we'd also like to serve him with this Criminal Complaint for Criminal Invasion of Privacy under 942.09, for capturing nude images without the consent of the person depicted. We're also moving to amend the cases against Mr. Franks and Mr. Calandro *in abstentia* for conspiracy to commit the same crime."

Jason could hear Myron whispering to Earl, "Mice nuts."

Detective Rollins was already sworn in.

"Detective Rollins, did you investigate other suspects in this case besides Mr. Franks and Calandro?"

"Yes."

"Were those suspects who might have some grudges or issues with either Judge Erickson or Ms. Highsmith?"

"Yes."

"What about Tara's husband, Michael Highsmith? Did you look into him as a possible suspect?" Horner posed.

"Yes, we did investigate that possibility."

"What did you determine?"

"Obviously, there was a divorce pending, so that creates the possibility for all sorts of motives, from jealousy to financial gain," Detective Rollins testified. "As far as jealousy, Michael had a new romantic partner, and the divorce was initiated at his request."

"What about financial motives?"

"Tara had a five-hundred-thousand-dollar life insurance policy." Detective Rollins paused briefly, collecting her thoughts. "But she'd already changed the beneficiary from Michael to the Nature Conservancy, and Michael would likely have received notice of this change."

"Was their divorce final?"

"No."

"Wouldn't that provide an ongoing financial motive for Michael Highsmith?" Horner asked.

"Yes."

"Did you investigate the details of their financial situations as it related to the divorce proceeding?"

"To some extent, yes," Detective Rollins continued. "Their house was a joint asset worth three hundred forty-five thousand dollars, and Tara had some financial assets that she'd brought into the marriage, but those were frozen by the Temporary Order in the divorce case. She couldn't have changed the beneficiary even if she wanted to."

"Who was the beneficiary of those accounts?"

"Michael Highsmith," Detective Rollins said, staring right at Jason.

"Any idea of the amounts in those accounts?"

"I checked yesterday and there was approximately 3.74 million dollars in those brokerage accounts."

"In your work as a detective, is that an amount that could provide a motive for criminal activity?" Horner smiled.

Detective Rollins winced a bit. "Yes."

"With respect to the shooting itself, were you able to locate any video surveillance footage that aided you in your investigation?"

"Yes, we identified the same footage as Mr. Simpson," Detective Rollins replied. "In fact, we've had Mr. Simpson under surveillance since Judge Erickson identified him as the person who made the unlawful sex tape in La Crosse. Mr. Simpson led us to those responsible."

"And who is that?" Horner asked with a flourish.

"We agree that that trail led back to Michael Highsmith by way of Mr. Dale Lancaster, who we've taken into custody. He's been charged with Attempted First-Degree Murder in connection with the shooting of Judge Erickson. We have a Mr. Jon Lancaster, Dale's brother, in custody as well. Jon Lancaster has been charged with the Murder of Ms. Highsmith.

"Finally, just this morning, we took Mr. Michael Highsmith into custody in connection with both shootings. Dale Lancaster has been assisting us. The two brothers had been following both Judge Erickson and the deceased," Detective Rollins continued. "It seems that the manila envelope was designed to get Judge Erickson to go to the police, and they were trying to make the shootings look like contract killings.

We delayed informing the court, to make sure that we could have all three suspects in custody and to retain the element of surprise."

"Oh, you've surprised the court all right," said Judge Cole. "Let's take a break." After they were off the record, he added, "You all need to talk."

Horner and Rollins came over toward the table and led the whole group back into a quiet conference room.

"Why the hell didn't you give us this stuff?" Scott Horner asked. He was pissed. "We got it only because we were following your sleazy guy, Stan Simpson."

"I swear, we just got the footage last night," said a frightened-looking Myron. "You're going to dismiss, aren't you? We're ready to plea on the public corruption case and new conspiracy if you do."

"Four years?" offered Horner. "That work for you, Judge Erickson?"

Jason nodded. He was glad to see Earl was going to get time.

"That works," Jason replied. "So long as they hire a firm of our choosing to scrub all the photos and videos of Tara and me online."

Myron looked at Earl, frowning. Earl nodded.

"The Internet scrubbing is not a problem," Myron interposed. "How about two years, and this whole thing goes away and you can focus on the real murderers."

"Two won't do it." Horner shook his head.

Surprisingly, Earl spoke up. "I've always found that splitting the difference is a good way to settle things. Three years and I'm yours. You'll look good, because when people give you guff about it, you can say Earl Franks is in prison."

Jason nodded his agreement and then spoke. "Three years, so long as it's at Portage."

"Deal," said Myron.

When they came out of the conference room, they went back into the courtroom and put the deal on the record. When they were finished, Grace walked over to Jason and gave him a hug.

"It's over," she said, holding her embrace. "That's got to feel good."

"It does. For so many reasons." Jason sought out her eyes. "Thanks for your help."

"Please call me if you ever want to talk." Grace said. "Any time, day or night."

Jason smiled. "Thanks, Grace."

Justin and Ben came up to Jason, and Justin put his arm around him.

"Did you know that this was going to go down like that?" his brother asked.

"No, I had no clue."

"How does it leave you feeling?" Ben asked.

"I feel relieved that I won't have to testify again. And I guess some sense of relief that it wasn't Earl Franks who'd murdered her, but two lowlifes connected to Michael." Jason shook his head. "Damn, Michael had Tara murdered. It's hard to believe she could have married someone so evil."

Their blank stares were the only response. What was there to say?

After a pause, Ben said, "Come on, let me buy you brothers a drink."

PART THREE

THE BLUE SMELL
OF THE PINES

*"The blue smell of the pines must
be married to the green smell of the
plains, which are refreshed every
morning, with the smell of the stones,
the perfume of the distant marble."*

—PAUL CÉZANNE

Chapter Forty-Eight

~~~~~~~~~~~

BLUE LAKE REDUX

Shalom had given Jason a couple of assignments. At her urging, he scheduled crying sessions on weekday nights. At first two, and then one night a week. The idea was to feel some small bit of control over his grief and to save up the emotion for those sessions.

Then he was asked to make a list of his favorite places. In Madison, in Wisconsin, in the US, and in the world. He should think of them and go to them when possible and try to let them cheer him if they could. Jason was forty-five and already making his bucket list. Coming up with those lists was surprisingly hard—but the effort consumed whole evenings when he was very sad.

Then, another list assignment—where he'd been happiest with Tara. That was easy: in Blue Lake and in her arms.

"If you go there," Shalom said, "be prepared to cry."

"Do you think I should go?" Jason asked.

"Do you think it would help you to say goodbye?"

He shrugged.

But shortly after the trial, feeling a little safer knowing that there was no one still out there who wanted to kill him, Jason spent a Friday in Blue Lake. He stopped in at the Blue Lake Café and got a cup of their watery coffee served to him by the crabby waitress, who was doing her best to be solicitous.

"I was so sorry to hear about your friend," she said.

Jason nodded and waved her off. He missed Tara terribly.

One time when he was meeting her here, he'd been late. He'd come in to find Tara, in her light-tan-and-brown sweater, reading some fat literary or environmental book. She hadn't noticed him at first. He stood there for a minute, admiring her coffee-colored eyes, so deeply engrossed in her reading. Ideas no doubt flying like sparks in her head. In that gorgeous tan sweater. A bright scarf around her neck. He'd marveled at his friend a moment before she finally looked up and smiled.

"How long have you been standing there?" Tara had asked.

"Not long enough," he'd replied.

No, not long enough at all.

The grouchy waitress smiled at him as he got up to leave—were those tears in her eyes too? At the Blue Lake Café, at least, he was recognized as a tragic figure. Maybe next time he'd go to the tourist place, the Café Olé?

Jason headed out for a walk in the woods just north of the lake. How many times had he hiked the same path with Tara, among the red pines and white oak, following the little creek that flows into the lake? He sat on the same round, red rock where he'd sat with Tara, listening to the rustle of the wind in the trees, or following the flight of some fat songbird.

It was a sunny day in early March and the promise of spring was already in the northern air. The sun's warmth had some new sufficiency to it; the winds held some forgotten gentleness. A male cardinal had spring and mating on his mind. The cardinal sang out his mating call as Jason sat there. Always, the promise of intimacy and the reality of abiding loneliness.

Good luck, red bird!

A couple of times they'd even played cards here. Tara liked sitting beside Blue Lake and playing hearts or poker, something they'd both done as kids. The simple beauty of the blue water, the clearest he'd known, had helped to raise wild hopes for each of them. The natural world bewitched even as the life cycle betrayed. Inevitably.

After losing Tara, it was his choice to look at their time together as either the tragedy he could never live down, or as the very definition of what made life worth living. Jason knew which one Tara would have chosen for him.

There was some great continuity here, a literal chain of being at this place by this lake. Yes, a chain of trees and the sounds of the birds and the water and the taste and smell of the fish. A chain of people, too, from the native Ho-Chunk Nation to all of the people who'd shown up for the Christmas tree trial. People in canoes, people with troubles and regrets and hopes, were part of the picture too. All of these together were the environmental terroir that Tara had written about, the very spirit of the place. And Jason could feel something, what she would call her spirit, here too. It felt good to be back here with her.

He knew that he would come again.

Chapter Forty-Nine

~~~~~~~~

ENTRANCES AND EXITS

Jason liked hanging out with Grace. Their relationship had been building slowly over the nine months since the shootings. They lived more than two hours away from each other, but they talked on the phone fairly regularly.

And they'd previously done a trip to see Frank Lloyd Wright's headquarters, Taliesin, just outside Spring Green. A deranged handyman had killed Wright's mistress, Martha Borthwick Cheney, and her two children, then set Wright's northern masterpiece ablaze. The victims were the wife and children of one of Wright's clients, and the murderer a handyman Martha had just dismissed.

Taliesin had been restored but the place was still evocative. He and Grace had talked about violence, loss, and recovery there and then had a picnic at a nearby state park. But then Grace had driven back to La Crosse and Jason back to Madison.

A few weeks later, he'd gone to La Crosse after they realized that their fathers were buried in the same little cemetery on Highway 14 outside the city. They'd gone into the bluffy countryside together and held hands at the graves of each other's father there. And then they'd gone to lunch and walked the hills and tree-lined grounds of the nearby exact replica of the Shrine of Our Lady of Guadalupe.

They'd toasted each other's families with an excellent glass of pinot noir at the Culina Mariana Café there—those church bigshots knew their Santa Barbara wines. They'd kissed again on the lips as they parted ways.

Now, they'd planned a date, which meant spending the whole day together and would result in Grace going back to Madison with Jason. First, they were planning to hike at Devil's Lake and then go on to Aldo Leopold's nearby cabin, known as the Shack. Jason was then planning a solo trip to the prison at Portage, and then they were meeting up for the evening's performance of Shakespeare's *As You Like It,* Grace's favorite comedy, at an outdoor theater.

They greeted each other in the state park parking lot.

"It's a perfect day for our hike," Jason observed.

Grace embraced him and smiled. He was glad to see her. They went straight up the steep face of the bluff and only paused when they got to a lookout near the top.

"I forgot how beautiful it is here," Grace said.

"I love it here."

A young woman came by and asked Grace to take her picture. When Grace had finished, the woman asked if they wanted one on Grace's phone. Grace was ready to pass, but Jason said, "Sure, why not?"

Jason casually put his arm around her and could feel her shoulder blade rise up to greet him. It was their first picture together.

A group of turkey vultures circled in the sky between the lake and the top of the bluff near where she and Jason gawked at them. They walked along the bluff top and then down to the narrow trail that cut back to the visitor's center between the giant piles of purple rocks and the shore of Devil's Lake. There were still scattered pockets of the black lake flies as they made their way along the rocky trail.

"They're much worse in April," Jason said. "These guys are probably just the late bloomers."

"I think I've eaten a couple already," Grace said. "So, how are you doing with your grief?"

"It's like the weather. It comes and goes."

"How was the weather this week?" Grace asked.

"Honestly, mostly sunny, but a little nervous because of our date today."

Grace smiled. "So, this is a date."

"Of course it's a date."

"A marathon date. I even brought my toothbrush."

"Good." Jason smiled. "How do you feel about staying on in your building? Does it feel right?"

"It does. Thanks for asking. The season helps as well. May is my favorite month, when you still have the whole summer ahead of you. It was harder in February and March, when I would see that it was sunny and seventy somewhere else. But I'm so busy at work. My practice is thriving."

"Thanks for making time for this. I know it's farther for you, Grace, and I appreciate the effort."

Jason leaned in toward her and they kissed.

"I'm so glad I'm not going to have to either lie or testify about this kiss!"

He laughed and held her close. "I'm so sorry about all of that. I seem to leave a wake wherever I go."

They walked hand in hand to the parking lot and got into their separate cars, heading to Leopold's cabin. Jason had been a little anxious about going to Leopold's Shack because Aldo Leopold had meant so much to Tara. Leopold's *A Sand County Almanac* was the second book they'd read together, and it featured prominently in Tara's essay. Grace hadn't been at Tara's memorial or she likely wouldn't have suggested it.

But it wasn't triggering, except that he'd felt a little bit of the Emerson "all feeling" sitting down by the Wisconsin River with Grace. And Leopold's optimism was still engaging: "Once you learn to read the land, I have no fear of what you will do to it, or with it. And I know many pleasant things it will do to you." If only.

~~~~~~~

Grace offered to come too, but Jason decided to go alone to visit Earl Franks in prison. He'd come a long way toward forgiving himself for Tara's death. Did he want to forgive Franks as well? Why? More like, why not?

They said it was better for one's own health to forgive, but hating Franks seemed to fill some of the space that had formerly gone to loving Tara. He couldn't find a path into understanding Earl Franks. Franks was just there, lurking in the background, a phantom menace.

The new prison had a kind of eerie, futuristic beauty to it. If it had been set to music, it would have been some odd combination of high-tech and industrial sounds. Yet for all its Spartan modernism, it still had the gritty, body-odor smell of the old warehouse prisons. Nauseating cafeteria fare wafting above locker-room socks.

Jason used his judge ID to avoid everything but a wand search and a metal detector. He was shown into the waiting area, behind the bulletproof glass. Where there once had been a telephone, there was now a nifty little speaker system that amplified the voices only very locally.

Maybe it was all digitally recorded and downloaded somewhere to some great Kafkaesque listening center? As a victim, he almost hoped so. Though as a lawyer, it sickened him. The background thud of voices back and forth between the two sides of the glass, the side of freedom and of captivity, added another odd music.

Franks, thinner and appearing several years older already, seemed visibly disappointed to see him. Still, he called out heartily, "Hello, Judge." He sat down. "I thought you were someone else."

"Tommy C., maybe?"

"Nah, he's probably drinking limoncellos in Capri!" Franks smirked.

Jason found himself smiling again. Franks grinned for a second, too.

"You're probably right—that son of a bitch!"

Jason looked back toward the guard, watching within earshot.

"To what do I owe this honor?" Earl asked. "Why are you here?"

"You've been such a big part of my life. Let's be honest, you fucked it up royally! Yet I still have no clue what made you tick." Jason paused. "It's that banality-of-evil thing. Why'd you just go along? You didn't have to end up here."

"Owing scary people money just kind of snowballs. But, of course, there's more to it than just gambling." Earl seemed surprisingly willing to talk. "I've been thinking about things too. Not a helluva lot else to do if you're past the weight-lifting age here. I don't need a fucking hernia surgery from one of these prison butchers. But they have some decent books around. And I'm allowed two packages from Amazon Prime every month. I play the jailhouse lawyer card—keeps the Romeos off my back." Franks shook his head. "Literally. So, what is it you want to know?"

"I want to know everything."

Franks told Jason how he'd taken up with Courtney and how she'd fed him chicken soup when he had a cold. And about his regular trips to Vegas, and threatening Jason at the Water Law Conference. How doomed he felt when he saw what he called "the sickly, pig-eyed blonde woman" in the hallway in the courthouse in Lake Joseph. Earl was eager to tell him how he'd had nothing to do with the shooting, how bad he'd felt afterward when he thought he did, and how he'd seriously considered suicide.

"At that point, I really felt like I deserved to die."

"You don't deserve to die," Jason said bitterly. "But you do deserve this—hanging around in an orange jumpsuit doing favors for a bunch of mean guys."

Earl winced a little. "You know, I almost agree with you. I feel like I'm doing a sort of penance for all the stupid shit I've done over the past ten years. But prison, man, that's worth a bushel basket full of Hail Marys. Also, while you're here, I'd like to thank you for helping me get my freedom from Tommy Calandro and company." Franks smiled.

He *was* charming, Jason allowed. But was he ever sincere? What good was charm without sincerity? Nothing good ever came of it.

"You and Michael took Tara Highsmith from me, from her sister and her parents. How can I forgive that?" Jason thought about it a minute. "Frankly, Earl, I still hate your guts!"

"Well, I never hated yours. I told Calandro he was barking up the wrong tree."

"Don't try to charm me, Earl."

"It's never worked on you. Look, it's probably just empty words for you, but I am sorry. And I liked Tara. Her trial stories were always fair. She was funny. I feel like shit about it all," Earl confessed. "But I wasn't lying when I said I had nothing to do with shooting anyone. I thought I might even win the case."

"Oh, hell no!" Jason found himself smiling again. "Maybe if I'm really honest, maybe it's partly Schadenfreude that made me want to come here. I'm glad you're here."

"Well, I won't be forever. I'm gonna make it out of here. Be honest with me. Didn't you also feel a little relieved when it turned out that Michael and not Tommy C. had been the murderer?"

"A little. But we both know that Michael needed both your crimes and my failure to report them to carry out his plan."

"Maybe *this* plan, but he was a software engineer. He would've figured out something else without Tommy, much less me. Her husband, not me, gets your ninety percent of the blame this time."

Jason nodded. "Greed's still behind your ten and his ninety."

"For me, at that point, it was more about survival than greed. I'm not a murderer, I'm just an ordinary SOB!"

Just then, a prison guard came in and said their conversation was over.

"Thanks for coming, Jason," Franks called.

Jason turned around and nodded. He felt a little lighter.

Leaving the visiting lounge, Jason was stopped by a well-dressed young woman.

"Are you Jason Erickson?"

Jason nodded sheepishly. Mortified as he was so often these days when someone knew him but he didn't know them.

"Yes."

"I thought so. I'm Laurie Franks. Were you here to see my father?" She extended her hand. Jason recognized her father's broad nose in her pleasant face.

"Yes, I was here to see your father. Don't worry, I went pretty easy on him."

"Well, I know my father had a hand in messing up your life, but he's not all bad. I mean—"

"He seems to be faring well," Jason said, pretending to care.

Of everything Franks had said, the cruel way he talked about that woman from the bar disturbed Jason the most. Pig-eyed. Frightening. Franks could be endlessly cruel to her because he didn't know that she existed. She was Kant's means and not an end herself.

Jason thought he understood, at last, what was meant by the term the banality of evil.

"Your dad's still a big talker. Makes you wonder if there's any real there, there."

Laurie had her turn at looking mortified. "He's really popular here, with both the inmates and the staff. Everyone leaves him alone—hoping he'll help them with their case. He has helped a couple—he said he feels useful for the first time in"— Laurie stopped herself. "I'm going on and on about someone you probably detest."

"Well, good on you for still caring about your father." Jason turned to go.

The guard came back. "Ready for the next stop, Judge?"

"Yes, as ready as I'm going to be. This one will be brief, so please stick around if you can."

The deafening sounds of doors opening hit him. The sauerkraut smell, then down through the terrifying warren that led to the maximum-security cells. Nineteenth century. Dungeons, almost. They were set a good foot below the hallway floor.

"Highsmith's down there. I'm guessing you don't want to go in?" the guard asked.

"Nah, just want to say hello."

Tara's murderous husband looked just like a guy at Jason's gym. Thin, balding a bit, and athletic, but now with that pale yellow-gray pallor of an inmate. Highsmith spoke first. "Why are you here?"

"You look like shit, dude," Jason observed happily. "Somehow, that makes me feel better about the whole universe."

"Glad to be of assistance," Michael said.

"Screw you! May you rot in this hell without the possibility of parole for what you did to Tara. I loved her!" Jason cried. "By the way, I'm suing you for every penny. Guard, I'm ready to go!"

"I figured," the guard said, leading him back. "I'd hate him too! Followed your case on TV."

Jason drove off back toward Spring Green and the American Players Theatre, where he was meeting Grace. The prison, that hell of concrete and razor-wire, settled into his subconscious gloom. It was mid-afternoon and the sky, too, was dark gray.

The warming seas across the planet sent ever more ominous rain-heavy cumulonimbus bands across the skies. Jason drove on the state highway he always took, but came to a sign that said, "Bridge Out, Detour Soon."

Everywhere, the waters were rising and the clouds were oppressively low and dark gray. The millennial floods, the Biblical-scale rains, came with the sinking recognition that climate change was here and was catastrophic. Go figure. The experts had been right all along. Selfish idiots had kept them from acting.

In North Carolina, the CAFO pig-shit pits and coal-ash storage areas had been swept away by Hurricane Florence flooding, leading to massive dead spots along the coast. The idiots had reduced regulation and filled wetlands, and given exemptions for pig and chicken farms in low-lying floodplains.

The same thing was happening from Wisconsin dairy CAFOs, which had created similar lifeless areas along a huge stretch of Lake Michigan. Madison streets and homes were flooded, and just last month an architectural historian had been swept away into a culvert in the flash floods.

Jason pulled over when he came to the bridge and got out of his car. The black floodwaters had not only taken down the bridge but also a huge section of the banks on either side. Halfway down the crater, there was a piece of concrete with exposed rebar that dangled helplessly. He had to keep going—had to set his grief down and pick up his sword—to keep fighting the good and urgent fight. Tara's parents and he had agreed to jointly sue Michael to claim some of Tara's brokerage funds to set up a foundation to do just that.

Jason thought of all that as he drove the detour on to the outdoor theater. He met up with Grace in the parking lot and, as they unpacked their picnic, told her about the bridge being out.

"Yeah, I had that same problem," she replied. "We're probably going to have to get used to it." She told him about the Floodplain Conference and the way the experts were having to reengineer work they'd done in the past five years. She stopped suddenly and smiled. "But look, the sky is turning blue."

"Purple, at least. Wow. It's been weeks." It was true. The sun had poked through the clouds enough that Jason wished he had his sunglasses. "So, why is *As You Like It* your favorite Shakespeare play, Grace?"

"Because of Rosalind, of course! Probably his greatest female character. She's witty and self-aware, romantic and skeptical to the point of being almost cynical. But she also takes charge of things and is pretty androgynous as well. A thoroughly modern character and play." She paused for a second, choosing her words carefully. "Bad things happen to people in the comedies, but they just find a way to laugh through their tears."

"That's my goal, as I'm sure you know." Grace's enthusiasms and ideas—and there were many—were contagious. "I love your enthusiasm."

"I was a theater geek as a kid, which my parents encouraged because they thought it would fit with law." She shook her head. Her blonde hair was flying in five directions in the breeze. "Damn. It just occurred to me that I'm living out my parents' hopes for me as a kid. They always wanted me to take over my uncle's practice."

Jason was moved by her whole life story. "How does that make you feel?" he asked.

"Just fine, really. I feel really okay with things now. I mean, I can always sell my building if I feel too cramped. Just not for a million bucks."

Jason had packed a picnic basket with deli items and a good bottle of Chablis. He still couldn't drink chardonnay; Tara had loved it too much. They found a spot on a picnic table on the hill below the theater. Grace set up the food, and he opened the wine.

"It's a perfect night for it," Grace said. "Thanks for bringing all of this, Jason. You're sweet."

"You are too." They clinked glasses.

Some roaming musicians played chamber music for the picnickers, mostly older married couples. It was all very romantic. Were they romantic? It might take until midnight, or the next morning, for them to know. A trumpet summoned them to head up to the large outdoor theater.

They took their basket back to the car and hiked up the hill with scores of others.

The Forest of Arden design was nearly as grand as the summer night itself had become. They looked at each other and smiled. More trumpets, and some traveling musicians, called all eyes to the stage.

Grace was right; Rosalind was wonderful! Clueless Orlando, too. For the first time in months, Jason laughed.

Now, here was Jacque's famous "all the world's a stage" speech. All men and women have their entrances and exits. Yes, Jason sighed. And then the seven ages of man.

Which one was Jason in now? A new one, since he'd found a measure of justice for Tara. Keeping up her efforts, her faith in making things better, most of all.

In Hollywood, as in so much of the culture, the story was always that the person who loses a great love can never recover. It was to be taken as some final act of love (rather than defeat) when they said, "He or she never remarried." But here, in the Forest of Arden, there was another possibility.

Grace and he had lost great loves, but still had their own time left on the stage to fill. Their own entrances and exits. Their own lives to lead. Later, after another glass of wine at intermission, he held her hand.

He could feel her pulse, beating out the rhythm of her life, and even portending something tragic in the half-second between heartbeats. The moon and stars were now clearly visible above them. The distant pine trees added their silent dignity, their blue smell, as the crickets and actors sang out.

EPILOGUE

They say that time heals wounds but, for Jason, as for Grace before him, it was more that time dulled the pain of loss. There was his life with Tara in it and his life without her, and these were two profoundly different things. Without all of the romance and hopes that she'd inspired, the second life was a lesser one.

In his conversations and time with Tara, there'd always been a sense of trying to figure the world out together. From the start of their book club, they'd been on a shared quest for meaning. Then, later, for sharing itself.

But time kept moving forward. He was alive and she was dead. And his own life was not uneventful. President Trump took office in 2017, and the whole Wisconsin experience of disrespect for the rule of law went national, went global.

A couple of years later, Wisconsin elected a progressive new governor—one for whom both Jason and Grace had held fundraisers. Jason was still something of a public figure in the state. The new governor asked Jason to join the new administration and to help it set environmental policy, as the climate changed, as Environmental Legal Counsel.

Jason agreed. The job was made more difficult by the outgoing governor and the gerrymandered state legislature. They'd done their best to limit the power of the newly elected governor in one final, obedient bow to the billionaires who bankrolled their campaigns and wrote most of the laws for them. The losers opposed everything the people had voted for the new governor to accomplish. Now, it seemed to be loser-keep-all. This, too, became a theme in national politics, coming to a violent head on January 6, 2021.

But working on the forest-not-the-trees environmental policy and litigation against bad actors was both a wonderful way to honor Tara and a healing piece of work for Jason in its own right. Jason was grateful for the opportunity and worked very hard and productively even if the challenges sometimes seemed overwhelming.

Grace had lost her husband while still in law school. She was wise and patient. Jason had been moving closer to her, and slowly they'd become something like romantic partners. As close as two people who live two and a half hours away from each other could expect to be.

Grace's practice in La Crosse was thriving and her confidence in herself as a lawyer had become a part of her personality in a very appealing way. She was happy with the way things had evolved between them, and was reluctant to press their luck any further by having one of them move to the other's city. It worked for the moment.

Meanwhile, Courtney Sharpe had become the managing shareholder of Earl Franks's old firm in Chicago. For a while she toyed around with some of the new associates, male and female, as she'd been toyed with herself. But then she settled in with one of them, Steve Olson, who had worked with Earl on the Lake Joseph case after Courtney had dumped him. She and Steve were both ruthlessly ambitious and made a relentless and hard-charging team.

Earl got out of prison after just twenty-seven months. He often said he felt "like a new old man" since he retired to his cottage on Blue Lake. He still had some deferred compensation and Social Security to live on, and it was enough and more to fuss a bit with the furnishings and to fix the windows and insulation to make it a year-round residence.

The sunlight that reflected on the bluest lake in the world still poured in the back window in the morning. Laurie and her kids were regular visitors in the summer. They called him Paw-Paw, which he secretly hated, but Laurie joked it was better Paw-Paw than Out-Law!

There was still seemingly time for Earl to do something positive and productive with his life, but for now, he was content to sit on his ass, pass gas, and fish for walleye. He shared the sitting and the fishing with the widow Betty Franklin, whose rear end he'd admired for more than thirty years. "She was," he said to whomever would listen, "quite an old pistol, who still wore bikinis and drank martinis on the beach."

Betty gave as good as she got and actually seemed to enjoy Earl's notoriety after her very tame and sickly pastor husband had finally passed. Their motto together was: seize the decade!

Earl, after all, as he also was fond of saying, hadn't killed anyone.

But Michael Highsmith had, and he was still at the maximum-security facility in Portage serving a life sentence plus sixty years without the possibility of parole. The two morons who did the shooting were up there too.

ACKNOWLEDGMENTS

I would like to thank my daughters Allie and Anna for their inspiring love and support of me and my writing; and the terrific fiction mentors who made my Augsburg MFA such a growth experience: Stephan Eirik Clark and Cass Dalglish, who provided insights into early drafts, and Ted Thompson and Lindsay Starck, who helped me refine both the story and the writing; also invaluable were editors Meagan Thompson, Lisa Huempfner, Elizabeth Ridley, and Aaron Teel; thanks as well to friends and family who read early drafts—Marc Vitale, Gary Wilson, Jim Scully, and Laurence Boldt. Finally, thanks to the River Grove team in Austin, especially Jessica Reyes for her editorial insights and Chase Quarterman for the beautiful cover art.

ABOUT THE AUTHOR

JEFFREY D. BOLDT's credits include: *Great River Review, Berkeley Poetry Review, Blueline, Interim, The J Journal, Tikkun, and Agave.* His poems have been included in numerous anthologies. Six of his short stories have recently appeared in *The Missing Slate, The MacGuffin, Mistake House, Rosebud,* and *The Fictional Café.*

Boldt is a graduate of the University of Wisconsin and its School of Law. After a career focusing on environmental law, Boldt received his MFA in Fiction from Augsburg University in 2019. *Blue Lake* is his first published novel.

CPSIA information can be obtained
at www.ICGtesting.com
Printed in the USA
LVHW101245220822
726557LV00002B/37